BACKSTORY

BEHIND THE SCENES OF A FAMOUS FILM-THRILLER

PAT DUNLAP EVANS

PUBLISHER'S NOTES

Copyright © 2020 Pat Dunlap Evans
March 10, 2024, updated bio and made minor text changes
Published in the United States of America, by
A.M. Chai Literary

Due to publishing software limitations, excerpts depicting screenplays are not formatted to exact specifications. This novel has been digitally produced. In case a typographical error escaped our editors' eyes, please notify the author at Promos@PatDunlapEvans.com.

Cover Assistance: Pam Roberts
Cover Photo: © Aina Jameela/Shutterstock

ISBN: 978-0-9968822-6-2 (Print Paperback)
ISBN: 978-0-9968822-7-9 (Kindle MOBI)
ISBN: 978-0-9968822-8-6 (E-Pub)

DEDICATION

To my readers: This one is for you.

It's not an ordinary story, nor told in a standard format.

I call it an experiential thriller.

Please take your time as you ride along

with Merry Mayfield, and keep an open eye and mind.

FORWARD

To the Reader,

Throughout the life of famed screenwriter Meredith Mayfield, one saying proved true. Life imitates art. Several decades after Ms. Mayfield's film thriller *Those Who Try* was nominated for best original dramatic screenplay at the 1992 Academy Awards, this collection of her writings reveals the backstory of her first successful work.

Readers will encounter varied formats, including personal letters, screenplay scenes, this *Foreword*, and an *Afterword* by the editors. Dated 1988 to 1990, Ms. Mayfield's letters speak candidly to Roland Holmes, her film professor at Columbia University, where she earned an MFA. The screenplay excerpts are from *Those Who Try*. For screenplay terms, we provide a brief glossary:

```
ALL CAPS — Indicate scenes, signs, first
appearance of characters, sounds, or shot.
INT. / EXT. — Interior or exterior location.
INSERT — A camera shot of an object or text.
INTERCUT — Alternating characters or scenes.
O.S. — A voice heard off screen.
M.O.S. — Without sound.
SUPER — Superimpose, usually text.
V.O. — An unseen narrator.
```

Never fear, there isn't a test at the end. However, each section appears in a different format for a reason.

RH and JH,
Editors

SCENE 1

FADE IN:

INT. AUSTIN POLICE STATION — 1990 — NIGHT

SIGN: "City of Austin Police Facility"

In a dingy interview room, a hotshot young
DETECTIVE paces in front of a distraught MERRY
MAYFIELD, 38, still pretty with black bobbed
hair. She sobs into her quivering hands.

>   DETECTIVE
>   Ms. Mayfield ... I realize this is a
>   trying situation, but I need you to
>   calm down.

Merry valiantly tries to stop crying.

Detective hands her a box of tissues.

She blows her nose, then inhales in a deep
shudder.

>   MERRY
>   A nightmare of nights ... I'd give
>   anything for you to go away.

                         DETECTIVE
          You mean me, or what happened
          tonight?

                           MERRY
          Too many nights. But especially
          tonight. Oh, my baby ...

Letter One
August 3, 1988

Dear Roland,

Well, I made it through my first week in Austin, Texas. There's much I've wanted to tell you, but I delayed writing so I could get a grip.

I can just hear you shouting, "Don't just put words on paper. That's typing. Ask yourself what you feel about what you think. Art is emotion!"

I do try, Professor Brilliance.

✉ ✉ ✉

My father died three days before I moved. Our dear friend Sigrid likely told you about that, but you didn't care enough to express your sympathy. You with those liquid-blue eyes that ignited my spirit with the revelations I craved, you could not call to say, "I am sorry about your father."

No.

The cause of death was esophageal varices, cirrhosis of the liver, and acute emphysema—a horrifying list of conditions meaning that the blood vessels in Dad's throat had burst because he drank a gallon of vodka each day, and his lungs had so many holes from chain smoking that he gasped, gasped, and gasped.

From this rather biting description, you can tell I didn't adore my dad. I've always envied women who had a classic "first love" relationship with their father. But my dad was an oddball, darkly handsome and brilliant, but an alcoholic, a booming-voiced loner obsessed with his own maleness. He could lecture me for hours about testosterone and estrogen, and why men were strong and women were weak. This trait was fueled in part by the booze, one drink every hour, or so he bragged to us at one of the many family intervention sessions I attended when my brother Brandon or Mom tried to get Dad to stop drinking.

That's why Dad's death added an even greater jumble of emotions to our moving day that included a cacophony of eureka moments, oh-no's, and angst. But since truth is stranger than fiction, Dad's death and our wild journey have produced several new scenes for me to include in my comedy-drama screenplay—yes, still working-titled, "Those Who Try."

As for the lead actress, imagine the adorable Demi Moore as me.

The story begins with my optimistic plan: Drive from Greenwich, Connecticut, to my dad's house on Cedar Creek Lake in two and a half days. We'd stop first in Knoxville, Tennessee, then mush on to Dad's lake house for the night before heading to Austin and the funeral Brandon insisted on having.

The travel time was totally possible. Eleven hours to Knoxville. Twelve more to the lake house, which is about an hour and a half southeast of Dallas. The kids would take turns driving. My oldest daughter Nora wasn't bad behind the wheel, and my fourteen-year-old, Claire, had her learner's permit. Once at the lake, we would gather the things we wanted from Dad's house, load them into a U-Haul truck, then drive this now-three-vehicle caravan to Austin in time for Dad's memorial service, to be held at the Eternal Spirit Center the following day.

A carefully crafted plan, but overzealous because life got in the way.

When we finally drove away from the Greenwich house, there was stuff crammed window to window inside both cars. I was driving a metallic-brown 1976 Very Used Olds Cutlass Supreme with a light-tan vinyl top. It's not a bad looking car, but I'm sure you'll remember when I drove only new Mercedes. (I had to sell mine so we could eat.) Trailing behind the Cutlass was our twenty-six-foot ski boat on a double-axle trailer—a ridiculous contraption to haul, but more about that later.

My angry seventeen-year-old, Nora, who is blond and blue-eyed like her father, was driving her blue-and-white 1978 Volkswagen van with our two huge red setters, Edith and Louis, on the third back seat. The veterinarian had given us pet tranquilizers to keep the dogs calm. Perched in that seat, the two looked like a pair of redheaded hippies wigged out on some *primo* stuff.

Of course, the weather gods decided to storm on us the first day of our trip. From dawn to sunset, dark clouds, lightning bolts, and thunder rumbled across the sky, while rain pummeled both cars. This delayed us terribly. Also, of course, the boat trailer broke down at precisely midnight, fifty miles east of Knoxville. In the rain, rain, rain, storm, storm, storm.

A kindly trucker stopped to help. "Bad wheel bearings in that right front wheel, little lady. Good thaaang you got a double-axle trailer, or you'da lost the whole rig."

There was no way to fix the wheel bearings that night, so the kids watched from the van as I stooped in my blue rain hoodie and held the trucker's yellow flashlight in the rain, rain, rain, while he hunched in his yellow slicker, jacked up the trailer, and took off the right front tire. He put that tire under the boat cover, and then he chained the front axle to the trailer frame and jacked it high enough so the right wheel rim wouldn't hit the pavement. That meant the left-front wheel couldn't touch the ground. Lastly, he added air to the trailer's back two tires so as to carry the additional load.

"You can head on down the highway now, little lady. Those back tires'll hold 'er."

Where is it written that kindly truckers actually know what they are talking about? After I pulled out on the highway with the kids following in the van, the over-pumped back tires on the trailer swelled from the added pressure and started scraping and screeching against the trailer body. That spewed a rocket trail of steam and smoke from singed rubber—so much so, I could barely see Nora's VW behind me, that is, until she started beeping madly and flashing her lights.

I pulled over. Of course, it was still raining. Black as death. 1:00 a.m.

Scottie, my twelve-year-old son, kept hollering, "This is the most horrible thing that has ever happened to me, and I have my own mother to thank for it."

I parked the Very Used Cutlass and the boat trailer on the highway shoulder, turned on the flashers, then ran back to the van, where I squeezed between the slobbering dogs and tried not to cry. Nora drove us into Knoxville, where we checked into a Quality Inn. So exhausted I couldn't sleep, I sat in a desk chair and nursed a paper cup of gin, listening to Edith and Louis pant and the children breathe.

All night long, I tried to figure out how to get to Dad's funeral on time. I'd have to find a mechanic to fix the boat trailer, then put Edith and Louis in a kennel (they'd probably have nervous breakdowns), drive the van to the airport, take a plane with the kids to Austin, endure Dad's funeral service, fly back to Knoxville, retrieve the van, rescue Edith and Louis, hope the boat trailer was fixed by then, and drive the rest of the way to Dad's house. This was my determined plan.

My brother Brandon was not going to have this to hang over my head for the next half-century. He is the hero child that families of alcoholics often have. A control freak, intent on making things happen the way he demands they should, instead of the way they will happen because life has its own way.

Then it hit me. Dad would have been furious that he was having any funeral, especially one officiated by Brandon's evangelical-minister wife, Deanna, at her Eternal Spirit Center. Although our dear mother had reared us kids as Catholics, Dad was an agnostic—if not a downright atheist—who always refused to say whatever step Alcoholics Anonymous requires drunks to spout about there being a higher power. In spite of this, Brandon had pronounced that Dad's funeral would be an Eternal Spirit ceremony, because that was the kind of service Brandon would have if he died right then.

So, as the sunrise peeked under the Quality Inn vinyl drapes, my determination to get to Dad's funeral diffused into reality. Call it Godot, call it common sense, call it Dad's spirit. But as I listened to three adolescents and old two dogs sleeping deeply, I had my eureka moment.

"I am risking my children's lives and my sanity to get to a ritual that Dad wouldn't stand for if he were alive."

I called Dear Pluppy Brandon. I could just see him on the other end of the line—his dark-mustached mouth huffing and puffing, his mud-brown eyes a frenzy of neurotic overcompensation, and his still-tenor voice annoyingly abuzz with plans.

"Merry, you're exhausted, confused, and under stress. You shouldn't make decisions now that you'll regret for the rest of your life. I will fly to Knoxville and help you get the trailer fixed. You'll never forgive yourself if you don't come to Dad's service."

That's Brandon—ready to tell me what I need to feel and do.

"I've been having some nice talks with Dad. He knows why I can't be at his funeral."

Brandon didn't laugh. "Merry, let me speak to Nora."

"She's asleep."

"Merry, I insist."

I shouldn't have let him.

As Nora told me later, "Uncle Brandon thinks you're going nuts. He said, 'If your mother continues to hear voices or if she starts acting weird, call me or a doctor.'"

Damn Brandon! He is forever laying out neurotic paths for me to follow. But I said no to Brandon's nervous breakdown. I did not go to my father's funeral. Instead, I spent that next day locating a mechanic to fix the boat trailer, but he couldn't do it until the following day. So the kids and I drove Nora's van back to the Cutlass and boat trailer. I got in and slowly drove on the highway shoulder until we got to the exit for the Quality Inn. The kids drove behind me in the van, flashing security lights. Going that slow, we made it to Knoxville without singed rubber and smoke.

The next morning, the mechanic arrived in a beat-up yellow pickup with his wife and baby. When he got out, I realized he had only one arm and a patch over an eye. Goodness, how could this one-armed, one-eyed man fix my trailer?

Turns out, his wife was his missing body parts. She held their baby on one hip and hoisted a wrench or jack with the free hand. Neither of them said much—just nodded toward this or that tool until the job was done.

After I paid them the three hundred dollars I couldn't afford, the kids and I, Cutlass, boat trailer, and Nora's van with the dogs headed back on the highway. The sky was still cloudy, but at least the highway was dry. From then on, we seemed to float mile after mile, until about the time of Dad's funeral service, when the sun broke through and basked us in the golden light of a most beautiful summer day. We even got to see a glorious, huge red Texas sunset before nightfall, when we arrived at Dad and Mom's house about 10:00 p.m.

It was spookier than hell pulling into that driveway, now that nobody lived in my parents' home. As I walked in the front door, I had a tremendous case of *déjà vu*, since I had experienced a similar life event only six months before—the death of my mother—which Sigrid probably told you about too, but I won't bore you with the details now. Maybe later, if I can dredge up the feelings. You'll notice how I'm avoiding pain in this bit of caustic prose. And yet, as I turned on the lights, I felt the joy and comfort of being at home, this time without the annoyances of the unhappy people who had lived there—the loud, alcoholic father; the martyred mother; the overbearing brother. And I, who was so exasperated by them all.

The house was lakefront, so after I fixed a martini and made a late-night snack of chicken soup and peanut-butter crackers for the kids, we went down to the dock and took a moonlight swim in the warm summer waters. Gliding along in the midnight waves, I felt a glorious sense of victory, as though we were the lone survivors of a hundred-year war we had won.

"This trip has been the most horrible thing that ever happened to me, and I have my own mother to thank for it," my son pronounced again.

Shades of his Uncle Brandon's mantra, repainting gloom.

"My dear Scottie, be glad if this remains the most horrible thing. And count your blessings that you are safe. In some species, mothers have been known to eat their offspring."

"Gross, Mom," all three said simultaneously, followed by huge sighs.

For revenge, I made them take showers at 1:00 a.m. Then we played rock, paper, scissors to choose beds. Needless to say, none would pick my father's bed.

"His ghost will probably wander around that room," my fourteen-year-old Claire hollered.

So, I did it. Donning my nightgown, I went into my parents' bedroom, sensing the aromas of an old man's mustiness and my mother's tears. Then, so tired I could barely see, I crawled in my dead father's bed and whispered,"Good night, Dad. I hope you are now at peace."

As I pulled up the covers, I felt his spirit envelop me. I slept soundly, flat on my back, spread-eagled like I'd seen my father sleep. I awoke the next morning in the very same position.

After breakfast, the kids and I rented a U-Haul truck to hold some of the furniture I wanted from my parents' house. We loaded the truck until noon, then locked up the house and headed south again.

Roland, you would have been astonished at this incredible caravan. I drove the white-and-orange U-Haul, Nora drove the Cutlass hauling the boat trailer, and Claire drove the van on her learner's permit—heaven help her—learning how to drive a stick shift the hard way.

Turns out, my U-Haul didn't have first or second gears, so I had to start off in third, and the fucker kept dying. The air conditioner on the VW van ceased to exhale cold air somewhere south of Corsicana, so the kids transferred Edith and Louis to the back seat of the Very Used Cutlass. Then the AC on the Cutlass quit near Waco. Apparently, we had burned up the transmission by hauling a boat trailer such a long way.

But what the hell. We made it to Austin. Samuel Beckett would have been proud of us. As would the ever-bizarre Jean Genet.

My only regret in missing my father's funeral was that I did not see the ethereal Deanna in action as minister or preacher—whatever she calls herself. Dear Pluppy Brandon videotaped the event and has delivered a black-plastic VHS cassette, which stares at me with its white-reel eyes. I have not played it. Maybe never will.

Regardless, we're moved in. Not unpacked. But in. It's lonelier than hell. I so miss the times spent with you, my dear pal Sigrid, and others I refuse to name.

More later in the delightful comedy drama, *Those Who Try*.

Love,
Merry

SCENE 2

INT. MERRY'S DUPLEX OFFICE — NIGHT — 1988

At her father's old desk, Merry sits in a filmy nightie, urgently typing a long letter on a 1983 MACINTOSH SE. She finishes, takes a final sip of a MARTINI, and chews the olives.

INSERT — TEXT ON MAC SCREEN:

More later in the delightful comedy drama, *Those Who Try*.

Love,
Merry

She expertly prints the pages on an APPLE LASERWRITER, gets up to retrieve them, and then hand-addresses an ENVELOPE to:

"Roland Holmes, Film Program, Columbia University"

Merry folds and stuffs the pages into the envelope, seals it, and checks to see if her door is still closed before she hides the envelope in the back of a file CABINET.

                         MERRY
          No one will find it here. Then again,
          the kids seem to find everything,
          even my vibrators.

She smiles wanly at her own joke, then gazes
out a dark window. A pair of HEADLIGHTS float
into a space in the complex's parking lot.
Merry hears a CAR DOOR close.

                         MERRY
          I don't know one adult in this town
          except Brandon and Deanna. That's
          like not knowing anybody at all.

EXT. MERRY'S DUPLEX — 1988 — NIGHT

Bending low to hide behind the thick bushes
under Merry's office window, GLENN, about 30,
handsome but scruffy, quietly scoots into
place. Silently, he rises enough to peer in.

THROUGH THE WINDOW

Merry's back is turned. Her filmy nightie
reveals a lovely derriere.

Glenn's eyes gleam with a dark urgency that
goes far beyond lust.

He pulls out a CAMERA and takes a few shots of
Merry, just before she turns out the light and
opens her office door.

Letter Two
August 6, 1988

Dear Roland,

To help you envision my life's cast of characters, I'll tell you a bit about my sister-in-law—tall, big-nosed, flame-haired Deanna. When she and Brandon became engaged, she pronounced that she would convert to Catholicism, our family's faith. This pleased Mother greatly, and she rewarded the young couple with a full-mass Catholic wedding, since Deanna's parents could not afford one. But right after Mom died— just six months before Dad—Deanna announced she was becoming a minister for the Eternal Spirit Center, a dome-topped megachurch on Highway 290 in Oak Hill. It's a grungy suburb that is light years from the snooty area of West Lake Hills, where Deanna and Brandon live.

Deanna told me, "I have found my true calling in the Eternal Spirit faith, to serve those in need. I think your mother would understand the change. She was a woman of deep faith."

Instead of being upset at Deanna's failure to honor her engagement promise, Brandon pronounced, "The girls and I are converting to the Eternal Spirit faith too. The Catholic Church has nothing to offer us."

This is so typical of Brandon, to make sudden pronouncements as if they are the true light and way. Even more, he insisted I fly down for Deanna's "Vision of Holiness" ceremony, her ordination. "It's important for our family show to support for Deanna's ministry. After all, Dad won't come, and you're all we've got, now that Mother ..."

I fell for Brandon's guilt-inducing plea because it was a way to escape my job—if you can call it that—selling auto insurance from a beige fiberglass booth outside the appliance department at Sears. This is what happens to film and drama majors after they earn their master's degree.

Since they have no skills for many professions, they wind up selling something.

My slimy boss, Harold Beardsley, was a sniveling thief who kept writing his name as agent on my new clients' applications. When I discovered he was stealing my commissions, I fantasized about canceling all of Harold's policies. I could have done that, you know. Within a few hours, I could have screwed up hundreds of lives.

Would that have been it—my Genet-inspired, irrational, intuitive, gratuitous act you preached to us in Contemporary and Modern Drama—the act that proves I indeed exist?

✉ ✉ ✉

I digress.

Deanna's ordination was held inside the vast Eternal Spirit Center, with a white-beamed dome ceiling and skylight above the altar. As my kids and I took our first-row seats beside Brandon, I glanced at the pews behind us, which were packed with the same sort of folks you might see at Walmart on Saturday nights. In that sea of aliens, Deanna looked rather heavenly as she floated from the wings, draped in a white-satin robe. Her long strawberry hair was curly and ethereal. If Deanna didn't have such a misshapen hooter, she might have been beautiful—kind of a Barbara Streisand problem.

Leading off, Brother Malcolm, a burly, bald, gray-bearded guy with electric-green eyes, delivered an hour-long exhortation for the congregation to open our hearts to the spirits that supposedly circle above us and govern our earthly lives. Then Brother Malcolm laid both hands on Deanna's shoulders, pressed his forehead to hers, and shouted into her face for five minutes, exhorting the eternal spirits to bring their precious blood her way.

Before long, Deanna started shouting too, only hers was more of a screech. "I am awash in the Eternal Spirits. Touch me, brothers and sisters, and ye shall touch them too."

Suddenly, Brother Malcolm jolted up, stretched his arms wide, and yelled, "I felt their touch! The Spirits are among us and will bless us all!"

With tears streaming, Deanna trembled as she arose and slowly walked down the aisles like the winner of the Miss America contest. As the loony congregants pawed at her robes, I could not believe my brother, a former altar boy, thought this was okay. I leaned near and whispered, "What's a good Catholic boy like you doing in a place like this?" My hope was for a wink, a bit of recognition of our shared Sundays spent miserably humble on our knees.

Instead, Brandon gave me a dismayed-at-Merry look and refused to make eye contact for the rest of my visit. Even when he took me back to the airport, he hugged me lightly and murmured, "I hope you can get your life in order, Merry."

After Deanna's ordination, she went on a six-month internship to convert the unbaptized in Zimbabwe. So, during those three weeks Dad spent dying, Brandon kept calling Deanna, hoping she would fly to the VA Hospital in Dallas and work a miracle. But he couldn't get through.

That lucky intervention spared me from Deanna's preaching over Dad's cantaloupe balls twenty-four hours a day. You see, during one of our many weekend visits to Dad before he died, Brandon and I were stationed in chairs beside the hospital bed, not saying much, just watching Dad gasp and swell.

But then Brandon suddenly blurted, "Gosh, Father's balls are the size of cantaloupes. They must weigh three pounds."

I sighed. "Don't tell me you have the same obsession as Dad."

Brandon gave me one of his dismayed-at-Merry looks.

He couldn't know I was referring to a time I saw my father weigh the darn things. His testicles. I must have been twelve. Dad had a history of parading about the house *au natural*, no matter who was there. He frequently said the male body was "too beautiful to cover, although females should keep their equipment draped so we males won't be senselessly aroused." Dad also expounded on the topic of testosterone vs. estrogen, saying things like, "Women simply don't have the right juice."

So this one morning when Dad waltzed into the kitchen with not even a towel around him, my prepubescent eyes desperately tried, but could not avoid his thick shrub of black pubic hair and bluish penis dangling like an Italian sausage over a pair of roasted meatballs. He didn't seem at all flustered that his young daughter was there, fervently pretending to pour a glass of lemonade. He got out a kitchen scale and put it on the counter. Then he mounted a step stool, flopped his balls on the scale, and held up his dick so the weight wouldn't count in the tally.

"Come read this, Merry. I don't have my readers."

You can imagine the horrified mind of a girl as she desperately aims her eyes at the dial, except they betray her and instead focus on the hairy, wrinkled blobs of animality.

In case you're wondering, Dad's balls weighed ten ounces.

Disappointed, he muttered, "I thought they'd weigh at least a pound."

That was Dad in a nutshell (hah!).

After Brandon's "cantaloupe balls" comment at the hospital, he seemed to give up on his determination to save Dad. About twenty times, Brandon had driven between Austin and Dallas to meet with specialists and discuss revolutionary treatments. For days, he stood by Dad's bed, held his hand, and urged him, "You can do it, Father. Fight. Fight." Dutiful alcoholic's son.

I admit that my neurotic brother was a more devoted child than I.

Boom! So, a six-pack of guilt is what I give myself tonight. Well, let me modify that by saying I did put forth major effort, flying as often as I could afford between Greenwich and Dallas.

Brandon drove up from Austin each time and picked me up at the airport. In the huge crowd awaiting my packed flight, I didn't even have to search for him. He was in my face, a man on a mission, out of breath from his forty pounds overweight. His eyes bored holes in mine. "Don't worry, we are going to save Father. I've got power of attorney. We can hire the best doctors, and I can do anything I want with Father's assets."

You'll notice that the "we" in "we are going to save Father" did not include my name related to financial matters.

On the long ride around Loop 12 to the grim VA Hospital with blue and green walls, just south of downtown Dallas, we whizzed past rusty junkyards, poor man's liquor stores, and summer-bleached grasses. Brandon urgently elaborated his plan to liquidate Dad's assets (my future assets) and use the proceeds to slam Dad into yet another rehab hospital, number six or eight—I can't recall.

Brandon has always been in charge of details like that, but his exuberance met with my resistance, since I am the rebel child who says things like, "Dad might be better off dead. The man has been drunk for forty-five years."

Now that he's gone, I eat those words for breakfast, lunch, and dinner guilt.

On my first hospital visit, Dad was having the DTs (*delirium tremens*). He sat lurching, wild-eyed. His thick black hair—without a strand of gray despite his seventy-one years—clumped in storm clouds above his pillow. An oxygen mask pressed around his nose and mouth. He gurgled when he tried to speak. His eyes stared through me, seeing things beyond.

"Look out, Merry! It's ... look out!" he blared.

Brandon patted Dad's hand. "It's all right, Father. We're going to take care of you."

"Stupid son of a bitch. Get the bedpan. I'm going to crap!"

I ran and got a nurse, then escaped to the waiting room for a while.

Brandon came to get me later. "He's calm now. He asked for you."

I shook my head no. "I'll let you handle this part," I snapped, but in retrospect I should have gone back, because that weekend was the last time Dad would be able speak to us. Only a week later, Brandon warned me by phone that things had gone downhill.

Fearful of what I might encounter on my next visit, I waited outside Dad's hospital room and steeled myself with the determination that no matter how difficult this scene, I would have courage. I would not move.

When I looked in, Dad's face was so puffy he looked like he might explode. His kidneys were failing, and his body had become a puffball. When you touched him, you felt seepage—as if the stuff of life wanted to escape the beast. A ventilator tube was jammed down his throat. His eyes were open but rolled back, displaying only the whites. The nurses had warned me he was blind. But within seconds after I walked in, those beeping monitors that display numbers connected to the heart rose thirty points.

"Look, Merry, Father knows you're here." That was profound for Brandon.

Yes, dammit. Dad knew I was there. He was still fighting.

That's when I realized he didn't want to die; I wanted him to. Several times I got so desperate to end Dad's suffering, I went to the hospital chapel, got on my knees, feverishly crossed myself, and begged Godot to end this horrid scene.

Meanwhile, Brandon probably was praying that Dad would live. Like always, the two of us canceled each other out.

In spite of both of us, Dad died when neither Brandon nor I were there—July 29, Dad's seventy-second birthday. I was in Greenwich, packing for my move, when the doctor called.

Brandon was back in Austin when he got the news. He was crying when he phoned me. "I guess you've heard. He's gone, Merry."

I envisioned the two of us at opposite ends of the phone lines— Brandon crying, me trying to disguise the enormity of my relief.

Well, in spite of all aims, I've gone weepy with this journaling exercise. I shall take a break and reconnoiter so I won't ramble inconsequentially.

Love,
Merry

SCENE 3

EXT. MERRY'S DUPLEX — NIGHT — 1988

Glenn is hiding in the bushes again. Through
the office window, Glenn watches Merry typing
intently. Beside her is a half-full MARTINI
GLASS with one OLIVE.

Glenn leers and grins luridly as he
creepily unzips his jeans and slowly starts
masturbating.

INT. MERRY'S DUPLEX OFFICE — NIGHT — 1988

Merry prints the pages, then folds, stuffs, and
seals them in another white envelope.

Again, she addresses the envelope to:

"Roland Holmes, Columbia University Film
Program."

She files the envelope with the earlier one,
just as Merry's oldest teen NORA silently
opens the door and peeks in.

Merry doesn't realize Nora is there.

> MERRY
> (to herself)
> If Brandon ever sees these, he would
> poop a brick. Hopefully, he'll die
> first. After all, he's three years
> older. One can hope.

> NORA
> Talking to yourself, Mom?

> MERRY
> Sane mothers do this to keep from
> killing their teenagers.

> NORA
> Good one, Mom. Shall I call Uncle
> Brandon about your mental state?

> MERRY
> That would be your final phone call.

Nora grins sarcastically and DRUMS her fingers
on the door.

> MERRY (CONT'D)
> And please tell your brother and
> sister to get to bed. You've got
> student orientation tomorrow.

> NORA
> I know, Mom. Thanks again for making
> me start my senior year in a new
> town. Just because you grew up in
> Texas doesn't mean I had to. I could
> have stayed in Greenwich with Dad.

> MERRY
> Someday I may tell you more, but
> there was no way for you to stay.

Nora leaves with a SLAM of the door.

Merry rolls her eyes and SIGHS.

EXT. MERRY'S DUPLEX — NIGHT

Still behind the bushes, Glenn scoots down the
way to

NORA'S BEDROOM WINDOW

Glenn shinnies up to watch as Nora takes off
her jeans, revealing an athletic teen body in
only her panties.

Glenn's eyes glaze as he pumps and shudders in
an orgasmic release.

Letter Three
August 19, 1988

Dear Roland,

Brandon's latest obsession is that I'm not gainfully employed. At lunch last week, we met at Chuy's, a Tex-Mex joint on Barton Springs Road near Brandon's office. Chuy's is a dive you would love, decorated in Elvis memorabilia, Mexican flying fish, and hubcaps on the ceiling.

Over an Elvis Presley Memorial Combo of beef, cheese, and chicken enchiladas, a crispy taco, and *chile con queso*, Brandon puffed, "What do you do all day?"

I lied. "I take out the boat and sunbathe in the nude."

He rolled his sausage-patty eyes, trying flattery this time. "Merry, with your looks and personality you should go into real estate."

"If you'll recall, Dad left me enough to make it a year or two—that is, if I live in a cruddy duplex. In the meantime, I'm going to write a screenplay, set in this town you made me move to."

His eyes got beady. "Merry, no one pressured you to move here. As I recall, you said you'd love to get away from the cold." He takes a sip of iced tea, gathering courage. "I have a good friend who's a manager with B. J. Hathaway Real Estate. I can get you an interview."

"Why don't you go into real estate yourself? With Deanna's preacher megabucks, you wouldn't have to worry about immediate income."

Brandon wiped queso off his mustache. His eyes squinted. "First off, Deanna does not earn megabucks. Secondly, I'm only trying to help."

"Only trying to help? Then encourage me to write."

"Merry, get a job."

Comments like that have always made me wonder if Mom's woodpile had an extramarital log in it while Dad was drinking his way through

World War II. He was a lieutenant commander on a ship in the Pacific and, as the story goes, he came home on leave to visit Mom.

Brandon was born eight months later, weighing nine pounds.

A scrapbook Mom kept had a V-mail from Dad, datelined "Samoa." In tiny print he wrote, "Hefty weight for eight months. I wish I could have been there for the birth—that is, if I was there at conception. Right?"

I also submit that Brandon does not look a bit like my father—especially Brandon's mud-brown eyes. Mom had wide-set green eyes, which could be bright with fun whenever she forgot the pain of being married to Dad. He had bowling-ball-sized eyes that ignited whenever he was interrupted by what he saw as Mom's bothersome questions.

I always that the existence of a genetic question like Brandon was the reason Dad drank. Once, I even mentioned to Brandon that Mom might have had a lover while Dad was off to sea.

"Merry, that's disrespectful. Mother was a good Catholic and would've never had an affair!"

Good old Brandon. He ignored my allegations that he was the result of Mom's indiscretion and blindly defended her morals.

Oh, perhaps my accusation that Brandon is not a fruit of Dad's loins is a low blow. As a teen, he fretted that he had too much of an overbite, or that his eyes were too round, legs too short, waist too long, hair too thin. All of it was. He desperately tried not to, but remained jealous that his little sister, I, was blessed with Dad's thick black hair, Mom's green cat eyes, and any other asset Brandon wanted but I got.

"Eat your heart out," I as much said when I invaded Brandon's world in 1949, three years after he was born.

In retaliation, he scolded me for breaking his toy train. He railed to Mom that I was a messy brat. He tattled when I drew pictures on walls, cut holes in his shirts, or splattered paints over his bedroom floor. "Mother, do something with that child!"

But Mom would smile, I would laugh, and Brandon would run wounded to his room and slam the door—frustrated that the darling of the family had won yet another round.

Nowadays, my brother's job is executive director of Austin Search for Knowledge, ASK—get it? It's a non-profit aimed at helping the underprivileged learn job skills, so they won't steal cars. It's a noble cause, but I don't think Brandon's heart is in it. His salary has reached the city cap. Maybe he's pushing me to try real estate so he can try it vicariously.

How could I expect Brandon to understand that after six years under your intellectual spell, I am simply ruined for conventional occupations? Other than screenwriting, what am I good for in today's demanding culture of occupation?

When someone asks what you do for a living, that means, "What do you have to do, instead of what you want to do?"

✉   ✉   ✉

Dear Roland, what would you think—you in your empire as professor emeritus (despite your rapscallion behavior), film program, Columbia University—if you knew I was unburdening my soul, my anger, my sadness to you? You who opened my world, my eyes. You gave me definition. Was Genet right? You called me "writer." Therefore I am? What shall I do for my irrational, intuitive, and gratuitous act to prove it?

I still remember that June day, after classes were over and I was no longer officially a student, we met at the Raven Bar, that grizzly personification of a campus hangout. Face-to-face we sat, you in your gray cord jacket and me, overdressed professional golfer's wife. I did not have enough guts to look you in the eye ... those noon-sky eyes that twinkled behind your wire-rimmed lenses. The question was pregnant. Now that my education was complete, would we be friends? Lovers? Mentor and protégé?

You blushed and got flustered. I blushed and got flustered. Once again, we were too shy to bare our souls. I still think we at least could have made it to friendship if we had spent that evening without the intrusion of you know who. But there she came. Jillian. Tall, frazzle-haired, persistent Jillian Saunders, who swooped in at the wrong time and ruined the pregnant moment for me and us, but not for her.

I refuse to say more about Jillian at this time.

Love,
Merry

SCENE 4

INT. BRANDON'S BATHROOM — 1988 — NIGHT

BRANDON, 43, paunchy and balding, brushes his teeth. In the mirror, he seeks answers to unspoken questions.

> DEANNA (O.S.)
> Are you clean and shiny for me?

> BRANDON
> (mimicking)
> Clean and shiny?

> DEANNA (O.S.)
> Brandon, did you hear me?

> BRANDON
> Yes, dear, I heard you.

Brandon wipes toothpaste from his thick brown mustache and pats his fat tummy in dismay.

INT. BRANDON'S BEDROOM — NIGHT

In a lush bed with satin sheets and pillows, redheaded DEANNA, 40s, with a huge nose, reads an Eternal Spirit MAGAZINE.

Wrapped in only a towel, Brandon enters from
the bathroom. Beside a dresser, he fidgets
indecisively.

                    DEANNA
          I thought we might snuggle-wuggle.

                    BRANDON
          It's pretty late.

                    DEANNA
          It's been a while.

Brandon hides behind his towel as he looks for
a t-shirt and shorts in the dresser.

                    DEANNA
          Why are you being so prudish? Is
          something wrong?

                    BRANDON
          What do you mean?

                    DEANNA
          I've been in Africa for six months!
          I would think you'd want to make
          love to me.

                    BRANDON
          I have a lot on my mind. Dad dying.
          Mom. Merry.

                    DEANNA
          Sex can release pent-up tensions.

                    BRANDON
          Sex can't change the fact that Merry
          is a malingerer.

                    DEANNA
          Give her time. She's had a lot.

                    BRANDON
          Says she's writing a movie. Won't
          make a dime.

                    DEANNA
          Do you want me to talk to her?

                    BRANDON
          She's not religious. Seems amoral.

                    DEANNA
          Is she drinking?

                    BRANDON
          Had three Mexican martinis at lunch.

                    DEANNA
          Does she have your father's disease?

                    BRANDON
          For all I know.

                    DEANNA
          Come to bed. I've missed you. We can
          just snuggle if you're not in the
          mood to wuggle.

Brandon gives up pretense, drops his towel,
and pulls on boxers, shorts, and a t-shirt.

                    BRANDON
     I've got work to make up ... all
     that time off from Father's illness
     and Mother's ...

                    DEANNA
     But it's late.

                    BRANDON
     I'm sorry, but I just can't ...

Without a glance or kiss goodbye, Brandon
leaves hurriedly.

Deanna curls into a ball and cries.

Letter Four
August 20, 1988

Dear Roland,

Mom always told me, "Everything will be hunky-dory," but the only hunky-dory thing that's happened during the past six months was my overdue divorce from Doug Garner and the legal return of my maiden name "Mayfield," which Sigrid must have told you about, but you didn't care about that either. You always seemed intimidated by my marriage to a professional golfer, jokingly referring to him as Merry's One Iron because, as you put it, "He seems of so little use to you."

Good little martyr, I would reply with something like, "Doug's a pretty good guy when you get down to it." Shit. The truth was, I spent nineteen years serving as a mere spike cleaner for Doug's alligator golf shoes, until he revealed his true character in a global gambling scam, got kicked off the PGA tour, and then ran off with a barmaid with two kids.

Sigrid told me by phone last week that Doug is now working as a loading-dock foreman, paying the barmaid's rent and taking her kids to McDonald's—although he hasn't sent child support since I moved here.

I remember you once scoffed, "Divorce isn't enough. Only mutilation will do."

I fantasize about shooting Doug in the testicles with the Glock 27 I inherited from Dad, a semi-automatic pistol that scares the life out of me. That's why I hide it in the file cabinet behind these ramblings. Deanna wouldn't allow Brandon to have it, so Brandon urged me to "take it for protection, now that you're all alone," he reminded me.

Would shooting Doug in the balls make me an existential hero?

Perhaps I'd better take a break until I can control this piece of art— my emotion for you.

⊠   ⊠   ⊠

I am back. Odd little metaphor above, my emotion, my art, eh?

"The unconscious mind has immense power. Like icebergs, most of your mind's operation remains out of sight." That's what you retorted after I naively asked whether major writers planned each metaphor before writing their works. Or were these dreamed up later by film professors who had nothing to do but have affairs with tall, frizzy-haired divorcées?

There I go again. I want only good feelings.

⊠   ⊠   ⊠

I will now tell you about my wild experience at Aqua Fest, an annual festival of Austin's water. Contrary to the notions of an Ivy Leaguer like you, Texas has many rivers and lakes. And Central Texas has a 150-mile stretch of six clear, deep, lovely Highland Lakes, nestled between green rolling hills that are lush with juniper and oak—a forest of green that turns to a violet haze at sundown. The Violet Crown they call it, an atmospheric phenomenon.

The six lakes are formed by a series of dams on the Colorado River—not the one out West; this Colorado River begins and ends in Texas. Evidently, some tequila-riddled mapmakers confused it with another river, so this one wound up named "Colorado," which means reddish in Spanish, even though the river is not red at all.

There's a patriotic movement to rename our Colorado River the Texas River. I don't feel Texan, yet. You may have ruined me for that.

I read about Aqua Fest in the *Austin American-Statesman* newspaper. The article said I should head downtown for the Light Parade at Town Lake—a calm, wide, dark-green stretch through the city that is lined by trails, parks, and hotels. Because the newspaper predicted a crowd of fifty thousand, I wondered if the Light Parade might be a good place to bump into a wealthy prince of a man who could save me from financial doom.

So I donned a slinky red sundress with matching red sandals and bag, hopped in the VU Cutlass, and stopped off at a 7-Eleven to buy a gold plastic Skipper Pin (this gets you inside various venues). Then I went to the Hyatt Hotel, parked in the lot, and walked inside to the atrium. It was 5:00 p.m. The Light Parade didn't start until 9:00 p.m. What to do? I perched at the bar between tall, potted ficus trees, flashed my Skipper Pin for the drink discount, and ordered a martini. And another.

For a while, I chatted with a rather cute University of Texas engineering student who sidled up beside me at the bar. I think his name was Glenn. At age twenty-nine, he was a late-blooming student but nine years too young for me. Still, he was funny, and we had a good chat.

Off in a corner, a band twanged, "Wasting Away in Margaritaville." Glenn and I laughed at that, since we were wasting away quickly. Then he gave me that flirtatious twinkle you guys always do, but as I said, he seemed too young for my thirty-eight years.

By 8:30 p.m. crowds were swarming into the lobby. I desperately needed to go potty, so I asked Glenn to save my spot while I clutched my now third martini in search of a bathroom, not comprehending for the life of me, that I was slap-dab in the middle of the famous-to-everybody-but-me Aqua Fest Commodore's Gala Flotilla.

As my search for a potty continued, I spotted a thin silver-blond man with wire-rimmed glasses. He was dressed in a mustard-yellow uniform like an old-style Manhattan doorman might wear, with white pom-poms on each shoulder and a dark gold, braided baldric across his chest. In my martini'd wisdom, I assumed that this blond fellow was the Hyatt doorman.

"Excuse me, but where's the ladies' restroom?"

He peered from behind his glasses and scoffed. "Ma'am, I have absolutely no idea."

Even in my stupor, I realized I had offended him somehow, but I didn't understand why, until I wandered through the huge crowd and noticed that there were about a hundred of these similarly costumed doormen, shaking hands and calling each other "commodore."

One waved and shouted, "Bob! Admiral Redford!"

As the silver-blond turned and grinned widely, my foggy comprehension lifted. My doorman was megastar Robert Redford! Why hadn't I recognized him? His face was in the newspaper that morning as Honorary Admiral of Aqua Fest. The article said he used to spend summers in Austin as a child.

And so, my gin-infused brain had asked Robert Redford where I could go tee-tee.

Gads.

Drunkenly, I decided I must apologize to this megastar, but as I approached, he and the crowd began surging through the atrium and out the hotel's back doors, then across a patio and down steps toward the shores of Town Lake.

In a fever, I followed the crush. By the time I reached the water's edge, Robert Redford had boarded a speedboat that suddenly was roaring off. I stood near the dock while the rest of the crowd—probably a hundred drunken commodores, and another hundred of their similarly drunken ladies—boarded about twenty-five large speedboats.

Each boat driver revved his engine, trying to impress the others or themselves. Water flumed behind propellers. Waves splashed into other boats. Drivers, commodores, and ladies laughed and wiped off the spray. Then each boat zoomed off to join Robert Redford. And I was left standing on the dock.

"Aren't you going with them?"

I turned. The voice belonged to a muscled Hispanic policeman.

He gave me a flirtatious grin. "They can't leave you onshore. You're prettier than the rest."

I was just about to tell him I wasn't with the group, when a speedboat suddenly zoomed back.

The driver steered beside the dock. "They sent me back to get you!"

Oh dear, the commodores thought they had left me behind. I glanced at the cop. He motioned me forward, as if to say, "Here, beautiful and obviously important lady, I, a hunky Austin Police officer, shall help you rejoin the honored movie star's party."

Maybe it was the gin. Maybe I have no grip on reality. Or maybe I'm an actor in some film yet to be produced, but I took the policeman's arm and stepped onto the boat.

It tipped a bit, and I teetered from seat to seat until I managed to plop beside the driver without falling or, more importantly, spilling my martini. As he revved the engine, I waved an Elizabethan hand to the cop on shore. Then vroom, my boat headed beyond the city lights where Town Lake's waters loomed dark and wide.

I had no idea why I was on this boat, where we were going, or what I would do when I got there, but I simply grinned and told myself, "Act."

My boat's driver, a rather grizzly man with a cigarette hanging from his lips, shouted above the engine roar, "Sorry you got left behind."

"I didn't want to intrude," I shouted back.

"Yeah, we're all a little drunk out here."

Lines from a Pinter play?

Our boat rounded a bend to the east, where we rendezvoused with the twenty other speedboats, each loaded with commodores and sundressed women. The group cheered when my boat arrived.

"We couldn't start until you got here," someone shouted.

"It's about time, Goddess," someone else called out.

I didn't know who they thought I was, but I smiled and waved to these wonderful new friends who, like me, probably didn't know each other but were afraid to admit it.

In the darkness, I searched for Robert Redford, but I couldn't see more than silhouettes of doorman suits.

Then somebody shouted, "Let's get this show on the road!"

Chaos ensued. Engines revved, accompanied by "Whoops," "Holy shits," and "Goddamns!" as all the boats got in line.

Just beyond our boats, much larger shapes loomed on the water. These turned out to be the parade floats. As my boat slowly idled, the other speedboats hooked one-by-one to an assigned float. Then the driver attached an electrical cord of some kind, and the float's lights blinked on. After that, the boat pulled the float westward on the lake.

Aha! A "Light Parade."

The first float was a blinking replica of the University of Texas Tower. When the tower's orange lights flashed on, a huge crowd along the shores burst into cheers. The University of Texas band must have been somewhere, because you could hear them blasting another annoying rendition of "The Eyes of Texas Are Upon You."

When the second float's lights flipped on, I could see it was a replica of the Alamo in San Antonio. Then another float flashed on—a gigantic longhorn steer, the UT mascot. And another was a huge red, white, and blue Lone Star flag. On and on this went, a lighted display of Texana floating down Town Lake behind the commodores' boats.

As my driver idled our boat and I sipped my martini, I wondered which float my boat was supposed to pull, until there was only one float left. Guess whose float turned out to be the *pièce de résistance* of the Aqua Fest Light Parade!

Roland, you would get such a laugh out of this. My float was a massive replica of the Texas State Capitol. It looks just like the capitol in Washington, DC, except the Texas version is made of pink granite from the Texas Hill Country. It also has a silver-white goddess on top that holds aloft the Lone Star.

My driver revved the engine and steered us next to the float. "There you go, honey." He gestured for me to step overboard.

"Who, me?"

"Just step on over. Here, I'll help you."

Double martini and red purse in hand, I took his arm and teetered onto the float. In an opposite reaction, the float almost threw me back, which might have been a blessing, but I managed to retain enough coordination to stay upright. As I wondered what to do next, the driver hooked my float to the back of his boat. Then, he hooked up the cords, and the lights flashed on.

They were bright *pink*, Roland, bathing the float in color like the pink granite capitol in midtown. And here I had worn a *red* dress.

My driver pointed me to a ladder at the back of the capitol, so I climbed to a platform where I saw an entry to the dome. Inside it, a second ladder led me to a smaller platform at the dome's tip-top, where I saw a pole with a flashing gold Lone Star. That's when I realized I was supposed to be the Goddess of the Capitol.

No telling what happened to the woman who was supposed to be me, but surely she was somewhere, wearing an all-white gown that a real goddess might have worn for such an occasion.

Feeling surreal, I took my position—gold star in one hand, martini in the other—and waved my star at the silhouettes shadowing the shores.

Overhead, fireworks started bursting as people cheered, and the UT band played "Deep in the Heart of Texas."

I got a bang out of this absurdity and started shrieking in laughter, with the boat engine thankfully drowning my din. Can you imagine this scene? Me, the Goddess of the Capitol, floating on a wide river through downtown Austin, waving to a hundred thousand people on the banks, while magnificent fireworks boomed in orgasms above. Meredith Mayfield, prodigal daughter, had come home to Texas.

I slugged the last of my martini and hurled the glass overboard in an irrational gesture that said, "I am; therefore, fuck yourself."

As the float reached the center of downtown, I melted into the moment—my emotions vacillating between *Franny and Zooey*'s heights of glee and *Grendel*'s despair. I stared beyond the fireworks, recalling the losses of my parents, husband, money, home, and the you I never had.

"Little Merry's had an accident, deep in the heart of Texas," my cries echoed, as my float passed under Congress Avenue Bridge toward First Street, then west to the Lamar Bridge. Dissolving in tears, I bravely waved my gold star until my float reached Zilker Park. There, each float's lights went dark, and each speedboat unhooked from its float and circled toward the middle of the river.

Through my mascara-bled eyes, I spied Robert Redford in his admiral costume, standing in the bow of the lead boat, looking like a thin George Washington. I would have waved, but I had cried off my makeup. And since our vain Merry Mayfield could not reveal to a megastar and hundreds of commodores that the Goddess of the Texas Capitol was actually an impostor, I panicked. From my high perch, I gripped my purse and took a flying leap.

Floosh! My red sundress floated around my ears. Cold, slick, and thick, the water sucked me down. For a brief moment, it occurred to me that if this were an art film, I'd stay under forever. But good existential heroine that you made of me, I kicked upward until I broke surface and grabbed for breath. Then, in a stunned, silent breaststroke, I swam ashore—astounding the beer-saturated, whoopee crowd who gawked as I struggled uphill in my dripping red dress.

"Lordy, look what slithered out of the lake," one drunk said.

His girlfriend swatted him. "Hush, Charlie. She fell off a damn boat. Honey, need some help?"

"No thanks. I just ... well ..."

As they stared, I decided to make a run for it—no guts, no balls to pretend now. I urgently stumbled uphill as people gathered blankets, coolers, and beer cans. Doggedly, I clambered in my wet red sandals across the Lamar Bridge and back to the Hyatt, where my Very Used Chariot awaited.

Luckily, I'd had enough sense to hold on to my purse. I somehow made it home alive, slithered past the kids, showered, and crashed. A death-like hangover was my penance Sunday morning.

But there was redemption: my picture was on the front page of Sunday's newspaper, a half-page full-color photo of my pink capitol float alight on the glimmering water, while fireworks blasted above. I could just make out a faint image of my black bobbed hair and bare arms raised, one holding the star, the other the martini.

I sent a clip to Sigrid, knowing she will show it to you. Will you call?

Love,
Merry

SCENE 5

EXT. GLENN'S TRAILER PARK — 1988 — DAY

Glenn's small aluminum trailer is one of many
lined up in a student-housing complex on the
shores of Lake Austin.

INT. GLENN'S TRAILER — DAY

IN BACK OFFICE

Glenn uses scissors to cut out a NEWSPAPER
PHOTO of Merry on the Aqua Fest float. He tacks
it to a cork board.

Also on the cork board, there are numerous
PHOTOS showing Merry in only a nightie or
undies.

                    GLENN
          Delicious, it's time for us to meet
          again.

Letter Five
September 10, 1988

Dear Roland,

I got laid for the first time since my divorce! I picked him up at a singles bar, or he picked me up, not sure who picked up whom, but I definitely had a need. Prior to doing it, I had felt so alienated. Just to talk to someone, I have phoned our pal Sigrid at odd hours—although she spends most of my long-distance charges complaining about her tepid sex life with that pathetic actor pal of yours, Frank Huber.

So, with this kind of non-life going on, I decided to get laid. (I can see you scowling.) Yes, I am rationalizing, primarily because I know you would be disappointed in my method of jolting myself out of a funk, i.e., to fuck out of a funk!

At least I made him use a condom. This AIDS thing is scary.

His name is Glenn. Meeting him was a coincidence because he was the same engineering student I met at the Hyatt bar during Aqua Fest. Only this time, I ran into him at Donn's Depot, a piano bar on Fifth Street, built from several old railroad cars and a caboose. The interior is dark-cocktail-lounge red: carpet, draperies, and flocked wallpaper. Donn is the star singer. He plays piano and sings every popular Elvis song you know. Vegas-lounge stuff with a three-piece band. Except Donn's voice is quite good. I usually sit at the piano bar, get maudlin, and sing along. It's cathartic. Sometimes I try to harmonize with Donn, but one time, he grimaced and whispered to his guitarist, "Oh no. There she goes again."

Glenn is shorter than I like and, as I've said, nine years younger, but he is cute. Brown hair, wicked brown eyes, thankfully clean shaven. His eyes have a way of penetrating the conversation, as if everything he says means something beyond the words.

His opening line was, "This time, maybe you won't run off?"

We slow danced. Very close. Then he took me to a back table where we told our life stories until closing time.

"I've left Alaska forever. Had to."

"That doesn't sound good."

"Six years ago, a girl I was dating wasn't quite sixteen, but she'd told me she was eighteen. A couple of cops caught us in my van one night and hauled me in for statutory rape. It wasn't fair, but it was the fact."

"That's why you had to leave?"

"Felony rape conviction with probation. Hard to get a decent job with that on your record. So I decided to go back to school, study geological engineering, maybe start an oil company. I inherited a bit of money."

We danced the last dance, "An American Trilogy," that inspirational piece. It's a slow one that builds, ending with "Glory, Glory, Hallelujah," and you feel like marching off to war or to bed and you don't care which.

As Glenn's thigh pressed into my crotch, I melted into the moment, enjoying the sensation of being held and inhaling a man's scent. After the lights came on and the bartenders told us, "You don't have to go home, but you can't stay here," we walked outside to my VU Cutlass, where Glenn asked me to drive with him back to his place. When I said no, he asked for my number. I handed him one of my new cards with my title, "Meredith Mayfield, Screenwriter."

He said, "I'll call you tomorrow."

I wasn't sure I wanted him to, but when I got inside and closed my car door, Glenn stood and stared through my windshield. It was like that scene in *Body Heat*, remember, when William Hurt lusts after Kathleen Turner outside her glass front door, and she stands inside, fearful, yet daring and beckoning.

What can I say? To avoid broken glass, I opened the car door.

We threw ourselves at one another.

Unlike you, Glenn was a wonderful kisser, which we engaged in for probably at least a half hour. Then we spent the next hour coitally interacting every way humans can imagine in a Very Used Cutlass. Yes, right there in Donn's parking lot. We floundered in the front seat, in the back, then over the seats. The car windows were so steamed it looked like a thunderstorm was going on inside.

Although we were at it for an hour, Glenn claimed the quarters were too close, so he asked me to come (accidental play on words) back to his place, which was nearby. We didn't bother putting on clothes. Glenn drove my Cutlass fifty buck-naked miles an hour down Lake Austin Blvd., while I curled in his lap and toyed with his stiffly swaying apparatus.

Can you imagine what some policeman would have done to us?

After the Cutlass jolted into the gravel driveway of what turned out to be a student trailer park beside Lake Austin, we ran like nymphs into Glenn's trailer. Inside, it was existentially sparse but not too grungy. Glenn was at least neat, having spent time in the marines before getting in trouble with the fifteen-year-old in Alaska.

His black Doberman named Natasha jumped on Glenn with joy. He grabbed a robe and took the dog outside. Poor thing had been locked in all evening. While they were gone, I found a towel to wrap my nakedness in, then sat on Glenn's bed, not sure whether I should be there.

After he came inside, he closed the bedroom door, but Natasha kept scratching and barking. So he let her in and told her to "sit-stay" while we flailed onto the bed and resumed our thrashing. Natasha obediently watched but added the occasional growl that intimidated the hell out of me. I wasn't getting anywhere sexually, and Glenn took forever to come. It was one of those drunken ordeals women go through, where you hang on to the mattress while the fellow whams away.

When he finally shouted, "I'm coming!" I was so relieved, I laughed.

Afterward, he rolled off in exhaustion. Total time must have been three hours. Yet, I did not manage one orgasm. Couldn't with six martinis in my bloodstream and a Doberman poised to give me an episiotomy. Don't get me wrong. I enjoyed the act, the drama, and athleticism of the event. I even got quite tingly when I managed to forget Natasha.

I suppose I wanted to tell you this to make you jealous. I also hoped to document that I am alive. Sex is self-confirmation, Roland. I think it's a darn shame you didn't have enough gonads to self-confirm with me.

✉   ✉   ✉

Now I ask: What is a writer to do with such material? Is this something for a film that would be important enough for scholars like you to decree it a masterpiece? Perhaps I could use it to enhance your cynical philosophies about males and females.

"The biggest mistake men and women make in marriage is not that they have sex with each other, but they try to do it for a lifetime," you once spouted to our class while discussing Edward Albee's *Who's Afraid of Virginia Woolf?*

Bah! Spoken by a man who probably can't get it up.

Regardless, I will discover how to use this scene (and Natasha) in my screenplay *Those Who Try*. Yes, that's the title. And I will find a producer. At least I am trying. Better than staying in a bad marriage, like you do. Better than the way Jillian feeds off being your mistress.

My goodness, you've spent twenty-plus years trying to write a masterpiece for the stage. Did your affair with Jillian begin after you realized you were on a slow slide into failure, that all your scholarship and brains couldn't make a successful writer out of you because art is emotion and you're afraid to feel anything, so how in the hell can you portray it?

"Those who can't do, teach. Those who try are the true existential heroes."

Your words back at you—you intellectual chickenshit.

Love,
Merry

SCENE 6

INT. MERRY'S DUPLEX — 1988 — DAY

IN THE KITCHEN

A clock shows 5:30 p.m. Merry is doggedly cooking dinner when she hears a DOORBELL.

From down the hall, Nora calls out.

> NORA (O.S)
> I've got it, Mom. Wonder who it is.

IN THE FOYER

Nora in tight jeans and a low-cut t-shirt opens the door.

Standing outside, also in jeans, Glenn smiles widely and gives Nora a flirtatious once over.

> GLENN
> You must be Nora. You don't look a bit like your mom. How'd you wind up so tall and blond?

Before Nora can answer, Merry comes to the door, but her smile quickly turns to concern.

> MERRY
Glenn! What are you doing here?

> GLENN
Is that how you greet a friend?

> MERRY
Nora, I've got this.

> NORA
Mom!

> MERRY
Nora, please wash up. Dinner's
almost ready.

> NORA
Excuse me, Glenn, but my mother is
rudely sending me down the hall.

Nora sullenly walks away but turns to give
Glenn a playful smile.

> NORA
Nice to meet you, Glenn.

> MERRY
Nora ...

> GLENN
Sounds like I'm right on time.

> MERRY
Glenn, I didn't invite you to
dinner.

                    GLENN
     But I'm here. Aren't you going to
     ask me in?

Merry glances to see if Nora can hear. She's
just around a corner, but Merry can't see her.

                    MERRY
     Look, I enjoyed meeting you, but
     you're too young for me.

                    GLENN
     You didn't act that way the other
     night. I thought we had a good time.

Eyebrows raised, Nora leans closer to hear
better.

                    MERRY
               (whispering)
     Glenn, it was a wild, crazy night. I
     drank too much, that's all.

                    GLENN
     I'll call you later to talk.

                    MERRY
     I don't think that's a good idea.

                    GLENN
     I'll call you later.

                    MERRY
     Glenn, I don't mean to be rude...

As Merry attempts to close the door, Glenn extends a foot to stop it.

Merry gives him daring glare.

                    MERRY
          Nora, Claire, Scottie, dinner!

The three kids shuffle by the front door on their way to the kitchen, but each gives Glenn a curious glance.

Frustrated, Glenn backs away but gives Merry a look that says he's not through with her.

Merry closes the door, locks it in relief.

IN THE KITCHEN

The kids gather at a small dining table.

                    CLAIRE
          Who was that, Mom?

                    MERRY
          Definitely not my prince. He's too
          young.

                    NORA
          I thought he was cute.

                    MERRY
          Nora, he's not your prince either.

Letter Six
September 13, 1988

Dear Roland,

Darn it, that guy Glenn called me last night. Evidently, he cannot take no for an answer. I lied and told him I was seeing someone, but he murmured "Uh, huh?" as if he didn't believe me. I was polite but firm.

Hopefully, he won't call again. I have enough to deal with.

Deanna dropped by this morning. I was still in my nightgown, hair a mess. Still am, as I write this to you. I had gone back to bed after driving the kids to school at 7:00 a.m. They start school so early these days. So, I crawled in bed and must have sunk into a stupor. A few too many last night, but I awoke dreaming about a doorbell ringing. And I could hear Deanna's high-pitched voice. "Merry? Is this your side of the duplex? I'm not sure I'm ringing the correct doorbell."

Phooey. It wasn't a dream.

I let her in. "If you'd let me know you were coming ..."

She smiled like a fake friend. "Got a cup of coffee, sister?"

I was stuck. So I threw on a robe, made coffee, and we went to my tiny living room. Deanna was spiffed up in a black clerical blouse and white priest's collar. That set me back. Was this a minister's call?

To delay, I opened the drapes to view what was a gloomy, rainy day. "Austin always needs rain, but I don't like the gloom when we actually get a storm."

Apparently, Deanna was not interested in pleasantries. She began, "Brandon and I are concerned about your lack of spiritual faith."

Boom.

My first impulse was to run to my bedroom and slam the door, but if I did, Deanna would tell Brandon, and he would give me holy shit. So I replied as pleasantly as I could, "You might say I'm in a period of agnostic existentialism, and I like it that way."

"Brandon's heart would break if he heard you say that. He has high hopes for you."

"I have high hopes for me too, Deanna."

"That's a positive. Brandon and I want you to join us for Sunday services."

"I'm not sure the Eternal Spirit Center is where I need to be. Not with my attitude about organized religion, good ol' God, and the universe."

"The video of your father's funeral was a good sample of the Eternal Spirit service."

"I haven't seen the video."

"Don't you think you should at least watch it? Brandon filmed it for your benefit, since you couldn't see your way clear to attend."

"See my way clear? My trailer broke down in a raging storm."

"Most people don't haul boats to their father's funeral."

"Let's not forget the timing. I was in the middle of a fifteen-hundred-mile move. Brandon insisted on having a religious service, although my father was an atheist. I tried to attend the service but was unable to get there without causing my children, my dogs, and myself debilitating stress."

"Brandon said he would have helped you."

"Deanna, I will not discuss this further. I'm simply not ready to view the video. I'm sure you did a great job of sanctifying our father's spirit whether he wanted it sanctified or not."

Deanna adjusted her collar. "Brandon paid $1,000 for that videotape. And I officiated *gratis*. I should think you'd feel an obligation."

"Obligation? Tell me, Deanna, during Dad's funeral, did you ever wonder how your Eternal Spirit mumbo-jumbo and Brandon's $1,000 could make one holy difference in the disposition of Dad's soul when the man didn't believe in God?"

"Merry, Merry, Merry. I realize you're adjusting to all that's happened. But you're misdirecting your anger at me instead of putting your energy into positive goals. Brandon told me you were considering real estate. I think that would be a good career for you. Brandon has a friend who is a manager for B. J. Hathaway, and Brandon said—"

"Now it's you too? Real estate! Good God."

"You don't have to take the Lord's name in vain."

She went on, but I remained silent until she got the idea I was done with her sermon. So, she thanked me for the coffee and left. I know she'll tell Brandon I was rude.

⊠   ⊠   ⊠

No, I did not make a martini. I'm drinking coffee to cure my hangover.

I must admit that Deanna was partly right. Instead of going back to bed this morning, I could be sitting at an open house and showing people where the master bedroom is, maybe even making a sales commission. Better yet, instead of writing to you, I could be working on my script, trying to be the writer you taught me to be. Trying to impress you but never knowing if I did. Wondering always how you felt. Never knowing. Just observing your behaviors.

Oh, how I watched you. It only took me one session of your Creative Writing History class before I was obsessed. You came in ten minutes late, angled your corduroyed rear upon a desk, and said, "Forgive my tardiness, but I've just returned from a summer on Majorca, and I'm suffering from jet lag, cultural shock, and an intense hangover."

I was the only student who laughed—most of the class were nineteen-year-old preppies.

But I was quickly spellbound as your lyrical tenor dissected this stage play, that novel, or those films in a way I had no idea anyone could or would. After that first class, I brought a recorder to tape your every word—not so I could learn more but so I could hear your voice whenever I wanted. I was determined to know you.

One day, I stood by a hallway fountain after class and bent to the spout every few minutes, peeking under my armpit for a glimpse of you. After five minutes of this posturing, you came out and headed toward the stairs. I sucked down another mouthful and listened. When I heard your shoes hit the first landing, I followed down the steps to the second-floor alcove while you went on down.

In that alcove, there is a high octagonal window—ever notice it? I stood on tiptoes and peered over the dusty stone sill to see if you would exit the first-floor below. I was giddy when that worked—within seconds, you were outside, you in your olive tweed jacket, tan cords, and tweed ivy cap. You bounded down the steps, angled across a walkway, then jogged down Broadway. I watched your cap rhythmically bob until you entered a red brick building one full block away.

Now I knew where you went after class. Elated, I followed your path until I saw the sign. Columbia University Film Program. Ha! This was the first time I knew where the offices were.

The next class, instead of parking in a student garage, I arrived a half hour early and parked near your office. It took forever to find a space, but through my windshield, I watched for fifteen agonizing minutes until I saw you drive by, then turn into a faculty garage.

I almost shrieked. Your car was a scarred black Jeep CJ-7 with a tattered black-vinyl top and plastic back windows. A beat-up Jeep. To me, that symbolized you were human. Approachable. Possible.

Can you imagine someone getting such a charge out of this?

I watched you go inside the film office, then later come out and head up Broadway toward class. I silently got out of my car but lagged behind, trembling that you would see me. Surely you could hear my heart pounding through my *faux* leopard jacket. Could you feel my excitement? Art is emotion, isn't it? Couldn't you feel me there?

I was so out of breath; I could barely make it up the block, or up three flights after you. By the time I got to the classroom, I took a desk in the back. You weren't there yet. I tried to calm my breathing. Moments later, the door opened. You rushed in and scanned the room. When your eyes got to mine, I panicked. Surely you knew I had been spying.

"Yes, my dears. What were we discussing? Stoppard? Mamet? Genet? No. Mere wishful thought. We've been wallowing in Henry James's *The American* all week. Bah! Our only consolation is that Henry is so dead he cannot bore us anymore. Now, shall we turn to Act 3?"

All through your lecture, I could not focus. I was so full of my success as a spy.

When class ended, I rushed out while you bantered with a student. I went down a flight to the second-floor alcove and waited as students jostled by. Five minutes must have passed before I heard your voice echo above, wittily chatting with someone as you began down the stairs.

You were coming.

I started down. At the ground floor, I opened the door, went outside, and fumbled with my purse—pretending to look for my car keys. I felt so transparent. I took small, deliberate steps until I heard your laughter. I walked slowly, making sure, of course, from peripheral glances, that you saw me.

You took the bait. I repeated this behavior after each class, and within a week, you caught up and passed me, saying something silly like, "Well, if it isn't Columbia's own Barbara Nicklaus." That was the first of your sarcastic jokes about my being a pro golfer's wife, admitted only because you asked students to reveal something others might not know.

Your sarcasm got my goat. But it didn't take much longer before we were walking side by side, always accidentally on purpose. We did that for the next six years, all the way through my MFA. Six years!

But I wanted more. I wanted to know you.

So after classes I started waiting in my car, watching until your Jeep roared out of the faculty garage. Then I would follow until you took an exit to Jersey.

But one afternoon, your Jeep led me to the Raven, the notorious campus bar I'd heard about. This was perfect! I could saunter inside like any film student, and you could not possibly imagine I had followed you. So I parked across from the Raven and waited for you to go inside. But—ah, so typically contrary to my plans—you nervously paced on the sidewalk out front, until a tall, thin, frizzy-headed, but unfortunately pretty brunette in a street-length black hooded cape got out of a cab. You two hugged fondly, like lovers of long standing.

Shit. A golf ball in my gut—this was the woman I'd seen after class. You would say, "Well, hello," as though sardonically surprised to see her, and the two of you would head downstairs, leaving me to walk alone. I blindly assumed she was a faculty colleague. But now I could see that she was your girlfriend. Your mistress!

That killed me. And yet, I dredged up enough courage to go inside the Raven. Although the interior was dimly lit, I spotted you and Jillian in a back corner booth. Rather than walk your way, I sat at the bar and ordered a martini, glancing toward your booth now and then.

You were gesturing as you always do. Spouting dramatically.

I was euphoric. Spying in person was participation. I uneasily sipped my martini and waited until I couldn't stand it another second, then I got up and waltzed by your booth on the way to the ladies' room, pretending I had no idea you were there. In my peripheral vision, I could see your head turn to follow me, and I could feel your eyes as they zeroed in.

I went inside the restroom and stood in front of the mirror. To hell with your having a mistress. I leaned in and announced, "This will be." Then, with eyes focused straight ahead, I walked out and swished by your table, almost levitating with delight.

Back at my barstool, I could feel you coming. In my peripheral vision, I saw a blur, and then you were standing two feet to my right. To get my attention, you loudly ordered, "Two Guinness drafts, my good man." And then, even though the bartender was drawing your beers, you shouted louder, "Two Guinness, my good man?"

That was for my ears.

At first, I refused to turn your way. But then, you started whistling a funny tweet to get my attention, and I realized I would have to be the one. So I feigned a double-take and said, "Of all the gin joints in all the towns of the world ..."

"Well, hello, Mrs. Garner," you grinned with feigned surprise.

Two actors in a silly scene, written and produced by me.

The bartender handed you two dripping mugs. You took one in each hand, but the movement jostled your eyeglasses off-kilter, down to the bulbous end of your nose. You looked so nutty-professor-ish, I giggled.

"Mrs. Garner, I would stay for a chat, but I'm about to drop my eyeglasses, not to mention these two necessary beers." Then you tossed your head back in an attempt to levitate your glasses, except you spilled beer onto your shoes. "Drunken sot!" you shouted at yourself.

"Professor Holmes, let me help." While you held your beers, I slid off my stool and pushed your glasses up where they belonged—giving you an eyeball-to-eyeball shot of my eyes to yours. The spark between us was dynamic.

"Thank you, Mrs. Garner. Remind me to give you an A on your test."

We exchanged a flirtatious smile. Then back you went to your nervous Jillian. And back I went to my barstool. But I was neck-deep in glee.

The next time our class met, you were lecturing on *Our Town*.

"If you're looking for a romantic theme, Thornton Wilder seems to say that it's impossible for men and women to sustain the romantic passion that unites them in the first place. Yet, we humans insist on trying. We giddily marry, then bore each other with the ordinariness of life, only to mourn our losses when we look back upon our lives."

Unexpectedly, your lightning eyes centered on me. "No wonder so many unhappy Greenwich housewives take film courses and hang their hips out at the Raven."

Zap! My mind whirled. You thought I was taking film courses because I was unhappy? Maybe so. But you also thought I'd been at the Raven to meet any man who'd have me? Shit. Apparently, I'd been too good at stalking you, so you jumped to conclusions and insulted me with an alliterative line, likely dreamed up in the shower that morning.

Your insult stung. Swelled and bled for days. I sat on the back row for a week after that and didn't wait for you after class. But eventually I realized that in order to gain the respect of the brilliant Roland Holmes, I had to do it another way than hanging my hip out at the Raven. So, I became an analytic observer rather than a participatory spy. I watched you and listened for another whole semester. And, finally, from all your lectures and comedic asides, I realized that the only thing you cared about was writing for the stage and film. That's when my evolution to "screenwriter" began.

Before then, I didn't know I could be the one who imagines the magic.

Love,
Merry

SCENE 7

INT. MERRY'S DUPLEX — DAY — 1988

IN THE OFFICE

A clock says 1:00 p.m. but Merry is still
in her bathrobe and her hair is a mess. She
writes on a 1983 MACINTOSH SE, between sips
from her martini.

PHONE RINGS. Merry groans at the interruption
but picks it up.

                    MERRY
     Hello?

INT. GLENN'S TRAILER — DAY

IN BACK OFFICE

Glenn paces, a wall phone to his ear.

PHOTOS OF NORA are now tacked on the cork
bulletin board, alongside Merry's photos.

                    GLENN
     Good morning, Sexy.

INTERCUT — TELEPHONE CONVERSATION

> MERRY
>
> Who is this?

> GLENN
>
> Don't you recognize my voice by now?

> MERRY
>
> Glenn?

> GLENN
>
> That's my girl. Natasha misses you.

> MERRY
> (sighing heavily)
> Glenn, I've told you. It was just a
> wild fling.

> GLENN
>
> You women sometimes say "no" when
> you mean "yes."

> MERRY
>
> Maybe that girl in Alaska meant no.

> GLENN
> (shouting)
> That girl lied to me.

> MERRY
>
> Glenn, I'm sorry you've had
> problems, but I can't see you
> anymore. I really must insist ...
> do not call me or come to my house
> again. Do you understand?

Glenn angrily hangs up. He sets his eyes on Merry's photo.

                    GLENN
          Any more orders, Mommy?

INT. MERRY'S DUPLEX — 1988 — DAY

IN MERRY'S OFFICE

Merry hangs up the phone in dismay.

                    MERRY
          Oh dear, I think I messed up.

Letter Seven
September 13, 1988 (Cont'd.)

Dear Roland,

I'm continuing my morning entry. I actually worked on my screenplay most of today, stopping only to make dinner and guide the kids through homework, baths, and beds. But Sigrid called about an hour ago, and we both giggled ourselves silly remembering a night last May at the Raven.

"Did you ever hear more? Remember when Jillian hinted that Roland had problems in bed?" I asked.

"Enough to make me wonder," she replied.

That night in question, the Raven was packed with collegiate bodies pressed against our wooden booth. Sigrid and Frank were there, along with your conniving Jillian. We were the oh-so-smug MFA and PhD crowd, the men in tweed jackets, cord pants, and ivy caps, and the women in dark, fuzzy sweaters, plaid skirts, and knee-high leather boots. We were drunk enough, and it was late enough that you had reached your patented finger-raising stage—this time on the topic of sex.

"Ah yes, sex—the baby boomers' soma tablet. We five have the privilege of fucking our way through a revolution, this time with AIDS as our avenging god. Simply use a condom, and we can screw our hearts out. Yet, we still wake in the night and wonder why we're so miserable."

Jillian fiddled with a tendril that had escaped her French twist. "Roland, your cynicism is open. Zip it." We four giggled, but then (aha!) Jillian added, rather bitingly, "Sex can't give you a dopamine high if your lover isn't competent in the bedroom."

Zot! Things got quiet as hell. You shot her a disheartened look. She fiddled with her tendril. Abruptly, the confrontation-avoidant Frank and Sigrid stood, patted you on the shoulder, and left. Perhaps I should have left, too, but I wouldn't have missed a disagreement between you and Jillian for anything. She had pointed the finger at you, our Godot of theater arts—you weren't good in bed. At least not with her.

Pissed that this scene was playing on your stage, you stared off in dramatic pause. After a moment, you directed a comment more toward the air than to Jillian and me. "As my good friend Frank tells me, 'You can't think. You just have to do it.'" Then, dramatically, you turned to me, your eyes droplets of the Mediterranean Sea. "What about you, Merry? Would you forgive a man his occasional inadequacies?"

Wow! Before I could conjure a reply, you dashed from the table in a Tony Award exit, leaving Jillian with me, although neither of us cared for that to continue. She fidgeted, desperate for an excuse to leave, so that you two could go to her apartment and try to get yours up, which you clearly could not do on certain occasions—and I hoped this would be another.

Was that the reason? You not only were impotent as a writer but also as a lover? That would explain many things—like our next Thursday night at the Raven, when we five gathered again. Seated next to you, Jillian suffered along while you and I, a pair of riotous drunks, laughed so hard at our own jokes Jillian stood with an exasperated sigh.

"I cannot endure another 'Merry and Roland Comedy Hour.'" Then she donned her coquettish black cape and ran out.

Uh-oh. I caught your eye.

You gave me a wry smile.

Would you stay with me or follow Jillian? What did you feel for me?

Frank and Sigrid quickly excused themselves, so for once it was the two of us. We talked, laughed, and flirted until closing time. Your eyes were alight. Arm in arm, we waltzed our boozy infatuation to the Raven's icy parking lot, where we pretended to be Dutch skaters. The night was cold and moonless. We arrived at your black Jeep and climbed inside, not knowing what each expected. We giggled and shivered.

You clumsily attempted a kiss, but it was more a closed-lip peck than a kiss—were you leaving that to me? Darn. I wanted you to take me in your arms, kiss me deeply, possess me, dammit. Disappointed, I pulled back, wondering what to do, but I heard myself murmur, "Good night," which I didn't want to say, instead of, "I can't believe that was the way you kissed me," which I felt. Something between those two lines would have kept me in the car so we could figure this out, but I ran away.

You whispered, "Good night," with a bewildered smile.

I shrugged and closed the Jeep door. Scooting across the frozen lot, I made it to my Mercedes, but after I got inside, I was so stunned by your inept kiss and my escape, I couldn't feel my body. Why did I run? I started my car and let it warm up—angry at myself for lacking the courage to force the issue. If we at least attempted to make love, even if you were horrible in bed, then having you in your impotency would have been better than not knowing you at all. Wouldn't it?

What was it you said to our drama class about men and women? "In order for men and women to be friends, they have to be lovers first."

How many of us were there, naive students who enrolled at Columbia or Barnard with no idea what to study or even who we were until we met you? How many would-be writers, actors, directors, and producers have been spawned because they fell in love with your intellect the first week of Creative Writing History, a class they signed up for because it sounded like fun?

You with your balding big brain and brilliant wit. You with the ability to articulate amazing ideas about the works we studied, except you could express those thoughts while we sat like dried sponges and wondered how you knew all that.

"Art is emotion! There are oh-so many feelings in this world—pain, sorrow, love, hate, anger, despair, elation, desire, orgasm. On and on. Don't worry about your story's plot—ack! I can barely stand to say the word. Remember, there are only seven of them. But when you can jump inside each character's mind and heart, and feel along with them, you might understand what the writer was trying to express. Just don't ever say that I told you what that was."

Damn. Ever obtuse. Intimidating. Elusive.

Love,
Merry

SCENE 8

EXT. ANCHORAGE PARKING LOT — 1987 — NIGHT

1980s commercial van has Alaska LICENSE PLATE.

On the van's side, a sign says, "Dry Cleaning for Alaska's Best Pressed".

INSIDE BACK OF VAN

Between rows of plastic covered HANGING CLOTHES, Glenn lustily kisses and fondles a pretty TEEN GIRL. She's only 15, but she's wearing heavy makeup.

Glenn reaches for her jeans zipper. He smiles at Teen Girl with a question on his lips.

                    GLENN
          Wanna help me steam up the clothes?

                    TEEN GIRL
          What do you mean?

                    GLENN
          Don't play dumb. Do you want to make
          love? You know. Have sex.

>   TEEN GIRL
> I've never done it before. Not all
> the way.

>   GLENN
> How old did you say you were?

>   TEEN GIRL
> Eighteen.

>   GLENN
> But you've never had sex?

>   TEEN GIRL
> Guess everybody has a first time.

Glenn gives her a dubious look but kisses her
again—testing. The two grow more ardent, until
Glenn yanks open her jeans, and Teen Girl
pulls away.

>   TEEN GIRL
> I don't know if I want to do this.

Glenn silently ignores her and mounts
abruptly, abusively.

Teen Girl looks frightened and in pain. She
struggles to push Glenn off, but he grasps her
and violently rams away.

OUTSIDE VAN

Anchorage POLICE quietly drive in and park
beside the van.

OFFICER 1 and OFFICER 2 get out. Both hear
Teen Girl crying inside the van. They turn on
FLASHLIGHTS.

                    TEEN GIRL (O.S.)
          Stop. You're hurting me.

                    GLENN (O.S.)
               (grunting with ardor)
          Can't stop now, can't ...

                    TEEN GIRL (O.S.)
          Please. You're hurting me! Stop.

                    OFFICER 2
          Open the back.

Officer 1 opens the van door and startles Glenn
and Teen Girl with his light.

INSIDE BACK OF VAN

                    GLENN
          What the fuck?

Officer 2 shines light into girl's face.

                    OFFICER 2
          How old are you, ma'am? You got ID?

                    TEEN GIRL
          Just my Learner's Permit.

She fumbles for her PURSE and gives an ID CARD
to Officer 2.

                    OFFICER 2
        This says you're fifteen.

                    GLENN
        Goddamn it! She told me she's
        eighteen.

                    OFFICER 1
        But she also told you to stop.

                    GLENN
        You know how it is. A guy can't
        stop—

                    OFFICER 2
        Yeah, sure. We've got to take you
        two downtown. Honey, you can call
        your parents from there.

                    TEEN GIRL
        Don't tell my parents. I don't want
        them to know. They'll kill me.

                    OFFICER 2
        State law, young lady. Age of
        consent in Alaska is sixteen.

IN PARKING LOT

Officer 2 holds a WALKIE-TALKIE.

                    OFFICER 2
        Unit 657. We need backup to take
        a young girl downtown. Rape case.
        Parking lot at Valley of the Moon.

INSIDE BACK OF VAN

> GLENN
> Goddamn cunt said she was eighteen.

> OFFICER 1
> Keep your yap shut and put your
> clothes on. We'll read you your
> rights on the way downtown.

Glenn angrily puts on his clothes.

IN PARKING LOT

Officer 1 leads Glenn to police car, cuffs him,
puts him in back, slams door. Officer 1 gets in
the driver's side but leaves that door open.

INSIDE BACK OF VAN

Teen Girl shivers and cries as she dresses.

> OFFICER 2
> Honey, he won't hurt you anymore.

INSIDE POLICE CAR

> GLENN
> I wasn't hurting her. She wanted it.

> OFFICER 1
> Take my advice. When she hollers,
> "Stop. You're hurting me,"
> something's not right.

Letter Eight
October 1, 1988

Dear Roland,

This eats my gut each time I let the realization penetrate. First off, Brandon lied.

"Merry, I'd like to take you to lunch. I'd like to spend time with my very own sister, get to know you better. We're all that's left, you know."

That's what he said, anyway. Dear Pluppy Brandon is good at guilt.

We met at Las Palomas, a Mexican restaurant in West Lake Hills. DPB was all smiles as he greeted me, then led me to a table where—how could I have envisioned a scene otherwise—his friend awaited, the manager for B. J. Hathaway Real Estate.

Jack Carleton's smile was one you would expect from a recruitment manager in search of fresh meat.

⊠   ⊠   ⊠

INT. MEXICAN RESTAURANT — DAY

Brandon escorts Merry to a table, where he gives Merry an optimistic nod.

Greeting them, JACK, about 40, smiles lewdly.

                    BRANDON
        Merry, I'd like you to meet Jack
        Carleton, recruitment manager for B.
        J. Hathaway in West Lake Hills.

Jack shakes Merry's hand but fondles her palm
with his fingers.

Merry yanks her hand away and wipes it on her
skirt, making a "eeeeuuuuu" face.

As all three take a seat, Merry shoots Brandon
a glare.

A WAITER hands out menus.

> BRANDON
> Well now, let's peruse the menu
> before we talk business. I highly
> recommend the *fajitas*. Or try
> the chicken *chile relleno*. It's
> fabulous! Save room for the *flan* too.

> MERRY
> (muttering)
> Brandon. Captain of the world.

> JACK
> What did she say?

Waiter interrupts and sets bowls of CHIPS and
SALSA on the table.

> WAITER
> What can I start you off with besides
> water?

> BRANDON
> Just iced teas for me and my sister.

                         MERRY
          I'll have two margaritas. No salt.

                        WAITER
          One of those days?

Brandon glares. Merry gives him an icy stare.

Waiter leaves to get drinks.

Brandon, Merry, and Jack look over menus.

Waiter returns, serves iced teas to the men
and two Margaritas with straws for Merry.

                         JACK
          So, Brandon tells me you want to
          join forces with the best real
          estate company in Austin.

Merry gleefully sucks down her first margarita.
Brandon squirms.

                        MERRY
          Jack, your remark is premature. I
          would be willing to hear a short
          presentation about real estate
          sales, but you should understand
          that this meeting was a surprise to
          me. I won't be so rude as to put you
          in the middle of my brother's quest
          to control my destiny, so why don't
          you say your speech and we can get
          the hell out of here?

As Brandon glares, Merry smiles smugly.

                    JACK
          Ah, Merry, let's keep an open
          mind. Real estate is the most
          vibrant industry in Austin. This
          town is a mecca for high-tech firms
          escaping the California price tag. I
          guarantee you'll make $80,000 your
          first year, especially if you work
          out of the West Lake Hills office.
          Who knows? With your looks, the
          sky's the limit, honey.

                    MERRY
          I don't like to be called honey.

                    BRANDON
          Merry ...

                    MERRY
          I must add that making money is not
          my only goal.

                    JACK
          Who doesn't like money?

                    MERRY
          My creative interests take priority.
          Thanks to a small inheritance,
          and if I live in a rented duplex
          and drive an old car, I'll have
          enough funds to last two years.
          During that time, I am going to
          finish a screenplay. Yes, although
          Brandon will not acknowledge this,

```
I am trying to be a screenwriter,
not a real estate agent. And I am
determined that Brandon will not
stand in my way.
```

```
As the two men exchange disdainful glances,
Merry swills her second margarita. Then she
picks up the CHIPS and SALSA, and dumps both
bowls on Brandon's crotch.
```

✉ ✉ ✉

Okay, okay, okay. I did not verbally assault Jack and dump salsa on Brandon. However, I did have a couple of margaritas. Actually three.

Here's what really happened: Although Brandon tricked me into meeting him, I behaved like a good little sister and greeted Jack Carleton pleasantly. We had a lovely, controlled lunch, during which Jack told me everything that Brandon wanted to know about real estate and the B. J. Hathaway company.

I smiled, nodded, and said, "Oh yes, Jack. This sounds like something I might enjoy. Thanks so much for all you've done."

Why did I do this? Because I want to trick Brandon into thinking I am a responsible, sober, and mature woman. When he thinks that, he will be wrong. And I will have beaten him.

See?

To wit: I enrolled in my first real estate course at Austin Community College, which coincidentally is one block from Brandon's office at Austin Search for Knowledge (ASK). My class is called Fundamentals of Real Estate, and I promise I will hate it. But I'll do it. I might even drop by Brandon's office, take him to lunch, and drink cold-sober iced tea. That will show Brandon.

Perhaps I shall meet B. J. Hathaway in person someday and write a new screenplay called "Waiting for B. J. Hathaway." Aha! Then I shall truly be a screenwriter. I shall at last be?

✉ ✉ ✉

Ever since you gave my first one-act play a grade of C, I've tried so hard to define myself as "writer." That C was more like an F to you and to me. And the timing was so out of sync. You handed that play back to me on the very day you and I had our first "date."

I had finally gotten the courage to ask you for a drink. Now that I was in your writing class, you could see that I was not merely an unhappy housewife hanging her hip out at the Raven but a member of your elite Writing for the Screen and Stage.

That class was the ticket I should have bought all along.

I also took Shakespeare that semester, and Professor Clark Hundley insisted we attend an evening showing of Orson Welles's *Macbeth* in the theater screening room. As my Mercedes crunched up the icy drive into the faculty garage where Professor Hundley had gotten us passes, I spied your beat-up Jeep. My heart leapt. You were still there.

I had brought a thermos of martinis to get me through *Macbeth*, so after I saw your car, I wrote a cutesy note, "Although I fear that parking my Mercedes near your Jeep might give these two a chance to reproduce mutant offspring, I am trapped in the screening room with Professor Hundley and cannot do a thing to contracept it. I will head to the Raven afterward. Will I see you there?"

Imagine my excitement as I suffered through the film, imagining that you had been to your car by then. You had found my note. Soon, you and I would be you and me.

When I escaped the seminar, I rushed to my car, but lo and behold, your Jeep was still in the garage with my damn note on the windshield. That meant you were still inside. If I left for the Raven and you came out later to find the note, then my joke about our cars wouldn't make sense.

Just as I reached for the note on your windshield, your tenor echoed across the cold concrete. "Stop, thief. Get your hands off my car."

Flustered, I suffered through your silly accusations of car pandering, until you grabbed my note and read it loudly, your steamy breath rising into the cold air. "Ah, the Raven. Why yes! That would be wonderful."

Excitement!

"But not tonight. I operate a clandestine advertising agency and have a client waiting for these." You lifted a stack of fliers. "I figure the university owes me free copies for the salary they don't pay me. So, it will not be this time but another." You nodded a goodbye, and your glasses again fell to the end of your nose. You scoffed, pushed your rims in place, and slid into your Jeep. Then you looked at me intently. "Next Monday, after class."

Ziiiinnnnggg!

Foolishly, I dressed up in something red. Too much makeup. Demi Moore bobbed hair stiff with gel. But when I walked into the classroom, expecting to meet your eyes, I noticed a message scrawled on the chalkboard, written in a feminine script (Jillian's?). "Professor Holmes is being held for questioning by the Symbionese Liars' Army and cannot attend class today."

Clearly a joke on me, ha, ha, but I was crushed. I drove to the Raven, hoping to see your car, but your Jeep was a no-show there too. If I had known where Jillian lived, I would have driven there, such was my obsession. Damn you.

The next class was Wednesday. You reappeared but steadfastly refused to look me in the eye. Chickenshit.

So, then it, our first "date" was on Friday—the day you handed back my first attempt at a one-act play, only you had plastered a blazing-red C on it. A heart-crushing C that stood for cut! cut! through my heart.

The first day of writing class you had told us that you would never give a grade worse than a C. "If you at least try, you cannot fail," you said. But we all knew that a C meant we indeed had failed, since we had not written something A or B good.

I now realize that my first effort was amateurish, a story about a woman who wanted to be president of her bowling league. In retrospect, you should have given it an F. Yet, the very day you gave it back with a red C, you chose to follow me after class and say, "So, is it the Raven today?" As though you hadn't stood me up on Monday, ignored me on Wednesday, and humiliated me with a C moments earlier.

Shit. I considered saying no, but I had schemed for this first time together. I said, "See you there," but I was so nervous I couldn't breathe.

As I drove up Broadway, I wondered how I could impress you. I anxiously parked in the Raven lot and went inside, choosing a barstool in the middle. You came in five minutes later and slid on a stool beside me. We nodded hellos. Beyond that, I couldn't think of a thing to say.

"Well, Mrs. Garner. Tell me about the life of a pro golfer's wife."

"Oh, it's exciting when he makes the cut but depressing when he doesn't. I don't travel with him because, well, we have three kids. I think they need a stable environment. That's why Doug and I don't see much of each other. His travels."

Inane! Unhappy housewife hanging my hip out at the Raven. Why couldn't I have said something charming, intelligent, magical?

"Yes, I don't think men and women have a chance. If you'll recall my recent lecture, Wilder implied this in *Our Town*. We males puff up and beat our chests in anticipation of battles we're supposed to fight, but there aren't any, now that we've been domesticated. So we play golf and watch football, trying to placate the warrior within. And yet, what women really want is a man who will pay attention to *them*."

I nodded—dazed at the extent of your response to my boring remark. If I had one ounce of sophistication, I could have said something witty, meaningful. Anything!

Thankfully, you jumped in with another tirade. "But that's Genet, Pinter, Sartre, Beckett—any theater of the absurd writer, hell, toss in Andrei Tarkovsky and his *Stalker*. Males and females exist in zones of desire, nourished by our significant others. Yet this nourishment is entrapment; we crave to reach beyond and eventually venture to the outer limit, subconsciously putting space between ourselves and those we're leaving behind, until our yearning overwhelms us—and then we leap! We leap into a new zone, and within it, we encounter new others who also quickly entrap us. The cycle repeats. Zone to zone, awash in a sea of yearning for more."

That was you. Ever the professor, and I, ever your student. A student to whom you had given a C. Again, I was so insecure I could not even respond. And so, you went on.

"In order for me to thrive in this world, I must have my own place. I suppose you could call it my 'own zone,' an apartment in the Village. Just a room, kitchen, and bath. My wife doesn't even know about it. In fact, no one knows about it. I suppose I've just confided in you." You leaned nearer and peered through your wired rims with those starlit eyes.

Was I supposed to offer some dramatic allusion that indicated my understanding of your zone? Or was I supposed to ask you to show it to me? I didn't know what to do or say, so I blurted stupidly, "Do you have a bed?"

How crass! Here you were confiding in me, building a come-on, and relishing in it. And all I could say was, "Do you have a bed?"

Dismayed, you pulled back and mumbled, "Well yes, but I don't spend the night there." Then you turned and lifted your beer, sighing just a bit as you blew back the foam.

I had fucked it up.

I wasn't ready for you then. I had not waited for Godot. I had forced you and me beyond the moment when we should have begun. I had taken your writing class when I had absolutely no skill with which to impress you. I had put that note on your windshield before I had one word worth saying. I had been foolish, impatient, manipulative. Why?

I was so fucking empty.

✉   ✉   ✉

Oh, here we go. Back to my vacuum of a marriage. Please save us from that diatribe. To change the subject, I must tell you about an unexpected moment—a scene so surprising I couldn't have made it up.

I was downtown yesterday, driving along after my real estate class. I got to a stoplight at Sixth and Congress. Out of the corner of my eye, I noticed a man staring at me from the sidewalk. I looked, and guess who it was? Robert Redford. The movie star.

When my light turned green and I drove by, do you know what he did? He whistled. Wheet-whew! And waved at me in my VU Cutlass.

Even Robert Redford is looking for something, but he doesn't know what it is.

Love,
Merry

SCENE 9

INT. BRANDON'S BEDROOM — 1988 — NIGHT

Deanna, in fluffy pink lingerie, reads a
CHRISTIANITY TODAY magazine in bed.

Standing beside the dresser in boxer shorts,
Brandon dons plaid pj's.

> BRANDON
> At least Merry enrolled in real
> estate classes.

> DEANNA
> Guess my little talk helped.

> BRANDON
> Your talk? I took her to lunch with
> Jack Carleton of B. J. Hathaway. He
> basically offered her a job.

> DEANNA
> I told you about our heart-to-heart
> a few weeks ago.

> BRANDON
> So, you're taking credit for Merry
> going into real estate?

                        DEANNA
          Sometimes it takes a second voice to
          bring change. I counsel families all
          the time—

                        BRANDON
          There you go again. Always your
          ministry. Your success. You don't
          give me credit for anything!

                        DEANNA
          Brandon ... I'm sorry. I must've
          hurt your feelings.
                    (trying to sound sexy)
          Let me make up for it. Maybe a back
          rub. Maybe a ...

Deanna gets out of bed, takes off her gown, and
beckons Brandon with her eyes. In spite of her
nose, she has a lovely figure.

Brandon does a double take, tries to resist.

                        BRANDON
          I don't know if I'm in the mood.
          Tough day.

                        DEANNA
          Let me give you a back rub. Lie down
          beside me.

Brandon reluctantly lies on his stomach.

Deanna straddles him from behind, massages his
back, then rubs her breasts across it.

Then she moves down, presses her muff against his buttocks.

> DEANNA
>
> Now turn over.

At first Brandon hesitates, but he eventually yields and turns.

As Deanna goes down on him, he gains an erection.

> DEANNA
>
> That's perking up well.

Deanna moves upward and eagerly mounts. Her passions grow. Within seconds she's shouting.

> DEANNA
>
> Oh, Jesus, how I love you, Jesus.

Brandon glares at her in astonishment.

> BRANDON
>
> Why do I feel like you just committed adultery?

> DEANNA
>
> What do you mean? That was wonderful.

> BRANDON
>
> But you had an orgasm in ten seconds and shouted, "Oh, Jesus, how I love you, Jesus."

                    DEANNA
A woman in the throes cannot be
held responsible for what she might
scream.

                    BRANDON
My name is Brandon. If there is a
next time, you might want to shout
my name when you come.

Brandon rolls off the bed, then fumbles through
the dresser for clothes, again getting ready
to leave.

                    BRANDON
I need to clear my head.

                    DEANNA
Brandon, you don't need to go
anywhere. I didn't mean anything.

Brandon heads out.

Lying on her back, Deanna hears his CAR
ENGINE. She sighs, looks heavenward, reaches
out, and smiles amorously.

Letter Nine
October 21, 1988

Dear Roland,

It is almost midnight. I cannot sleep. Dear Pluppy Brandon (DPB) has done it again. Why do I try to maintain contact with such a man?

Today was my birthday. Thirty-nine—the final birthday before I am a Very Used Woman. My kids, bless their hearts, baked a cake, ordered a bucket from the colonel, and hosted a party—including Brandon, Deanna, and their three redheaded girls. Okay, so the guest list was slim, since the kids didn't know anyone else to invite other than my neighbor—a short, plump blonde named Pamela who might be about my age. She and I say hi, but I don't think that's cause for her to come to my birthday party.

Luckily, they did not invite (shudder) Glenn. Oh, I didn't tell you, but he called again! When I told Glenn one more time that I would not go out with him, he had the balls to ask me if Nora was dating anybody.

I exploded, "She's way too young for you!" and hung up.

I hope Glenn is not a stalker.

✉ ✉ ✉

Back to the party ... although it was small, I was in an expansive mood, even sober by the time DPB and his holy gang arrived.

Brandon gave me a bloodhound's sniff. "Well, this is a happy birthday." He nodded to Deanna, as if to convey, "Our prayers have been answered. Merry's sober."

Deanna rushed to give me a hug. "My, you smell wonderful, Merry. What is that perfume you're wearing?"

They are a disgusting pair.

Before I could think of a snide reply, the doorbell rang one more time than I expected it to. The kids raced to open it.

Claire proudly led in a Tom Selleck wannabe in a tuxedo. She frantically introduced him as Prince, then laughed hysterically.

You see, it has been the kids' joke since I divorced Doug that I would move to Texas and find my "prince"—a man who would take care of us emotionally the way Merry's One Iron did not and take care of us financially the way the Merry's One Iron once did. (Psychologists call this the Cinderella complex.)

As to this Tom Selleck look-alike, Brandon and Deanna appeared as bewildered as I.

Claire announced, "Mom's not doing so hot at finding a prince, so we ordered her one."

Deanna asked stupidly, "Did you kids buy enough chicken?"

"He's not staying for dinner," Nora said with a wry grin.

From that, I realized something was up, but it did not yet dawn on me that Prince was a stripper.

He took my arm and led me to the sofa, where he kissed me lightly, and whispered, "The batteries in my tape player went dead, but I assure you my other batteries are fully charged." He gave me a wink from the brightest pair of hazel eyes you could imagine. This guy was twinkling with erotic glee as he searched for an electrical outlet for his tape player.

At that point, I figured he was a Flashdance-style dancer.

Meanwhile, Brandon's eyes grew as wide as a shark's. He may have figured things out before I did. "What's going on here? Who is this man?"

"I don't know. It looks like we're going to have some dancing."

Brandon scowled. "What kind of dancing?"

"Merry, the girls and I must step down the hall. Our faith does not condone dancing."

"Deanna, please remember that my children and I are not of the Eternal Spirit faith. And neither was Brandon when you two married."

Then Deanna swooped out her arms like an avenging angel and shepherded her three girls down the hall into Scottie's bedroom.

Brandon stood beside a chair. "Deanna's right, Merry. This isn't appropriate—"

Suddenly, Prince's music blasted "Do You Love Me" by the Contours. My daughters crowded beside me and clapped in rhythm.

Scottie rolled his eyes and went down the hall, chiding, "I told the girls not to do this."

As Prince swiveled and bumped like Patrick Swayze, I was embarrassed by his gyrations. But I thought this was a cute idea the girls had. A dirty-dancing prince in a tuxedo. I blushed and laughed as my girls kept looking at me for reactions. It was only when Prince reached for his bow tie that I realized he was going to strip.

"You're not going to ...?" I asked innocently.

He gave me a sizzling nod and untied his tie.

My girls clapped madly and shouted, "Take it off, Prince; take it off!"

By that time, DPB's eyes were mud puddles of horror. "Stop this immediately! There are innocent children and faithful adults here!"

While my daughters cheered and I shrieked in embarrassment, Prince snatched pieces of ever-diminishing clothing from his tanned, muscular body until he was all but naked, wearing only a black-satin latex thong with the strap running between his buttocks, then upward in a protective cup over his bulging genitalia. Thank heavens for that cup. He gyrated in a grind that made volcanic eruptions of the protrusions beneath the satin latex (much larger bulges than you can manage, I'm sure).

Despite my embarrassment of having my girls see me so flustered— my cheeks must have been flaming red—I might have enjoyed this preposterous dance, except that DPB had turned into a hairy mammoth that stormed about the living room.

"Stop this smut! I should have known not to come here. I should have expected something like this from you people."

⊠　⊠　⊠

I must digress a bit to define the phrase "you people." To Brandon, this was yet another ordeal that his sinful sister Merry was putting him through—an ordeal in a long line of ordeals, of which Brandon keeps a detailed record.

The first occurred years ago when Brandon and Deanna visited Doug and me in Greenwich. Doug and I had dragged the pair to a

Fleetwood Mac concert against their will—Brandon didn't even know who Fleetwood Mac was. A group of friends had gotten us floor tickets at the New Haven Coliseum, so I decided to ignore Brandon and have a good time—or so I hoped, until, true to form, my dear husband chose that concert to get horribly drunk and sneak off to make out with a golf buddy's wife in the women's restroom.

I know this because I followed them. After the opening band's set, I saw Doug and—her name was Gloria—in the beer line, fondling and stealing furtive kisses. So, I watched as they went around a corner into the restroom. I spied their four boots in a cubicle when I walked in.

The foolish nerve—Doug's, that is.

The door was locked, so I took the next cubicle, listening to them pant and grunt about which clasp or zipper to undo until I'd had enough. I crouched down from my potty seat and scooted feet-first under the divider, shocking the hell out of them as I shinnied up between them.

"Merry, what the hell?!"

You should have seen the look on Doug's face when I slugged him. Blind, drunken incomprehension. I would have slugged Gloria, too, but she screamed and ran out. Then Doug, that asshole, bolted like a little boy on tiptoes into the men's restroom, where I refused to go—fearing I'd see a lineup of hairy fannies and gripped penises.

I waited outside, but Doug didn't come out. Eventually, I heard the announcer shouting, "Fleetwood Mac!" So, I gave up and went back to my seat beside Brandon, who would have known nothing, except he went into the men's restroom after the concert and found Doug passed out in a pool of vomit. Needless to say, he did not spare me the description.

From that point on, Brandon has recalled that visit as "Oh. The Fleetwood Mac concert." Then he finishes his remark with eyes rolled heavenward. In his mind, his sanctity would never have been tarnished by such sordid behavior but for his relationship to me.

Now this stripper in my living room was another ordeal for Brandon to mark in his book—another heathen incident that was my fault. And DPB will bring it up at all birthdays hence. "Oh, that birthday. The one with that stripper." Then he'll shudder and roll his eyes.

As for my birthday-party nightmare scene, Brandon kept shouting for Prince to stop stripping, but Prince kept doing his job, until Brandon lost it and body-slammed the poor guy toward the front door. "Not in front of my family. Not in front of me!"

All I could see of the tanned, rippled Prince were his hands fumbling to locate the door handle and his feet trying to keep the rest of him upright. Suddenly modest, Prince shouted, "I need my clothes. Get me my clothes."

As my girls gingerly fetched tuxedo parts from the living room and handed them to Prince, Claire kept saying, "I'm sorry, Prince. It's my fault for hiring you."

Scottie hollered from down the hall, "I told you girls not to do this." That's Scottie. The family's hindsight guru.

While Prince struggled to pull on his pants, Brandon pressed harder to throw him out.

"Sir, I'll be happy to leave if you'll allow me to put on my clothes. And get my tape player."

Instead, Brandon yanked open the door and shoved Prince out. The last image I saw was Prince's tanned bum as he hopped down the front walk, still trying to put on his pants.

After Brandon slammed the door, he glared as if I needed an exorcist. "Obscene. Disgusting. Only you would do this to me, Merry."

"It wasn't Mom's fault. We just thought it'd be funny," Claire said.

"It's a family joke. Prince is our nickname for—" Nora began.

I held up my hands. "Girls, he isn't worth your sweet humility."

Brandon didn't hear me anyway. He was stomping down the hall to retrieve Deanna and the girls. Moments later, the five filed out, while Deanna bobbed her red head and murmured benevolently, "Thank you for having us, children. We'll be in touch. Happy Birthday, Merry."

Hell. I am so pissed at DPB, I vow here and now to create a character like him in my screenplay. I'll have him sexually assaulted by a stripper with an absolutely elephantine penis.

Tell me, oh Professor Brilliance, why am I in Austin with my Holier Than Thou Brother?

Love,
Merry

Letter Ten
October 21, 1988 (Cont'd.)

Dear Roland,

Yes, it's still my damn birthday. It's almost midnight, but I remain so angry, I can't sleep. I'm locked in my office, playing one of your lecture tapes. I recorded as many as I could. Moments like these, when I'm lonelier than these expressions can soothe, I play your recorded voice, trailing on about existentialists and absurdists, your favorite Jean Genet. You can't hear this, but I'm playing the lecture when you asked me to read the part of Irma, the queen.

"Throughout Genet's life, he produced an impressive body of work devoted to his autobiographical experiences, as well as the wider social and political issues plaguing France. He intentionally dwelled in an environment of poverty and crime, and came by his topics honestly. His mother was a prostitute who put him up for adoption. He bounced between foster homes and later penal institutions. He also joined the French Foreign Legion at age eighteen but was dishonorably discharged after being caught in a homosexual act. From there, he became a vagabond, a thief, and a male prostitute all over Europe. He recounts these experience in *The Thief's Journal*. As a result, he cultivated writer friends like Jean Cocteau, Jean-Paul Sartre, and Michel Foucault, who shared Genet's passion for changing the world. In Genet's works, you can see how he turns good and evil on their heads. A true hippie, he became an activist during the 1960s, protesting the living conditions of immigrants in France. Genet's rebellious, illuminating texts have become influential to many writers today. Now, let's turn to page thirty-nine in *The Balcony*. Who will read Irma, the queen? Mrs. Garner? Shall we hear your interpretation?"

I remember blushing and staring at my desk. I was so new at this intellectual side of being.

"Mrs. Garner declines. Do we have a more courageous volunteer?"

Some Barnard girl said, "I'll do it if I can borrow your book."

Everybody laughed except me. Embarrassed, I grabbed my recorder and tiptoed out.

"Chicken!" you shouted after me.

Yet, I regained my courage to return for your next class, and the next. You opened my mind to new ways of seeing. Little did I know, but this has made me a misfit, nay, a renegade. I'm an observer. I see too much. I feel too much. I'm a writer.

"I wouldn't go around saying you're a writer until you've made $100,000 doing it."

Oh, hush. That's what you always used to say.

"Everybody's a writer. At every cocktail party, someone or the other brags, 'I'm working on a screenplay (or a stage play, novel, book of short stories, or book of poems).' But how many of those 'writers' have ever made $100,000 doing it?"

Certainly not you. You who wrote one off-Broadway play, *Move Over, Once for Me* and, after it closed within a month, switched to writing a documentary for a PBS affiliate about female students working their way through Barnard as prostitutes and topless dancers. That you didn't achieve financial success is not the shame. The shame is that you could not be satisfied with being a fabulous teacher, revered for your wit as you raved about the genius of Jean Genet and prodded our resistant minds.

"My dears, Genet was not as nuts as he might appear. He was more realistic than many of his contemporaries. If you don't think so, go out there and live it. Do you really think you can say, 'I am a screenwriter or an actor or even a professor,' without someone affirming that choice and defining you? Yes, I know ... Genet's world seems bleak, desolate, and far less hopeful than Beckett's Vladimir and Estragon. That patient little pair *Waiting for Godot* ... they did not move. In contrast, Genet would not wait. To him, hope, faith, and destiny culminate in the hero who will act, rage, react, irrationally, intuitively, gratuitously against the choices others make for him. To Genet, that is your only way to truly live!"

⊠   ⊠   ⊠

Okay, yes, I must get off Memory Lane.

I forgot to mention earlier that I took a break from my real estate class last week and went outside for a walk. Guess who I spotted in a brown sedan with a pretty olive-skinned brunette driving. Brandon. I shouted and waved, but he didn't see me. I assumed the woman is from his office. Hopefully a professional relationship, although maybe I should drop by to make Brandon nervous.

One last note. As the clock is about to strike midnight, I bought myself a birthday present. A Macintosh II, which cost well over $5,000 from my inheritance, but it is a far cry from the 1983 Macintosh SE and MacWrite program I've used since my collegiate studies with you. This new machine and the Microsoft Word program have been a joy to learn.

You would scoff at this purchase, since you once joked, "My friends are buying ever more powerful computers in the hope that this new machine will make them, at last, important writers." Then your laughter derided into scorn. "My dear students, writers write. That's what they do. If you can't write on an airplane napkin, or with a borrowed pen, or on a scrap of paper in the back of a taxi, you aren't a writer. No machine will change that. From chisels on stone to feather quills on papyrus, writers find a way to write. Period."

Despite your disdain for electronics, you might try one of these contraptions. Then you wouldn't need Jillian to type your manuscripts.

Love,
Merry

SCENE 10

EXT. MERRY'S DUPLEX — NIGHT — 1988

Glenn hides in the bushes below Nora's window.

THROUGH NORA'S WINDOW

Glenn watches Nora change into her pj's.

BEHIND HIM

Merry's neighbor PAMELA comes up the walk with two SACKS of groceries. She's about 40, blond, and pudgy. She catches Glenn peering.

                    PAMELA
         Hey, you. What are you doing?

Glenn quickly backs out of the bushes, acting like he's done nothing wrong.

                    GLENN
         Just checking the siding for
         carpenter ants.

                    PAMELA
         Got a business card?

                        GLENN
Didn't think I'd need one. Landlord
called about ants. Those buggers can
eat right through the wood framing.

                        PAMELA
I'm going to call the landlord.

Glenn uneasily backs toward the parking lot.

                        GLENN
Tell 'em the Bug Master was here.

                        PAMELA
What's your name?

                        GLENN
Harry Windsor, ma'am.

Glenn hurriedly gets in his car, starts the
engine, and drives away.

AT MERRY'S FRONT DOOR

Pamela knocks and waits until Merry opens.

                        PAMELA
Hi. I'm your neighbor. Pamela
Nichols.

                        MERRY
Merry Mayfield. Nice to meet you.

                        PAMELA
Well, you might not think so. I
caught a guy peeking in your window.

> MERRY
>
> My window?

> PAMELA
>
> That one there.

> MERRY
>
> That's my daughter's room. Maybe a
> kid from her high school?

> PAMELA
>
> This was no kid. Said his name was
> 'Harry Windsor.'

> MERRY
>
> Isn't that Queen Elizabeth's little
> boy? The redheaded one?

> PAMELA
>
> Dumb me. I didn't catch that. If I
> see him again, I'm calling the cops.

> MERRY
>
> I'll make sure Nora keeps her drapes
> closed. Thank you for letting us
> know.

INT. MERRY'S DUPLEX — 1988 — NIGHT

Merry closes the front door, then heads down
the hall to Nora's bedroom.

> MERRY
>
> Nora! We need to talk.

Letter Eleven
October 28, 1988

Dear Roland,

I guess Glenn has given up. Thankfully! I would have been worried if he kept calling, but I know the depths of obsession and how strong the pull is to make the desire a reality.

I've gotten to know my neighbor Pamela a bit better. Perhaps a new friend. She's very funny, but not as literate or articulate as Sigrid.

I talked to her last night ... Sigrid. She said she has broken up again with Frank; rather, he broke up with her.

"Frank actually said, 'It's time for us to explore different scenes. Perhaps our roles will intersect. Or not. It's all up to the script of life.'"

"Screw Frank. Couldn't he come up with better lines than that? Oh, I wish we could drown your sorrows at the Raven."

"The Raven is not the same without you. Truly. You and Roland kept me laughing for hours. Now that you and Frank are both gone, things get super intellectual. Roland rants about the dismal fate of the theater, while Jillian chimes in with sardonic lines."

"I never understood how you could love Frank," I blurted, although I shouldn't have.

"Thirty-eight and still pretending to be an actor, although he's really just a part-time instructor," she sighed, less angrily that I had expected.

But then, Sigrid never was concerned about money—not with her father being a Columbia trustee, and her mother coming from Upper East Side. Still, I think breaking up with Frank made Sigrid realize it's time to get on with it. She'll begin her doctoral studies in January.

"Getting my PhD may merely ensure I'll have an unmarketable future, but at least I'll be qualified to teach more than freshman English.

So, while Frank and I explore different scenes, I'll stay busy with good writers instead of the lousy actor I've been living with."

Poor baby. There was a hollowness in her voice, so I decided to entertain her with chatty news about my birthday party and the stripper, but I couldn't tell whether Sigrid was interested. You know Sigrid—she always seems interested.

I also told her I was writing to you. (Because I knew she would tell you so, and you will wait to receive a letter—only it won't come. Ha!)

Anyway, Sigrid is so dear. In that upper-crust accent, she said, "It's nice that you're writing him. Be sure to tell Roland hello for me!"

Isn't that Sigrid? You both teach at the same university, but she wants me to say hello to you for her.

✉   ✉   ✉

I'm pattering aimlessly. I must tell you a story. A set piece. Is all of life merely a series of connected set pieces?

I can see you shaking your finger. "Always plant your seeds in Act 1 so they will bear fruit in the final act."

And when we, your stupid pupils, asked, "But how can you plant seeds in the first act when you don't know how your story is going to end?" you tipped back on your beat-up suede lace-ups and twinkled at us through your wire rims.

"How could you even begin to write without knowing what each twist, each turn is going to be? Writing is a craft, dammit. Control it. It's not something that rambles inconsequentially!"

Okay, so I shall plant my seeds.

Morgan Crane was my hairdresser in Greenwich. A fabulous stylist and the reason I looked as good as I did and made you lust after me, if you truly did. He even looked a bit like you—blond and cute, with glasses like yours, and come to think of it, he also had blue eyes, slightly off kilter like yours. But he was slighter, effeminate, not so you would spot him on the street and say, "See that raving fag?" No. There was more heterosexual maleness to Morgan than that. But for whatever reason, whether Morgan had one too many X chromosomes or an abusive alcoholic father—who knows these things—he was gay.

Still, Morgan and I had a physical attraction for one another that I treasured. We never went to bed—how could we? For the better, we became good friends.

During my last two years in Greenwich, I didn't even go to his salon for a haircut. He would arrive at my house with scissors flourished, announcing, "Beauty on Wheels! Morgan, the Traveling Blade!"

But underneath his merry mask, he was pained to the point of hysteria about his homosexuality. One night after a few drinks, he gave me a passionate stare. "Merry, when I'm around you, I don't want to be gay. I hate this. But that's what I am." He hugged me, sobbing. "You don't know how much you mean to me. You just don't know."

Now I think I do. When we would flirt the way we did, when we would look into each other's eyes and feel that sizzling heterosexual attraction, I think Morgan felt like the heterosexual man he wished he could be.

His current beau was Hugh, a bookish-looking fellow who came to live at Morgan's condo. I went there for dinner a few times. Morgan had a Liberace side to home decor and had decorated with expensive crystal, figurines, and china—pretentiously placed in lighted hutches and cabinets. All in all, Morgan seemed happy, although he was drinking too much, as we all did. But abruptly, Morgan's beau Hugh accepted a new job in Phoenix. Morgan must have been in love with the guy because he sold his salon and fancy condo, then followed Hugh to Phoenix.

Ironically, this was the same week I moved to Austin. I had been so preoccupied with traveling to see Dad and, of course, moving, I didn't even know that Morgan had left Greenwich until last month, when he called me from Phoenix. We talked and laughed for hours. But he was having what a shrink would call identity problems. He couldn't get a job. No one knew his reputation. He was just a stylist with no client list.

Meanwhile, Hugh was meeting new people through work, so he invited them to parties at the condo Morgan had paid for. It had a view of Camelback and was fixed up with Morgan's fancy-foo things. That's what bothered him—Hugh kept showing off the house, but it was Morgan's house, Morgan's stuff.

"Those wenches take one look at the unemployed hairdresser and think, 'You whore!' And Hugh lets them think that. He leads them around as though all of this is his shit. But Hugh doesn't spend a dime on anything. He's the goddamn gigolo."

I tried to make Morgan feel better by saying, "Well, I guess I'm going to have to fly out to Phoenix to get a decent haircut."

"Oh do. Please do. We'll sit in the back and watch the sun drop behind the mountain. I love you, Merry. You know that, don't you?"

⊠   ⊠   ⊠

Seeds.

Three weeks ago, I was downtown for one of my real estate classes. Bored to death, I left mid-session and walked aimlessly through old West Austin—a lovely area, tree lined and peaceful, with quaint houses turned into law offices, bistros, and boutiques.

I noticed a dark blue house with a sign that said, "Aziz". Suddenly, I felt drawn into this place, as if caught by a magnet. I had no control. I went in and asked the balding male receptionist, "What is this?"

"We're Aziz. A hair salon. Would you like an appointment?"

"To tell you the truth, I was just wandering between classes. But while I'm here, well, who's your very best stylist?"

He laughed and smoothed his bare scalp. "As you can see, I don't need one." Then, in a knowing voice, he said, "You want Victor."

Two weeks later, I went back for my appointment. Victor turned out to be a tall, athletically built, but absolutely raving gay man with dyed red hair spiked in gelled points, and wispy bleached-blond bangs curling forward. We are talking odd. He also had a bushy, bleached-blond mustache twisted up in curlicues and held in place with blue aluminum hair clippies.

Victor noticed me gawking. "Oh, pardon!" He grabbed the clippies. "I'm so sorry. My previous client was deaf, but she could read lips amazingly well. So, I pinned up my mustache and she read my lips in the mirror."

"That was a great idea," I murmured, somewhat intimidated by this overly energetic man.

He took a step back and squinted. "Deary, do I know you?"

I restrained a laugh. "I don't think so."

"Why is it I feel so special about you? Come here. Give Victor a hug."

Gads. He reached with long, muscular arms, and we hugged violently for about a minute. I was doing it primarily to be polite. But Victor felt good. Manly. In fact, his hug turned me on a bit, although I'm not too selective these days.

He pulled back and stared. "I am definitely a wild and crazy guy today." He did a couple of silly arm pumps, then led me to the shampoo room. "Are you sure I don't know you?"

As he tipped my head back over the sink, Victor suddenly hiked his leg and straddled me, face forward, balancing his hands on the chair arms and his legs on either side of mine. He bent nearer, his face flush on top. His hazel eyes loomed not an inch away, and his nose pressed bulb to bulb against mine.

I felt a blast of electricity. You couldn't call it sexual. It was quite beyond.

"Something highly unusual is going on here!" Victor shouted toward another hairdresser who was shampooing a woman at the next sink. "Do you people see this? I am mounting a woman I've never even met. I am accosting her right here in the shampoo room! This is incredible. What in the hell is going on here?"

Although I realized this was part of his comedic persona, I did my best not to bolt while Victor washed and rinsed my hair. Then, while my conditioner soaked in, he excused himself for a bit and returned with two glasses of red wine.

He stood formally and toasted, "To a long and happy relationship."

I didn't know what to say but figured a glass of wine might help.

While Victor rinsed my hair, his frenetic energy calmed a bit as he asked the usual questions, such as who had been cutting my hair. So, I told him about my wonderful friend Morgan—how we both moved to different cities and I hadn't found anyone in Austin who could cut hair like my Morgan. I probably got a little carried away praising Morgan, but I was trying to let this guy Victor know that I was used to a wonderful and caring stylist.

Victor put his hands on his hips. "How can you expect me to cut your hair after hearing about the stylist king of Greenwich, C-T, and Phoenix, A-Z? But I'll try. And if you don't like what I've done, we can always shave it off. That's what Phillip wants me to do. Phillip absolutely loves bald guys."

Turns out Phillip was both Victor's receptionist and his beau—the bald fellow I had spoken to on that first day I wandered in.

While Victor cut and styled, we talked for at least two hours. To shorten, I'll summarize. Victor's mother was a religious fanatic from Oklahoma City who raised Victor to be a preacher/evangelist. (Coincidental shades of Deanna.) By age eighteen, Victor was preaching in tent revivals throughout the state. But he got arrested one night for preaching without a permit and landed in jail in Oklahoma City.

"By then, I already knew I was gay. Hell, I knew at age twelve. I also knew I wanted to be a hairdresser at a salon because that's where gay men worked. But Mother had made a preacher out of me. So here I was, a gay preacher in jail for forty-two days. Every night, I heard screams of men being raped. I prayed that my cellmates would rape me too, but the cops kept me in solitary. So after I got out, I gave up preaching. I figured if God would let a gay man go that long without getting screwed, I couldn't preach faith. Mother hasn't spoken to me since I left the ministry."

Between episodic blasts like that, I traded stories, not nearly as entertaining, but I tried. I told Victor about my one-nighter with Glenn, my trip down Town Lake on the pink float, my divorce from Merry's One Iron (the part about Doug getting caught in a gambling scam after betting on himself to win the US Open, instead of betting on somebody who could actually win the tournament), my dead mother (the story about Mom coming to sing to me after she died, something I have yet to write about), and about Deanna's Eternal Spirit ordination.

We got quite hysterical about Deanna. Victor had opened a second bottle of red, and I was having such a good time drinking wine and talking to Victor, I paid absolutely no attention to him cutting my hair. In fact, he had turned my chair so I could not see the mirror. But after Victor finished cutting, blowing, and styling, he whirled me around.

I looked in the mirror. Lightning bolts! We are talking psychic transport.

Victor had cut my hair exactly how my Morgan did. I mean, exactly. A short bob, full, thick, smooth, soft bangs, side part. Not one hair in a different place than Morgan would have styled it.

"Please like it."

"This is exactly the same way Morgan styled my hair."

Victor bounded around, shouting, "Phillip, she likes it! She loves us!"

We hugged, marveling at our coincidental connection.

After I paid, I was so excited about my haircut, Phillip offered Aziz's phone so I could call Morgan in Phoenix, but the number was disconnected. A computerized voice told me to call a different number for further information. So, I dialed that.

The answering "Hello" was effeminate but male.

"May I speak to Morgan?"

The voice hesitated. "Morgan's not here."

"Is this Hugh?"

"No."

"How can I reach Morgan Crane? I called his house and got a disconnected number."

"Morgan's ... well ..." Then the fellow called out, "Hugh? Can you come to the phone?"

Inexplicably, my body started shuddering in dread.

Hugh came on the line. "Who is this? Merry? Oh Merry. I'm so sorry. I thought someone would have told you. After the move, Morgan and I didn't get along. He was drinking—it was always the drinking. He'd have an interview for a stylist job, but he'd get drunk and screw it up. I couldn't take it. So, I left. Then, well, Morgan called and said he was going to do it, only I didn't believe him and refused to come over. But he did it, Merry. When I didn't hear from him for two days, I finally went over. He was dead in the car. In the garage. It was pretty bad."

I felt like my heart had come out of my chest. I started crying and couldn't talk.

Phillip hovered as Hugh kept asking, "Merry? Are you all right, Merry? I'm really sorry. I just assumed someone had told you."

I blubbered, "I guess Morgan did. He's been haunting a salon in Austin named Aziz."

Don't you see? Morgan's spirit had drawn me into that salon. Morgan's spirit made Victor feel something special about me and made me feel as if I knew Victor. And Morgan's spirit had hovered over Victor while he cut my hair.

Morgan had come to say goodbye. He loved me that much. I don't know whether I have ever been so honored by a friend.

Dear Brilliance, what shall I make of this? Is there room in drama for truth? You often said, "Truth intrudes on the suspended disbelief. Use truth only as a germ to harvest something different, something new."

Something new? I must save this until even I will know what to do.

Love,
Merry

SCENE 11

EXT. AZIZ HAIR SALON — 1988 — DAY

Tears streaming, Merry walks out of Aziz
Hair Salon and heads to her Cutlass. In her
peripheral vision, she notices a car and turns
to look. She recognizes Glenn seated in the
driver's seat. Merry quickly turns away.

INSIDE GLENN'S CAR

Glenn ogles Merry as she crosses the street.

Merry pretends to ignore him and walks quickly
to her car.

INT. 1976 OLDS CUTLASS — 1988 — DAY

Merry gets in, LOCKS her doors, then dabs at
her tears in the

REAR-VIEW MIRROR

where she sees Glenn staring back at her.

> MERRY
> (to herself)
> Maybe I should call the cops.

EXT. AZIZ HAIR SALON — 1988 — DAY

Glenn starts his ENGINE and slowly drives by
Merry's car, glaring determinedly at her.

INT. 1976 OLDS CUTLASS — 1988 — DAY

Merry pretends she doesn't see Glenn, but
she's jittery with nerves.

> MERRY
> What could I tell police? I think
> this guy is following me?
> > (scolding herself in mirror)
> Maybe this is payback because I
> stalked Roland. If he only knew how
> many times I followed him, he'd have
> never ... well, he didn't anyway.

Merry tries to shrug this off and puts her car
in gear.

Letter Twelve
November 5, 1988

Dear Roland,

I struggled all day on my screenplay. Too many scenes are autobiographical.

You taught us that it is okay to use circumstances as seeds to grow scenes, or to use people we know as models for characters, but my screenplay remains stuck in the mud of my life. Like you do.

Right after I first fell in obsession with you, I ran to the library to read *Move Over, Once for Me*, your failure of a stage play.

"My play was so far off-Broadway you had to enter through the alley," you self-deprecatingly referred to it in class.

Well, it was off—embarrassing, shocking for me to read. Your script revealed a you-as-protagonist I didn't want to know, a self-suffering wimp with a dark-haired mistress and neurotic fears of failure, stifled by the demands of a faded blond wife and four children.

Gads. You wrote the truth of your life—the very thing you taught us not to do. This was the writer you?

"Those who can't do, teach. Those who try are the true existential heroes."

You often said that with feigned humility, but your stage play was so awful, I started wondering if, nay I determined that I would have more success than you. Especially during grad school, a time when I drove by the Raven to see if your Jeep was there. It was. I nonchalantly walked in and sat at the bar, pretending I had no clue you were there. I ordered a Guinness, dropped my napkin on purpose, then leaned off my stool to pick it up. From your usual corner booth, you caught my eye and waved for me to join you, likely to Jillian's dismay.

Guinness after Guinness, you and I all but ignored her as she suffered in silence, until she steered the conversation to a topic she assumed only you and she could discuss.

Her dark eyes shone with a competitive glint. "Roland reviewed my favorite novel for the *Review*. Have you read James Salter's *Light Years*?"

Aha. I had her! "Yes, I read that in Lit II. I also read Roland's review."

You grinned. "Good for you. Jillian seems to think *Light Years* was an 'important work.' But I was dismayed at Salter's metaphoric superficiality related to Viri's vain quest for happiness."

"Oh, boo. *Light Years* was tender, joyful, and sensual. But in the end, yes, it was profoundly sad," Jillian said.

I gloated. "I wrote a paper on it. As I recall, reviews were mixed. The *Times* reviewer said it was ... let me see if I can remember the quote ... 'overwritten, *chichi*, and a rather silly novel.'"

Jillian glared. "Seems I'm an unenlightened moron."

Ha! With my enemy sulking, I played my grandest scene. "In your review, Roland, you called *Light Years* 'Viri's story.' But the narrative voice seemed more like that of his wife Nedra's. She may have died before Viri, but in my mind's eye, she was telling the story as if looking on from above. Kind of like Emily in *Our Town*."

Jillian lurched defensively. "But Roland was merely trying to say—"

You held up a finger. "Shh. Merry and I are talking about narrative voice, a writing technique you wouldn't understand. Let me think about this a moment."

Smack! Take that, Jillian, too busy typing manuscripts to write anything yourself.

I repeated (loving every delicious moment), "Salter began the novel with Nedra's voice."

You sat. Thinking. Then it came. The moment. "That's what I get for reviewing fiction. You are so right, Merry. I blew the fucking review."

Our wonderful moment. I had taught the teacher.

Our gaze held each other's, and from the glimmer in your eyes, I could see that you were impressed enough by my intellect to move into my zone. In fact, I know you tried.

Moments later, Jillian played her ace and stood to leave. You hesitated, but since you had driven her, your eyes and silent shrug conveyed you had no choice. As you two walked out, Jillian did not bother to give me one of her fake air kisses.

I sat alone in the booth for an hour, digesting the earlier scene. Digesting? Ha! I wallowed in delight. I had beaten Jillian at her intellectual game of *Light Years* and had impressed you, the teacher.

Abruptly, a waiter came. "Why didn't you answer that page?"

"What page?" I asked.

"You had a phone call," the waiter said.

"Why didn't you page me?"

"I did. But you didn't answer, so I thought you had left."

"Where's the phone?"

"He already hung up."

"Who?" I shouted, although I knew who had called.

"I don't know."

"What'd you tell him?"

"That you weren't here. You didn't answer your page."

"But I was here!"

"Probably too noisy. Sorry."

Could be a scene in *Waiting for Godot*. My chance blown. Shit.

The next day, I waited after class, but your eyes ricocheted past, as if I were a stranger.

I decided to press. I caught you before you went into the men's room. "Did you phone me at the Raven last night?"

"Not that I remember," you said as you scooted inside the door.

Chickenshit. You behaved as if there hadn't been a you and me the night before, as though our illuminations about *Light Years* were simply booze-induced silliness to be dismissed in the sober light of day.

"Not that I remember."

Oh, hell. How could you chuck everything for the frightening possibility that you and I should be you and me?

Goodnight, *Dear Diary*. I'm martini'd out now.

Love,
Merry

SCENE 12

EXT. RAVEN BAR, MANHATTAN — 1988 — DAY

STREET SIGN: "Broadway"

Above a funky bar, there's another

SIGN: "The Raven - a Bar"

INT. RAVEN BAR, MANHATTAN — 1988 — DAY

In a corner wooden booth, SIGRID, FRANK, JILLIAN, and ROLAND sit at a table littered with BEER CUPS of GUINNESS.

Jillian and Roland are in their late 40s. She's artistically pretty, dark, and frizzy haired. He's balding but enigmatic, with electric-blue eyes.

Sigrid and Frank are late 30s academic types, although Sigrid is fairly pretty. Frank is more theatrical, with a thin mustache.

                    SIGRID
          I talked to our dear Merry last
          night. She sends you each a fond
          hello. She's revising a screenplay.

JILLIAN
Why would anyone move to Texas?

SIGRID
Her brother lives there.

JILLIAN
How can a writer get a job in
Austin?

SIGRID
Merry says there's an active film
community. Even a film festival.

JILLIAN
That's what I call off-off-off.

FRANK
We have to start somewhere.

ROLAND
Best place is New York. The stage.
That's what David Mamet did. Now
look at him. Making bucks on the
gilded screen

JILLIAN
You know how competitive Merry is.

ROLAND
What does that mean?

JILLIAN
There's less competition in a town
like Austin. Merry can aim low.

                    SIGRID
          I don't know if that's fair.
          Divorce, death, family trauma.

                    ROLAND
          I understand the pull of living near
          family, but why waste an MFA from
          Columbia? As her thesis advisor, I
          feel like I've peed in the wind.

                    JILLIAN
          Not every student will be a success.
          Merry may not have what it takes.

                    ROLAND
          Oh, but Merry is very talented.

As Roland gazes off wistfully, Jillian pouts.

                    FRANK
          At least Merry got rid of the
          drunken golfer.

                    SIGRID
          I hear he works on a loading dock.

                    FRANK
          Now, there's a metaphor. Pro athlete
          sweats out days loading trucks.

                    JILLIAN
          A bit clichéd, Frank.

Roland is still disengaged. Jillian elbows
him. Roland raises his Guinness.

                              ROLAND
          To Merry, then.

Sigrid, Frank, and Roland toast. Reluctantly,
Jillian joins in.

                              SIGRID
          May we say we knew her when.

                          ROLAND, FRANK
          Here, here!

Jillian looks askance. Fumes.

Letter Thirteen
November 15, 1988

Dear Roland,

I have been too busy to write to you. Yes, I am doing things, rather than wallowing in memories of you, inhaling alcohol, and reeling in despair. First off, I've passed my real estate licensing test! To my chagrin, I am a State of Texas and B. J. Hathaway REALTOR®. (That's how they spell it. All caps with a circled R for registered trademark. Very official.)

Secondly, I had an interview with the manager of B. J. Hathaway's northwest office. Not that buddy of Dear Pluppy Brandon's. Jack Carleton manages the West Lake Hills office where DPB wants me to work because DPB lives in West Lake Hills, although I live ten miles away in Northwest Austin.

Instead, Erica Cooke is a hysterically haired woman of about fifty, who smells like last night's cigarettes. She's so middle-class she'd have her makeup done for free at the Lancôme counter, then not buy a thing.

In my interview, she did most of the talking. "B. J. is a hands-on leader. He's Mr. Big in the Austin community and a deacon at West Lake Hills Presbyterian Church. He expects all new agents to be on the job seven days a week."

Seven days a week? Erica and B. J. do not know the habits of Merry Mayfield well.

Thirdly, my Brilliance, I am diligently revising the self-absorbed screenplay that served as my master's thesis.

As you said, "Make the revisions, and you should land a producer."

Ever since I became a bona fide real estate agent, the fear of having that occupational definition has made me even more determined to finish. When it premieres to rave reviews—after much publicity hype—

and I make appearances on Leno, Letterman, and Oprah, where each of them adores me so much they ask me to return, I will shout to Brandon, "That's what you get for believing in B. J. Hathaway!"

I have not met B. J. yet. But I hear him on radio ads. He sounds like a cross between Billy Graham and J. R. Ewing. His slogan is, "The search is over." Problem is, I do not know what we're searching for.

But I will find it. If only to spite Brandon.

$$\boxtimes \quad \boxtimes \quad \boxtimes$$

From this, you can tell I'm in a better mood. I wouldn't call myself "happy." But the tone, the voice has moved beyond that depressed woman from my first narratives addressed to you in the file cabinet. Not only am I working but also, just this week, I may have seen my prince.

This all started at Maggie Mae's, my latest hangout, a Sixth St. warehouse pub that reverberates with throbbing music. During happy hours, it is populated by hordes of age thirty to fortyish professional types, looking for other thirty-to-fortyish humans to date. So last Thursday, I was approached by a gorgeous Yugoslavian named Zoran, who was a tall, curly blond, dressed in a gray-silk sport jacket and big-collared shirt. He had hooked his sunglasses into his open neckline, a la the singer Tom Jones, whom Zoran mentioned constantly.

"You can't keep a guy like Tom Jones down."

I laughed. "All I remember are his tight pants."

"Yes, everybody makes a thing about how he used to wear his pants so tight, but this man has such a great voice that if I could be a singer, I would be Tom Jones. He is a legend."

Occasionally, Zoran would break out in a blast of "Whoa Danny boy ... the pipes are calling ..." or "I-yi-yi-know what it means ..." All of this was in a thick Yugoslavian accent.

Because of the bar noise and the martinis swimming in my brain, I started thinking Zoran looked as sexy as Tom Jones, although I realized later that Zoran was merely an imitation, but well, I screwed up.

With troubles brewing in Yugoslavia, Zoran had emigrated to America by way of Switzerland. You have to admire his courage. He had that naive optimism so many immigrants have. I guess he would. He's making $90,000 teaching engineering at UT. Often, Zoran would stop in the middle of a sentence, raise his finger, and shout, "Only in America. God, I love this country!"

Regardless of that trait, I accepted his invitation to leave Maggie Mae's and go to Jeffrey's for dinner. The reason I accepted, other than the gin, was that I had read in *Texas Monthly* magazine—our version of the *New Yorker*—that Jeffrey's is the best in town. It also is very expensive.

We went in Zoran's car, a brown MG convertible with more character than class. The heater didn't work, so the chilly winds whistled through the cloth top as we headed west of downtown to a quaint neighborhood called Clarksville. It's hilly and green, with narrow streets—typically Austin, funky, arty—with older frame homes that are either gone to pot or else have been renovated and are now worth $2 million.

Jeffrey's is at 12th Street and West Lynn, in a white two-story building with a small red neon sign that simply says "Café." Surprisingly, the inside is rather sophisticated, a laid-back, continental ambiance, if you'll pardon this string of oxymorons. Very Austin—contemporary, country western, weird, high-tech, hick, arty, yuppie, Mexican, Junior League, cozy, *nouveau riche*, and funky. When I first arrived, I wondered where the upscale people went. Then I figured out that they're sitting next to me, wearing jeans and T-shirts, drinking Shiner Bocks, and propping their alligator boots on chairs.

Back to Jeffrey's. Zoran and I waited in an alcove until the *maître d'* led us to our table, where Zoran kept shouting, "Only in America!" and "God, I love this country," each time something simple happened—such as when the waiter poured water.

I was quickly embarrassed.

Even more awful, Zoran had decided I was going to be his sexual dessert. He kept giving me obvious leers after each swallow of wine.

But Zoran would not leer at me cheaply. In counterattack, I ordered the garlic-and-duck-liver pâté, the leek-and-mushroom soup, the Aransas redfish sautéed in chipotle butter, the chocolate intemperance, and a bottle of Dom Pérignon.

All during the meal, Zoran merely drank (no wonder he was so thin). I kept urging him to eat, but my words fell on a deaf palate. Although he was attractive physically, and he was spending a bundle on this dinner, he had the gall to presume that we were going to have sex before asking me how I felt about that plan.

Meanwhile—and this is far more important than my belabored description of Zoran—across the room, I spied a table of men dressed in three-piece suits, clearly a business dinner. The apparent leader was the most handsome of all—tall, olive skinned, with bushy dark eyebrows, a fortyish Gregory Peck, except with bright-green eyes. He caught my eye; I stared back. It was lust. We kept giving one another "the eye" while I ate my dinner and Zoran drank. Call it an escape from reality, I was overwhelmed by the intense determination that this dark, curly-haired man was the reason Godot had brought me to Austin.

Here was a Greek god of a man, and I had to do whatever it took to meet my prince.

After a half hour of our mutual lusting across the dining room, my prince got up and walked in an obvious detour around my chair. Pausing the slightest moment, he shot me a look that said, "Follow me."

Zoran was so drunk he didn't notice me nod yes with my eyebrows.

My prince grinned, then headed to the back of the restaurant where he went through two narrow, louvered doors.

Moments later, I excused myself to Zoran and followed.

He mumbled, "Be back soon, my sweet American pussy."

Beyond the louvered doors, a tiny alcove led to the restrooms. The curly-haired man must have been in the men's, so I decided to wait in that alcove for him to come out. But I didn't want him to know I was waiting, so I pretended I was just walking in. One foot ahead of the other, I poised in this ridiculous half-walk for about three minutes. My ears listened for the thunder of urine from beyond the men's door. In my psyche, I hoped to equate the strength of spray with the heft of the curly-haired man's penis, a silly bit of fantasy that sent me tittering into a giggle that turned into a shriek.

Eventually, I heard a faucet running and a towel dispensing. Aha! My prince would be out in a few seconds. Godot was coming. Then, the door opened and he was there, taller than I had thought, six-three or so, with eyes greener than I had imagined. Tall, dark, handsome, not one foot away. I poised in my stupid half gait and stared up at him. My tongue seemed to have metastasized and could not form words.

"Well, hello," he said, in a soothing announcer voice.

Can you believe what I pitifully said? "Here, let me get out of your way."

Talk about self-defeating behavior! I went inside the ladies' room, collapsed on a potty, and seethed, "Shit, shit, shit," until echoes bounced up to the walls. I was furious for chickening out.

This reminded me of you and me in the Jeep that night. In the face of uncertainty, I had panicked. But this time, I must have courage. I must try. Maybe my new prince was still waiting in the alcove—after all, Godot would wait for me, wouldn't he? It's not just one way, is it?

I peeked out the restroom door. No prince. Then I pushed through the louvered doors, back into Jeffrey's dining room, where my eyes searched. Aha! I spotted him at his table, glancing my way. I walked toward him. He nodded and waved a subtle, sensuous finger at me. I smiled. I would have stopped to say hello, but suddenly, that darn Zoran got up to escort me to our table.

"You know that man?" Zoran asked jealously as I sat.

"No."

"Then why did he wave at you?"

"Just Texas friendly, I suppose." I quickly changed the subject. "Why, Zoran, your duck is dying a cold death. Here, let me have some. Mmm. You really should try this. The sauce is incredible. And Zoran, I want you to know that I really do appreciate your bringing me here."

On and on I pattered to distract him. Disgusting.

Luckily, Zoran was easily placated. He slurred, "I like this place. It reminds me of a café in Switzerland. You been to Switzerland?"

I let Zoran ramble on about Switzerland, primarily because that gave me a chance to exchange more lustful glances with my prince, who, every minute or so, waved and smiled. But five waves and twenty smiles later, he paid his check and stood to leave.

I was desperate.

As he made his way to the front door, he again detoured behind my chair and touched my shoulder ever so lightly. Then he walked behind Zoran, paused, and gave me another look with his glittering green eyes. "I hope you have a wonderful evening," he said.

I practically put my chin into what was left of Zoran's duck.

Then, so perfectly, my prince turned his broad shoulders and walked to the front door. As the *maître d'* held it open, my prince turned. His eyes sought mine. We connected. He raised his hand, smiled wistfully, then turned and was gone.

I was sick with panic. How could I find him if I didn't know his name? I decided I must act. I excused myself again, then walked through a waiting area, where I tapped the lady *maître d'*.

"That man, the tall, dark man who just left. What is his name?"

"I don't know if I should say. He's a regular customer."

"Don't worry ... I met him at a party. We have mutual friends. I was embarrassed because I couldn't remember his name."

"I suppose it's okay. Everybody knows him, anyway. That's Arlen Wynnewood. He's a bigwig at Pecan Street ... I don't know his title."

"Of course, Arlen. I remembered the Wynnewood part, but I couldn't recall his first name. You know how that goes."

Arlen Wynnewood. The goddamn creative director of Pecan Street Theater, Roland, the largest theatrical company in Austin. Now you can see why I am in such a good mood. I will follow Arlen Wynnewood the same way I did you. Maybe he'll debut *Those Who Try* as a stage play. You always wanted me to start with the stage.

I'll send you a clip from the society page. "Arlen Wynnewood and Merry Mayfield—Austin's theatrical duo."

Now you can see why I am in better spirits. Perhaps a bit obsessive. Foolish. Tenuous. But when you're thirty-nine, broke, and lonely, tenuous is sometimes the best you can do.

✉ ✉ ✉

I'm forgetting Zoran. I want to forget Zoran.

When we left Jeffrey's in his MG, I was too distracted by my fantasies to remember my car until we were on MoPac freeway heading north, swerving all over the road. Then it hit me that Zoran was taking me to his condo. I shouted for him to drive me back to my car, but he drunkenly mumbled, "I have a special liqueur from Yugoslavia for you to try. Oh, Merry girl, the liqueur, the liqueur is calling you. God, I love this country."

I protested as strongly as I could without beating him up, but Zoran kept driving. And he somehow swerved us safely to his condo. When he pulled into his garage, I agreed to try his fucking liqueur, but only if he let me call a cab to drive me back downtown.

Up three flights, his condo was very yuppie, with mauve furnishings and accents. On his sofa, Zoran waited maybe .009 seconds after my first swallow of his liqueur before he pressed forward and kissed me. I would have pushed him away, except my lips suddenly realized that Zoran was a fabulous kisser—not like you—you tight-lipped academician.

And since I hadn't been kissed in a few months—Glenn was the only one—I thought I might enjoy more. But then Zoran tried to fondle some rather intimate body parts, and that made me frantic. So, I pushed him away and scampered to the condo's balcony. It overlooked the pool and hot tub below. The chilly air from that height was piercing.

Zoran zoomed after me and clamped his arms around my waist. He started sucking my neck. I slipped to the other side, where I folded my arms, trying to warm myself.

"I-yi-yi-know ... to be lost in a storm ..." Zoran sang in his Yugoslavian Tom Jones. He slid beside me again, while I pretended to be fascinated by the pool and hot tub below.

Thankfully, an escape plan hit. "Let's take a walk by the pool before you call me a cab."

His eyes ignited. "Let's take a hot tub. God, I love this country."

As Zoran and I went down to the hot tub, I continued to rebuff his pawing. I also refused to undress and get in the steamy water.

Giving me a "who cares" look, Zoran stripped to his birthday suit, displaying an uncircumcised wiener of notable size. He slipped into the tub and seemed to forget I was there.

This was a good thing. I figured I could find a pay phone, maybe in the cabana, but—this makes me sick to tell it—Zoran leaned back and commenced to thrashing his wiener, leering at me for inspiration, until the hot tub became a foaming cauldron. I was so stunned by his whacking; I could not move.

Not thirty seconds later, he elevated his rod through the swirling spa and shot Yugoslavian semen a foot into the air, shouting, "God, I love this country!"

☒ ☒ ☒

Martini relaxant in hand, there is no need to fear. Although Zoran the Yugoslavian was a self-gratifying pervert, and although I am a gosh-darn B. J. Hathaway real estate agent, I am not in despair. I have a new prince to consume my fantasies. Arlen Wynnewood.

In this fairytale, there cannot be a Jillian.

Love,
Merry

SCENE 13

EXT. OFFICE BUILDING — 1988 — DAY

SIGN above door: Austin Search for Knowledge

Brandon walks out front and glances to see if anybody's watching.

LUNA, his community-relations director, 30s and Hispanic, pulls up in a brown 1980 sedan. She's smiling.

Brandon gets inside and gives her a delighted peck on the cheek.

They drive away, clearly happy and in love.

EXT. LUNA'S APARTMENT BUILDING — 1988 — DAY

Luna and Brandon walk to her apartment.

INT. LUNA'S APARTMENT BEDROOM — 1988 — DAY

In a frenzy, Brandon whams away atop Luna.

She's enjoying it too.

He's huffing and puffing, almost at orgasm.

                          BRANDON
          Oh, Deanna, Deanna!

Luna jumps out from under him, gets out of
bed, and swats Brandon on his fat rear.

                           LUNA
          Screw you, Brandon!

Luna starts crying, then runs to bathroom. She
SLAMS the door.

Stunned on the bed, Brandon sighs heavily.

                          BRANDON
          Shit. My wife screams, "Jesus!" I
          scream, "Deanna!" I can't escape
          unhappy women, no matter where I
          stick it.

Letter Fourteen
December 24, 1988

Dear Roland,

It is Christmas Eve. Between martinis and writing to you, I am being entertained by fading stars on this year's televised "Solid Gold Christmas Special," starring Cybill Shepherd and Don Johnson. He's wearing a white linen suit, even though it's Christmas. That made me realize Zoran was doing a Don Johnson imitation, along with his Tom Jones.

Don and Cybill just introduced the four boyish middle-aged men who pretend to be The Monkees. Now they are singing, "It's lovely weather for a sleigh ride together with you."

Other than these characters frolicking on my Dad's TV that sits on my file cabinet, I am alone. The kids are spending the holiday week with their father and, I imagine, his girlfriend.

I called Nora this afternoon to ask how things were going.

"Okay," she said impatiently.

"Just okay?"

"What do you want, Mom? This is my life now, not yours." Then she hung up.

Smarty seventeen-ager! If I could, I would have wrung her neck through the phone line.

Even DPB and his ethereal wife Deanna have deserted me for an Eternal Spirit Convention in Tahoe or somewhere. They rented a condo, but DPB didn't give me any details or even say something thoughtful, like, "I hate to leave you alone on your first Christmas in Austin." Instead, he pronounced, "Deanna is preaching at the convention's Christmas Eve service. That's a coveted honor. She says it will be televised on the Truly Spiritual Network, so tune us in. I'll be in the front row, Merry!"

Quintessential Brandon. Needless to say, I'd rather watch the "Solid Gold Christmas Special" and give you a peek at a scene I wrote about you and Jillian this morning.

⊠   ⊠   ⊠

INT. JILLIAN'S BEDROOM — NIGHT

Roland and Jillian are trying to make love, but Roland cannot get an erection. Frustration is evident on both partners' faces.

Jillian quietly slides out from under Roland.

> JILLIAN
> Want to take a moment?

> ROLAND
> Too much thinking.

> JILLIAN
> As Frank says, 'Don't think. Just do it.'

> ROLAND
> Don't bring Frank into the room too.

Both laugh. Roland sighs.

> JILLIAN
> Try fantasizing about a movie star.

> ROLAND
> You want me to pretend I'm with someone other than you? What kind of woman are you?

                    JILLIAN
        A horny one.

Both chuckle sardonically and kiss lightly,
then more passionately. Eventually, Roland
gets going. Both enjoy this immensely until
Roland exclaims as he reaches orgasm.

                    ROLAND
        Oh, Merry! Merry! Merry!

                    JILLIAN
        Oh no. You didn't really say,
        "Merry, Merry, Merry."

                    ROLAND
        I'm afraid so.

                    JILLIAN
        I said, "movie star," you schmuck.

                    ROLAND
        I've never been good at fantasizing
        about movie stars.

                    JILLIAN
        But Merry? When will she be gone
        from my world?

                    ROLAND
        Next time I'll try Demi Moore.

                    JILLIAN
        Isn't she the actress Merry wants to
        star in her mythological screenplay
        that will never be produced?

                    ROLAND
          She may have mentioned that.

                    JILLIAN
          Too close for comfort.

                    ROLAND
          I can finish you up. Shall I get your
          vibrator?

                    JILLIAN
          I should say no, but in my current
          state, I can't be picky.

Still nude, Roland dutifully gets out of bed
and goes into the bathroom.

INT. JILLIAN'S BATHROOM — NIGHT

Roland closes the door and examines himself in
the mirror. In exasperation, he sighs.

                    ROLAND
          Get a grip. Merry's gone. You didn't
          act when you had the chance. So,
          accept what your cowardice produced.

                    ✉   ✉   ✉

   Take that, you impotent pontificator! Needless to say, I'll change all
names before that appears on-screen. (If.)

                    ✉   ✉   ✉

A martini break and subject change. I've been so lonely through this holiday season, I have called Sigrid three times this week. At first, she sounded glad to hear from me. The second time she sounded almost glad. The third time she sounded downright exasperated.

"Merry, doesn't this cost you a fortune?"

I was disappointed to hear she's back living with Frank in his tiny Village flat, but since it's the holidays, I suppose people need people. (Yes, I am a funny girl.)

"Merry, I don't have much time to talk. Frank and I are heading to MoMA's gift shop."

"Oh, I'm jealous. I ♡ MoMA's gift shop. I used to drop by after class."

"It is nice. Afterward, Frank has to stop at the film program office to pick up a script."

I smiled wistfully. "And then, beers at the Raven?"

"Maybe after the holidays. Frank asked Roland to help him rehearse for an audition. If he gets the part, he'd be financially secure for a while. Might not even have to teach."

"You're not quitting though."

"Never. But—quickly, since I do have to go—I thought you'd like to know, Roland received a Fulbright to Singapore but turned it down because he doesn't want to leave you-know-who alone."

"Did he mean Jillian or his wife?"

"I don't know." She giggled at that, then signed off, abandoning me.

She couldn't know I was facing my second Austin Christmas alone, since the kids are gone, and I don't know many souls here except my hairdresser Victor, my manager Cynthia, Zoran (shudder), and Glenn (shudder), whom I hope to have seen the last of, and Pamela next door.

"Christmas is for families," my mom always said.

Dad would murmur, "No matter how much they dislike each other."

Sarcastic prig.

Mom would put on a glitzy Christmas show anyway—complete with green, red, and white cookies; decorated tree; stuffed turkey or pineapple and brown sugar-glazed ham in the oven, and our stockings stuffed far above the brim. She was like that. She would ignore Dad's alcoholic melancholy, but not without subjecting us to her martyrdom. Christmas morning, there was the gift exchange, when I could tell Mom was disappointed by presents she received, whether from Dad or her kids. As a mom now, I understand, but I never thought I should give my family an elaborate celebration and expect something grand in return. Maybe I learned that through reverse osmosis.

✉   ✉   ✉

Oh no. I may regret this. I think I'm going to tell you about Mom.

Her voice was high and clear that October evening when she called over a year ago.

"Merry? I'm in the hospital in Dallas. Your father is in the hospital too. Not here. He's down in Kaufman. I can't see very well. I can't see." She started crying. Most people would cry when they see double because a malignant mass presses against their optic nerve.

"Do you need me to come down?" Stupid question. "I'll fly down."

I drove a rental car from the airport to the looming labyrinth called Baylor University Medical Center in Dallas. After about an hour of getting lost inside a frightening maze of beige hospital walls and dim corridors, I found Mom's room, appropriately bleak. When I saw her, I almost didn't recognize her because her skin was stretched so tightly across her swollen face. She was a Picasso titled "Someone Else's Mother."

I had brought her a chocolate bar. She couldn't focus on it or me, becoming nauseated trying to see. So I sat by her side, patted her hand, and shared the chocolate. Every now and then, she would rise to sit, but it made her dizzy to try.

"Just lie still, Mom. I'll sit here and read you the newspaper."

A relieved sigh. "It's so nice to have you here, dear."

I picked one of the humor columnists Mom would like, then read aloud, and nibbled chocolate. As I droned on and she drifted off, I stared out a dusty window and tried to pretend my mother was not dying.

Brandon drove in from Austin the next day. At that time, I hadn't seen him in years. It surprised me how plump he had gotten, balder, more crinkled around his muddy eyes. Not a blush of youth left. That scared me, since, if Brandon was old, I was not far behind. And that meant it really could be time for Mom to die.

Out in the hall, he whispered, "How does she look? Is it bad?"

"She has a mass on the brain. The lymphoma is out of control."

"But do you think she's going to die?"

"Yes, Brandon. I'm afraid I do."

He burst into tears, more child than man, and I patted him—although I didn't feel much of anything—just patted his shoulders and wondered why I didn't feel love for my only sibling.

Even more horrible than Mom's illness was the fact that our dear father had collapsed from cirrhosis, and was admitted to a different hospital near Mom and Dad's house on the lake. So Brandon and I spent the next week driving two hundred miles round trip each day, zooming across the flatlands between Dallas and Kaufman, trying to figure out what to do with Dad, since his Medicare coverage was limited, and what to do with Mom, because if she wasn't going to die right away, she couldn't handle Dad and his obsessive drinking.

A nurse recommended we put Dad in a nursing home. That sent Brandon and me on a futile quest to find a home with room for a man. It's a numbers game. You can place a man only if a male resident vacates. But since eighty percent of nursing home residents are women, there is a long list for every male vacancy.

Determined to find a slot, Brandon and I drove from one home to another, stupidly hoping that within the next seventy-two hours, all of the twenty males above Dad's name on each waiting list would die.

Oh, Roland. What horrible places. They should be called "dying" homes. The larger ones had hundreds of hospital-like rooms with elderly humans curled up like newborns or hunched in wheelchairs, holding teddy bears or dolls, babbling, begging, crying, sighing. One home had eight wings around a giant hub, with narrow corridors smelling of urine and ammonia. In one room, an old woman who was more skeleton than human was trying to get out of bed.

"Blanche! No, no, Blanche!" a nurse ran in and shouted.

In spite of the warnings, Blanche hit the floor with a whinny.

Brandon yanked me toward the front door. "We'll find the right place for Father. He's still got a chance. I know he does."

God bless the hero child. Thanks to Brandon's persistence, we found a place to put Dad—an alcoholic rehab center that cost $50,000 for three weeks. We got him in under Medicare. Since the Kaufman hospital was treating Dad for cirrhosis of the liver, the rehab place would treat him for alcoholism. So $50,000 of your tax dollars went toward my dad's refusal to admit he had to stop drinking or die.

"This program will work; I just know it," Brandon said.

Meanwhile, back in Dallas, Mom had radiation. The mass on her brain retreated enough for her to be released, although she had to wear an eye patch over one eye to focus.

"I get two of everything whether I want two or not."

Poor thing. Mom's name was Sylvia, so I called her Long John Sylvia because of her patch. My joke. That has been my role as an alcoholic's daughter. To make sad things funny.

Even before we pulled out of the hospital parking lot with Mom in the back seat, Brandon and I had an argument. Although it was early October, the outside temps were still hotter than hell, and Brandon's rental-car air conditioner wasn't working well.

"I cannot wait to get home," Mom murmured.

"We'll stop off at the rehab and let you visit Father."

I was incredulous. "No, we won't, Brandon. Take us to the lake house. I will cook Mom a nice supper, give her a warm bath, and put her to bed. She's got to be exhausted."

DPB put the car in drive, determined. "It's a family disease. They call it codependency. The rehab has a full schedule of classes this evening. We can all benefit."

"Brandon, is it necessary to rid the world of alcoholism today?" I strained toward the back seat. "How about you, Mom? As weary as you probably feel, wouldn't you like to hear Dad blame you one more time for his drinking?"

"Stop badgering Mother."

"Neither Mom nor I want to see that horrid man."

By that time, our mother had withered in the humid back seat, palms covering her face in a desperate attempt to stem the tears. But well, that flow was a pent-up river that didn't stop until we reached the turnoff to the lake. Thankfully, Brandon had yielded.

Mom sobbed, "Each time I get to this exit, it means I'm going home."

Oh dear. That made me feel like the shitty person Brandon thought I was, so I reached across to the back seat, and patted Mom's arm.

She eventually stifled her blubbering and managed a wan smile.

I turned to the front, not speaking to Brandon, who drove like a robot but with one ironic exception—after five minutes of silence, he and I both heaved major sighs. I glanced over. If Brandon had a sense of humor, we might have shared a forgiving brother-sister pat. But DPB insisted things remain gravely awful. No smile, no glimmer.

Goodness. The tension! DPB and I had been together for fifteen days. That's what I kept whining to poor Mom. "I've been down here fifteen days, Mom."

"My, my. Fifteen days," she said, sighing. Which meant, "I spent twenty years taking care of you and another twenty worrying about you, but you can't spend fifteen days with me?"

The problem was, I couldn't. Two weeks before Mom and Dad landed in the hospital, my marriage had fallen apart. THE END was rolling on-screen. Good old Merry's One Iron had plunged us into bankruptcy with gambling debts and legal fees in the hundreds of thousands. And since he refused to get a real job, even assistant pro at a country club, I was doing wild things like selling auto insurance while Doug played thirty-six holes of golf each day, screwed the barmaid, and drank himself into a stupor.

✉   ✉   ✉

Angry digression. Apologies. But I'm going to lay my mother to rest.

Although the mass on her brain retreated from her optic nerve and her vision eventually cleared, the damn lymphoma had spread throughout her body. She died last February after three horrible days going down, Dad told me later. She had vomited blood and fallen in the hall.

Dad was home from rehab by then and actually sober, thankfully. But I think his judgment was impaired. He decided—the asshole made the fucking decision—not to call me or Brandon. "I didn't want to bother you. I gave her a blanket and a pillow."

Mighty thoughtful, don't you think? He didn't call an ambulance until the next morning. Even then, he didn't go to the hospital with her. He'd been up all night and needed to rest. But the doctor called to tell him she didn't make it. She died alone. No husband. No family. No priest. She died alone with none of us around.

When he told me the news, I screamed into the phone, "Why didn't you call? I could have held her hand. I could have told her I loved her."

"Well, Merry, she knew that."

She knew that? The weekend before, she had called, doing her usual thing of making me feel guilty for not coming to see her, but she had no idea I couldn't afford a plane ticket.

"Bring Doug the next time you come down."

I didn't tell her I had filed for divorce. I dreaded telling her about the barmaid.

"Did Doug agree to let the kids be confirmed?"

There she went with the Church again. I hadn't attended mass, communion, or confession in years.

"Is everything all right, Merry? Your spirit seems so far away."

Stubborn child that I am, I refused to answer until even Mom realized she had pressed me too far.

She said weakly, "There I go again. Always trying to be the teacher."

Again, I refused to answer.

So, she said, "I love you, Merry."

It was more a guilt-laden question, so I didn't say I love you back. Instead I said, "Goodbye, Mom."

And that was it. She died a week later. I had refused to say I love you when I had the chance, but later demanded to know why I didn't have the chance to say it before she died.

"Well, Merry, she knew that."

⊠　⊠　⊠

Okay, this is depressing the hell out of everybody. I should not drink when I write. So, dear Roland, here is your cheery *denouement*.

Mom came to visit me after she died. She always said she would come back if she could find a way. In fact, after she died, I scoured her house looking for one final expression of a mother's love. She was like that. Always writing little notes that she would tuck in my lunch sack or put on top of lunch money. So I rummaged through drawers and closets, hoping. Each time I'd find a scrap of paper, I'd think, "Aha!" I'd press it to my chest in anticipation. But it turned out to be a grocery list. Nothing.

Then, months later, when I was back in Connecticut, I came home after trying to sell insurance and started peeling potatoes for dinner—rational, sober, simply peeling potatoes, not even fantasizing about castrating my boss Harold Beardsley. Then I heard Mom's voice, thin, high, and clear, singing an old lullaby, "Tura, lura, lura, tura lura lie."

Don't get me wrong—I didn't hear Mom's voice outside my head. The voice was internal. Clear as a bell. She sang that lullaby from beginning to end, just like she sang it to me so many years ago. Mom would hold me in a creaky rocking chair, while I cuddled, listening to her soprano and the chair's rhythmic creaking. That was my favorite time. I felt close to Mom, was able to love her, which was hard for me because of the unhappiness connected with Brandon and Dad.

Which leads me to wonder: Since I have been visited by my deceased mother and also by my stylist friend Morgan, and each has demonstrated a display of care, is someone, something trying to say that the existential voids you so vehemently preached—the nothingness painted by Beckett, Pinter, and Genet—are not truly black holes but rather tunnels to another side, that there *is* something beyond?

Oh, don't worry. You can't accuse me of regaining faith. It's just that these two supernatural visits cannot have been merely imagined. I'm not that talented.

The entire Solid Gold cast has gathered on stage to sing "Silent Night," their arms draped around each other. Don Johnson is crying.

Maybe I should tune in the Truly Spiritual Network to see if I can see Brandon.

Love,
Merry

SCENE 14

INT. MERRY'S DUPLEX — NIGHT — 1988

IN THE OFFICE

Merry turns off the TV and picks up an empty
martini glass, ready to head to the kitchen,
but she notices a reflection on the darkened TV
screen.

She looks toward the window and sees another
flash of movement.

She dashes over, peers out, and hears
RUSTLING. She urgently closes the drapes.

EXT. MERRY'S DUPLEX — NIGHT

Merry timidly opens the front door and looks
out. She doesn't see anything, so she ventures
out to the porch to look around.

                    MERRY
         Hello? Is someone there?

The neighbor's duplex door also opens. Pamela
comes out. She's wearing an ugly bathrobe, and
her hair is a disaster.

                    PAMELA
Merry Christmas ... if you celebrate
such things. One never knows.

                    MERRY
Yes. I just suffered through the
annual "Solid Gold Christmas
Special." Sorry to disturb you, but
I thought I heard something.

                    PAMELA
I did too, but I guess that was you.

                    MERRY
I saw movement out my window. Guess
I need to keep the drapes closed.

                    PAMELA
Think it was that same guy? Should
we call the cops?

                    MERRY
What would I say? "I saw something."

                    PAMELA
Could be a deer. One ate my potted
spruce. It was my pretend Christmas
tree. Well, guess we're safe now.
Merry Christmas.

                    MERRY
Such as it is.

                    PAMELA
That doesn't sound cheery.

>   MERRY
> Things haven't been going well.

>   PAMELA
> I realize it's late, and I'm a mess,
> but would you like a neighborly nog?
> Eggnog. You know. Booze.

>   MERRY
> I've already had a few.

>   PAMELA
> What's one more?

>   MERRY
> Far more than I need, but since it's
> Christmas Eve, why not? Let me get
> my key and lock up.

Merry heads in her side of the duplex, while
Pamela goes inside hers. Both doors are ajar.

Glenn slithers out from behind a bush. He
considers going inside Merry's open door.

>   GLENN
> Not yet. Be patient.

Glenn tiptoes to his car and gets inside.

FROM THE PARKING LOT

Glenn watches Merry come out and lock her
door. She KNOCKS on Pamela's door, then
timidly goes inside.

Glenn starts his ENGINE.

INT. GLENN'S CAR — NIGHT

                    GLENN

     Not tonight, but I will get you,
     Mommy Mayfield. You don't decide
     when. I do.

Letter Fifteen
January 13, 1989

Dear Roland,

It's 1989. Can you believe this? In only eleven years, you and I will see the turn of the century. One of my New Year's resolutions is to abolish depression. After all, I have a new friend in Pamela. Turns out, she is from Long Island, so we shared a bit of our New "Yawkah" history.

Although she has been in Austin for five years, she still speaks in Joan Rivers rasps that do not break for a reply. Appearance-wise, you might describe her as asexual, but if you said that to her face, she would sink her overbite into you. The rest of Pamela is plump, topped by dishwater-blond hair and gray eyes, like a pudgy Brownie who didn't get taller.

Career-wise, Pamela is also an oddball—for a female, that is. She spends her days inspecting elevators.

"When I decided to divorce Roger—my husband, long story—I knew I would have to support myself, so I did what all Long Island girls think they wanna be when they grow up: a nurse. Right? A friggin' nurse so they can marry a doctor. So here I am, age thirty-nine, and thirty-nine pounds overweight, trotting off to nursing school with a bunch of skinny twits who didn't want to learn anything but how to screw doctors. But the doctors are a bunch of pompous assholes, although most don't mind getting a piece off the nursing-school students. I mean—in the medical world, everybody is fucking everybody. Except me.

"I tell myself, Pamela, nobody here wants a thing you've got. So, I went to a career-counseling center. You know the kind, where two guys in suits tell you you're gonna be great if you'll simply plunk down $1,500 to take tests that will cost you another $1,500. Every test known to mankind, secret tests, the answers to which are known only to the two guys in the $1,500 suits you just paid for. And you know what they told me after I paid them $3,000 of Roger's money? They told me I was supposed to be either a military officer or an elevator inspector. 'It's your choice, Pamela,' they said. My choice?"

She laughed caustically.

Even though I didn't know this woman well, I understood her desperation. Frustration. She's about my age, educated before the women's movement, which means nobody had told Pamela she was supposed to make a living, that is, until she was thirty-nine and decided to live without being emotionally abused. And then two guys told her she was supposed to be a military officer or an elevator inspector.

"I called the military first, but they said I was too old. So that left the elevators. I studied for two years and got my QEI certification—that's what you need to get a job—then interned for a year, worked for Thyssen Elevators for a year, and started my own business. I don't make millions, and I have to travel too much, but I'm my own boss."

I was impressed by her resilience. Maybe I could learn a thing or two from her about making it on my own.

⊠   ⊠   ⊠

This is usually when I would retrieve a martini, except I am not drinking lately. I think that means I am not an alcoholic but an abuser of alcohol upon the wrong occasion.

Other than abolishing depression, my New Year's resolutions are:

(1) to finish my screenplay;

(2) to find new love, perhaps with Arlen Wynnewood;

(3) to succeed in real estate, that is, until I sell *Those Who Try* for a cool $2.1 million and become a regular on David Letterman's show; and

(4) last, but not least, to stop obsessing over you.

Amazingly enough, I have begun efforts to accomplish all the above.

"Merry's so much better these days, don't you think? Just another year in the home and maybe we can let her out on a trial basis."

That's what DPB would say. Screw Brandon.

⊠   ⊠   ⊠

(1) The script revision is going well. I am working on the final act, the one wherein my heroine decides to divorce her husband. It's difficult to write because the entire mess is autobiographical—your fault, since you were the one who suggested I write a screenplay centered on being a professional golfer's wife.

Your eyes had a glint of greed. "I'll be your editor and producer."

I always wondered if you meant that.

Regardless, in four more weeks, one month, the script will be done.

⊠   ⊠   ⊠

(2) As for the progress report on l-o-v-e: I spent fifteen hours last week parked in the Pecan Street Theater lot waiting for Arlen Wynnewood to come out during lunch. I arrived at 11:00 a.m., in case he was an early luncher, and I watched the door until 2:00 p.m., in case he was a late luncher. Evidently, Arlen Wynnewood is not a luncher. He was *there*, however, because I called his office from a nearby pay phone.

His secretary took my pretend name and told me, "Mr. Wynnewood will be out of his meeting shortly. I'll tell him you called."

My next stalking goal is to figure out which car the man drives, because then I could follow him after work the same way I tracked you. Will my pursuit of Arlen Wynnewood result in the same one-act?

Perhaps I also have learned a thing or two about forcing issues.

⊠   ⊠   ⊠

(3) As for real estate, I'm about to go broke getting into business. B. J. Hathaway requires female agents to wear a red-and-yellow striped polyester knit blazer that cost $275, and a red-polyester knit skirt that cost $190. I traded in the Cutlass for a new, albeit used car—a 1985 red Buick Electra 380 sedan. It has four doors so that clients may ride comfortably. Payment: $474.50 monthly, which, unlike days of yore, I cannot afford. I also had to buy two magnetic door signs, which cost $250 each. So far, the signs have not generated one client, although I did get a call from Brandon. He saw me driving by his office one day.

"You look great in red and yellow, Merry. You really blend right in."

What did that mean?

In today's training class, I learned how to compute a mortgage payment on my Texas Instruments Business Analyst II calculator ($99.95). Here we were, fifteen novice agents around a conference table, while Erica Cooke spent two hours passing out worksheets, scribbling on a blackboard, and scurrying from agent to agent in a fervent attempt to teach a calculator function geared to the IQ of the masses.

My brain kept screaming, "Would Genet ever compute a mortgage payment? I do not want to be so crushed by the system."

I glanced to see if any others, like me, were resistant, but the room was full of excited hopefuls who "ooh-ed" and "ahh-ed" when, after two hours of punching buttons, they derived an answer.

Even worse, tornado-haired Erica Cooke did not seem to notice that I was the only agent who got the correct number. She only seemed to care that the agents got an answer. Any fucking answer.

I wasn't going to let her ignore me. "But Erica, isn't there just one possible mortgage payment, given the figures you've presented?"

Erica glared. "Merry, we're not going to fault someone for getting an incorrect answer. We're trying to teach method."

I pressed. "So, it's okay to miscalculate a client's house payment?"

Erica glared. "The mortgage company does that anyway. This is just for estimates. Now, let's move on to closing costs."

(I don't think Erica will select me for outstanding student.)

✉   ✉   ✉

(4) As for obsessing about you, I have not wallowed on you (or Jillian) in this letter. Instead, you are simply *My Dear Diary*, a pathway to set down my disappointments, hopes, and confidences.

See? I'm trying. Hey, fella! Wanna buy a house?

Love,
Merry

SCENE 15

EXT. NORA'S HIGH SCHOOL — 1989 — DAY

IN THE PARKING LOT

Glenn parks his car to the left of Nora's 1978
VW VAN. Wearing a winter jacket, he gets out,
then checks to see if anybody's watching.
He pulls out a POCKET KNIFE, opens the main
blade, then stabs his car's right front tire.

The tire DEFLATES in a blast of steamy air.

Glenn puts the knife back in his pocket and
paces, watching for Nora.

AT THE SCHOOL DOOR

Nora walks out with a senior high FRIEND.
Both are in winter jackets. They chat MOS and
giggle like high-school girls do.

IN THE PARKING LOT

Glenn kneels and pretends to examine his flat
tire as Nora and Friend approach.

Nora waves goodbye to Friend.

                              NORA
         Call me later when you do your trig.

As Friend nods and waves, Nora goes to open
her van door, but Glenn is checking his flat,
blocking her way.

                              NORA
         Excuse me, sir. I need to get in.

Glenn rises. Gives Nora a wry smile.

                              GLENN
         "Sir"? Do I look like a geezer?

                              NORA
         Sorry. Didn't mean to.

Glenn pretends he just now recognizes Nora.

                              GLENN
         Say, aren't you Merry's daughter?

                              NORA
         How did you know that?

Glenn smiles to reassure her.

                              GLENN
         Maybe you don't remember. I thought
         your Mom had invited me to dinner.

                              NORA
         She said you're too young for her.
         That ought to make you feel better.

GLENN

I also remember you said I was cute.
Not that a guy wants to be 'cute.'

NORA

Handsome then. How's that?

GLENN

I'll take it.

NORA

Looks like you have a flat.

GLENN

Spare is flat too. I'll have to call
a cab from a payphone.

NORA

There's a tire store near our house.
I could give you a ride.

GLENN

Maybe you should call your Mom first.

NORA

I'm eighteen now. I don't have to
ask Mom for anything.

GLENN

How about you drive me to the tire
store, and I'll buy you a burger.

Nora smiles in delight. The two get in her van
and drive off.

Letter Sixteen
February 3, 1989

Dear Roland,

Brandon is a total prig. He calls me almost daily to pester me to view Dad's funeral video, but he does it under the guise of inquiring how my real estate career is doing. He begins by asking about my training. How long until I get my first client. Have I met B. J. Hathaway yet? Wouldn't I be better off in the West Lake Hills office?

But sooner or later, he says, "So ... Merry, what did you think about that video?"

"What video?" I say, baiting.

It doesn't matter. The answer is the same. "The video of Dad's memorial service. I spent $1,000 on that, Merry, and I should think—"

"Brandon, if you ask me again, I will hang up on you."

So he did call and ask again, and I hung up on him. Last night.

This led to my falling off the wagon, in spite of the fact I haven't been drinking much these days, what with my New Year's resolutions. But after hanging up on Brandon, I went to the kitchen for a martini, of which I took only one swig before I started to weep.

Oh dear. I could tell this would be one of my victimized-female gut wrenches. So, to hide from the kids—I mean, they really have put up with a lot—I grabbed a blanket and went to my tiny backyard.

It was colder than shit, even if this is the Sunbelt, and the frigid air seemed another affront. I collapsed in my white plastic-woven chaise and started sobbing. Not just about Brandon. About everything. Death. Divorce. Destitution. That's the way it works, isn't it? When you uncork a teeny hole in the dam, the lake crashes down on the village below, and everybody dies.

After a few minutes, I was gnashing so loud, I woke the neighbors—well Pamela anyway. She shouted out her sliding door, "If you're going to keep that up, you might as well come do it in my living room."

Mortified, I stuffed part of my blanket into my mouth and threw the rest over my head, feeling as if my insanity had been discovered.

Moments later, I heard Pamela's door slam, the fence gate creak, and leaves rustle as she walked into my yard. I heard her feet stop in a crunch.

"Merry, is that you under the blanket?"

"Yes," I managed.

She gently lifted the blanket off. Through my tears, I could see she was swallowed by a tomato-red terry bathrobe. "Your mother gave you that for Christmas, didn't she?"

Pamela glared. "Insulting someone is a defense mechanism. Something's very wrong out here. Tell me what or I'll call the loony bin to come get you."

"I'm having a meltdown."

"C'mon over. I got one hell of a gift bottle of Wild Turkey."

Ah, more booze. I didn't even attempt a polite protest. I gathered my blanket and trailed after Pamela's red robe. She opened her sliding door, and we went into her perfect little kitchen, where she poured me a stiff one, then sat across from me at her round breakfast table.

Reality time. I looked into this woman's deeply worried eyes and wondered how I could make her understand my anger toward DPB. I had already told her about the other painful chapters of my dreary life, although I've never told her about you. (I never tell anybody about you.) How could I ask Pamela to listen to more?

"I'm waiting."

I took a breath and spilled my guts. Ranted for an hour about how awful Brandon is, finishing with, "Why do I have to deal with a man who videotaped my father's funeral and gave me a copy so I would feel shitty for not being there?"

Pamela really perked up at that. "Videotaped a funeral? How was it?"

"What?"

"The funeral. The videotape."

"I haven't seen it."

"Why?"

"I haven't wanted to."

"Why?"

"I don't know. Maybe because I don't want to relive it, maybe because of ... dread. Plain old dread."

"Let's have some dread with our whiskey. C'mon, go get the damn video. Aunt Pamela's whiskey will give you courage."

So that we wouldn't pique the kids' interest, we tiptoed to my side of the duplex, giggling silently like two girls at a slumber party. The kids heard us anyway and asked what in the hell we were doing. They were in the den watching TV, so I had to lie. "We're getting that PBS video. Pamela hasn't seen Plácido Domingo sing before."

"Yuck, that opera video you got?" Scottie said.

He didn't know that I had relabeled the video "PBS Opera Pagliacci— Plácido Domingo" because I knew they would never view it.

Pamela and I then giggled all the way back to her place, but when she put the cassette into the VCR player, I remembered this was not so darn funny. I felt the dread again. Dread that I could not handle more grief.

So while Pamela fiddled with the remote, I hid in her kitchen.

She shouted from the living room. "I got it loaded. Let's give it a try."

I reached for the Wild Turkey, but my hands, arms, lips, thighs, knees began trembling. This was the funeral that Godot had not allowed me to attend. And now, furious about having to exist in a world populated by neurotically pluppy people like my brother, I found myself perched on the rim of more despair—the videotape that Brandon had pronounced I must see.

"Hurry up. It's playing. I guess I can back it up. Is this Deanna? My word, she's wearing white satin. Is your brother the fat guy in the brown suit? Why does he keep smiling at the camera? He looks like he's waiting for Vanna White to ask what letters to turn."

I stayed in the kitchen, avoiding, until Pamela came to get me.

"What in the hell?"

I started blubbering between shrieks. "I don't know if I can ..."

"What do you think is on this video?"

"I don't want to see my father. I just don't want to see him anymore."

"You told me he was cremated."

"I mean, I don't want to see his hairy balls anymore."

"For heaven's sake, did he sexually abuse you?"

"No. He was just weird. He paraded around the house in the nude, and had this thing about weighing his balls."

Pamela grasped my elbow and firmly escorted me to her living room, crooning, "My dear, come to Aunt Pamela's Harmless Funeral Parlor and Video Playhouse." Then she plopped me on the sofa, tucked my blanket around, sat beside me, and restarted the videotape.

I watched the damn funeral.

After only the first few minutes, I realized I shouldn't have put myself through such dread. The video turned out to be like watching an absurd one-act comedy.

First off, the only people inside this massive church arena were Brandon, Deanna, their girls, and the video guy. And for most of the half hour, Deanna stood on an elevated platform that serves as the dais in the Eternal Spirit Center, where gigantic sunlit windows angled on the cathedral ceiling above. Her "raiment" was a super-duper white satin robe with wide bands of ornate gold and silver embroidered down her V neckline, hem, and belt.

Deanna groaned and beseeched about spirits "passing from this life but waiting wide-armed for us"—all those illogical things TV ministers spew on programs that appeal to desperate people. Except that Deanna was good at this. I was blown away with how much fervor she put into this service.

"Our beloved Virgil Mayfield—father to Brandon Mayfield here present and Merry Mayfield—our beloved sister who cannot be with us today, although we hold her near with us—our beloved Virgil Mayfield is now with his spiritual family in heaven and is welcomed as a new member. Hear ye, all spirits present and afar, do not despair. All life comes to this, as the scriptures have described, ashes to ashes. Dust to dust. Virgil, a sinner like us all, a man whose life was not what he dreamed, a man whose pain and heartache were dulled by addiction to the evils of alcohol, Virgil Mayfield, a man who questioned the existence of the Eternal Spirit, and yet through your benevolent mercy is now brother and disciple to our spiritual fathers and mothers, and a cousin to the angels and spirits who have passed before. He is at last home with his long-suffering wife, Sylvia ..."

On and on and on, the woman preached, punctuated with rhythmic and heavenly thrusts.

Although I appreciated her skills as an evangelist, two things about her performance eventually sent me teetering into laughter. At the beginning of the video, Deanna's strawberry hair was done up in a lovely French twist, but with her frenzied thrusting, curls kept erupting whenever she moved. By the end of the funeral, she looked like she had been laid.

Secondly, the whole time Deanna preached, her eyes veered into Neverland. Oh, they glistened with energy and passion, clear emeralds above her freckles and white-satin robes. But I swear, Roland, if anybody had tapped her on the shoulder—I don't care if it were a true spirit from heaven—Deanna would have continued preaching and beseeching with the same darn expression, because she was a woman possessed.

As for Brandon, all during the service, he kept turning around to smile at the camera. Spiffed up in a brown silk suit, with a white dress shirt and a wide striped tie that made him look like he was choking to death, he turned his pudgy mustached face to the camera and smiled.

Each time he did that, Pamela pounded the coffee table. "That asshole did this for himself, taped this so he could see himself on TV."

I'm really starting to like Pamela.

So, that was the dreaded video. Now I can stop hanging up on Brandon.

In retrospect, I couldn't help wondering what was so menacing about this funeral that Godot would keep me from attending it, unless it was to protect me from the conflicts I would have endured with Brandon. Maybe all of that would have been too overwhelming. Perhaps watching it on TV was the distance I needed from reality. I would have cared. Too much. About Dad and Mom and Doug and you and everything.

Until Pamela's Wild Turkey ran out at about 1:00 a.m., she and I replayed, fast-forwarded, slow-motioned, and freeze-framed that video, hooting and hollering, trying to find the most preposterous moment.

It came right after Deanna said, "Passing from this life is not a sad occasion, for he who has passed is forever reunited with his father, mother, and the eternal spirits." Then came one of her frenzied thrusts, and a red curl shot from her hair like a sunspot. At the same moment, Brandon smiled back toward the camera. It was perfect.

⊠   ⊠   ⊠

This morning, my head hurt so terribly from the Wild Turkey, my alcoholic's penance told me to channel the day into my New Year's resolutions. So, I made even more lists of things Merry can do to accomplish her goals. Although I have vowed in several entries to accomplish these same goals, I did not manage more than getting drunk last night.

But there is more. The second part of this *Dear Diary* entry is a progress report. Except I think I'm going to continue that tomorrow because I've written too much, and my fingers are tired.

To be continued ...

Love,
Merry

SCENE 16

EXT. GLENN'S TRAILER — 1989 — DAY

Nora's van pulls in the gravel lot. She parks and gets out, wearing jeans, boots, and a winter jacket.

When Nora knocks on the trailer door, NATASHA the Doberman BARKS from inside.

Glenn opens the door a crack and grins.

> GLENN
> Come on in, but I've got to walk Natasha before we go.

> NORA
> I'll stay out here. The movie starts in a bit.

Nora watches Glenn lead Natasha out. The dog jumps aggressively in Nora's direction.

> GLENN
> Down girl. Nora's a friend.

Nora gingerly pets Natasha on the head and smiles hesitantly at Glenn.

Glenn takes Nora's hand. The two walk the dog to a grassy area.

When Nora turns away for a bit, Glenn leers at her as if she's prime steak.

SCENE 17

INT. BRANDON'S KITCHEN — 1989 — DAY

While Brandon reads the morning NEWSPAPER,
Deanna blends SMOOTHIES, then pours two
glasses full, one for Brandon.

                    DEANNA
          This should help with your weight.

                    BRANDON
          You have a problem with my weight?

Deanna gently touches his round shoulder.

                    DEANNA
          We all need to keep an eye on our
          weight. I'm just trying to help you.

                    BRANDON
          You are always 'just trying to
          help.'

Brandon downs his smoothie and then grabs his
briefcase and a jacket.

                    DEANNA
          What, no kiss goodbye?

Brandon half-heartedly kisses Deanna on her
cheek.

> DEANNA
> Brandon, please wait a bit. We need
> to talk.

> BRANDON
> About what?

> DEANNA
> Since Merry moved here, you've been
> distant.

> BRANDON
> Merry has nothing to do with it.

> DEANNA
> So, you agree you've been distant.

> BRANDON
> There's a lot on my mind. Mom's
> death. Dad's. My job.

> DEANNA
> You keep saying that, but nothing
> improves between us. Can't you share
> with your wife what's bothering you?

> BRANDON
> Not now, Deanna. I've got to go.

> DEANNA
> Brandon, are you having an affair?

                    BRANDON
          An affair?!

                    DEANNA
          Yes. You work late or go to the
          office at odd hours. We've had sex
          once since Merry arrived.

                    BRANDON
          Merry has nothing to do with it.

                    DEANNA
          You're dodging the bullet!

Fuming, Brandon puts his smoothie down hard,
grabs his briefcase, and leaves.

After he exits, Deanna dissolves at the
kitchen table.

                    DEANNA
               (to herself, crying)
          My husband is having an affair.

Letter Seventeen
February 4, 1989

Dear Roland,

Yes, Professor Brilliance, here's the aforementioned progress report from yesterday's letter. I am almost a success at everything I am trying to be! First, I will share the details of what are probably the two more substantial items, and then, only then, I will reveal how I, Merry Mayfield, sleuth and temptress, have finally stalked down Arlen Wynnewood.

First, the script. As you know, it began as a stage play, primarily to please you. For some reason you ranked the stage several rungs above film, as though stage plays are more literary and therefore more meritorious. But I'm going for broke. I'm going for Hollywood. Call me crass, but I'd rather make some bucks than have my very literary stage play produced on an obscure stage so far off Broadway, you'd have to enter through the kitchen of some Ethiopian restaurant.

I remember how long it took me to finish the first two acts. You nagged, "Apply ass to chair. Writers write. They don't just talk about their great acts." But in those beginner days, it took me a full year under your watchful eye to get even two-thirds finished. Then all those things happened that I refuse to moan about again.

But since my resolutions, I sequestered in my office most evenings and wrote a gut-wrenching new ending. My sweet protagonist, Hope—who looks a bit like me—gets enough courage to leave her pro-golfer husband and marry her bisexual hairdresser, Morgan. Yes! It's a shocker ending—especially since Morgan reveals to Hope that he is HIV positive.

In the scene before this, however, Hope makes a final attempt to see if there's anything left of her marriage to Billy the golfer. She foolishly hopes she can persuade him to reach out to her.

But all during Hope's monologue, Billy putts balls into an electronic putting machine. Each ball plunks into the hole, plunks out, and rolls back to him—while Hope pleads for him to listen. Ignoring her, Billy silently continues to putt, until Hope gives up and walks away, leaving him putting, putting, putting.

In the next scene, well, here. I'll cut and paste this in.

⊠   ⊠   ⊠

EXT. MORGAN'S SALON — DAY

SIGN: Morgan's Hair and Beauty.
SMALL SIGN: We Are Now Closed.

INT. MORGAN'S SALON — DAY

Hope and Morgan are alone at his station. As
Morgan cuts her hair, he hesitates nervously.

                    MORGAN
        Hope, I need to tell you something.
        But you can't say anything until I'm
        done. Just sit and listen. Okay?

IN THE MIRROR

Hope looks worried.

                    HOPE
        You're scaring me. It's not the HIV.

                    MORGAN
        Hush. No, not the HIV. It's, well
        ... this is so hard for me. But for
        the past ten years, I've been in
        love with you. Did you know that?

                    HOPE
I've always known we were fond of
each other, that if you weren't—

                    MORGAN
Hush. I'm in love with you. Like
a chest-pounding, macho shithead,
heterosexual man loves a woman. But
there wasn't a way I could show my
love for you. Sexually. Oh, there
were times I'd pretend I was making
love to you.

AT STYLIST CHAIR

Morgan puts the scissors down and comes around
in front of Hope, who is a bit stunned.

                    MORGAN
You have to give me credit for being
creative. Now that I must accept the
fact that I shouldn't have sex with
anyone, male or female, and maybe
I'm even going to die of AIDS, I've
started wondering why I have wasted
time having sex with men I don't
love ... when I could have spent the
time loving you. Being with you.
Holding you. Talking to you. Doing
things with you. That's what love
is, isn't it? I know I'm asking you
to give up man-woman sex and give up
being Mrs. Rich Bitch, even though
that awful golfer made you sad. But
I'm asking.

Morgan gets down on one knee.

> MORGAN (CONT'D)
> I don't know how much time I have,
> but will you spend the rest of my
> life with me? I love you.

Hope reaches to Morgan, and both rise and hold
one another, crying in joy.

⊠ ⊠ ⊠

Next, we have three short scenes as Hope tries to make up her mind.
She talks to her friends, talks to Morgan, talks to herself. Everything is
left up in the air until the final scene.

⊠ ⊠ ⊠

INT. HOPE'S KITCHEN — DAY

Hope watches Billy walk out the back door with
several SUITCASES.

> HOPE
> (to herself)
> His career's over, just like our
> marriage. It's ironic that the two
> things died at the same time.

THROUGH A WINDOW

Hope watches Billy put his suitcases in the
car trunk. She looks expectantly to see if he
will come back to say goodbye, but he gets in
and drives off.

```
              HOPE (CONT'D)
I guess that's it. I'll miss how
we were when we were young ... how
he used to touch me. But that was
a dream. I'd rather have the love
Morgan can give, for as long as he
lives, than the kind of love I got
from a man who ignored me.
         (taking a big breath)
So here we go. Morgan and me. Best
friends together. It's odd how we
get where we're going. Isn't it?
```

FADE OUT.

                        ⊠   ⊠   ⊠

Okay, so I'm not writing *Hamlet*, but I don't think I stooped to dishonest sappiness. I was crying when I finished it. I was feeling.

As you always said, "If your characters are in love, you've got to feel their love. If they're angry, you've got to feel their rage. And if they're sad, you've got to cry all over your damn keyboard."

Well, I did.

Next step for this project is to join the Austin Film Society, get their list, and query producers. My log line pitch is "Caddy Shack Meets Steel Magnolias." Get it? Just pray that someone will produce it. If one does, I think I will get up the guts to call you.

                        ⊠   ⊠   ⊠

I yielded to a very light gin and tonic. I'm trying!

Update number two: On the most boring subject in the world, I have an actual real estate client. Oddly enough, it's Brandon.

In spite of my recent angry hang ups, he called one more time and said he wants to surprise Deanna with a new house, so he asked me to look up options on the MLS system. And I did. And we will go out next weekend to see properties. Maybe then I can prove to Brandon that I am worthy of his confidence.

Update number three, drum roll: Arlen Wynnewood. Last Tuesday, I parked in a crowded area of the Pecan Street Theater lot and glued my eyes to the front door. By 5:15 p.m., staffers in tight, colorful dresses and too-high heels giggled their goodbyes and drove off in their Hondas and Toyotas, leaving my car exposed. That made me wonder if I should move to a more camouflaged area, when suddenly—like in a spy film of which I am the heroine—there was Arlen Wynnewood: striding in a slick black pinstripe suit with the jacket unbuttoned erotically. He bounded down the steps and extended his long, lean legs (of course, I'm overwriting) toward a deep-red Mercedes 450 SL with a Texas "State of the Arts" vanity plate that said ARLEN. Is that perfection?

He got in and zoomed off. I roared after. Talk about obsessed. I was in a zone where no other could enter, although it was hell staying up with him. Arlen roared through green lights, zoomed through yellow ones, and ran a few red ones. He'd pause briefly, check for cross traffic, then zooooomm through the intersection.

Whenever Arlen changed lanes or turned, I changed lanes or turned, then floorboarded the LeSabre. I must have left a gallon of gasoline behind me on the pavement. Damn any car in my way. I ignored honking horns, screeching brakes, and shouts from open windows about what kind of stupid bitch I was.

After his Mercedes zoomed west of downtown two miles, it squealed into a graveled lot off First Street. I drove by slowly and noticed a small wooden building that had a neon-red flashing sign: BAR.

Aha! A bar. Do you see how things work if you have patience?

By the time I parked, touched up my makeup, and walked in, Arlen Wynnewood was at a table—his beautiful, broad back to me.

I took a barstool at the end and surveyed the surroundings. Inside, this "Bar" turned out to be dark, all wood, and funky—kind of like the Raven, a place I would expect to run into you. The female bartender was a cute, curvy brunette with pigtails that made her look younger than she probably was, which I guessed to be thirty-five.

"Hi, what'll you have?"

"Beefeater martini, up. Olives."

She smiled. "Is this your first time here? Our specialty is a jalapeño martini. Your option of gin or vodka. Tell you what—the first will be on me, and if you don't like it, I'll fix you that Yankee martini, on me too."

Would Merry Mayfield turn that down? "Gin, please."

The bartender poured ample Tanqueray and a dash of vermouth over ice in a silver shaker. Covered it, then shook it thirty times. Explicitly. Took off the top, poured the icy froth into a frozen martini glass, plopped in a long red plastic toothpick that held a piece of lime, an olive, and a slice of jalapeño pepper. She gave it to me with a grin.

"I hope you like it."

I took a sip and was instantly in love with this little bar and the world. The combination of the olive, lime, and jalapeño made this martini uniquely Texan.

Spare me the lecture. I have vowed to limit myself to two drinks per day. And I am sticking to that, unless I'm led astray.

While keeping an occasional eye on the back of Arlen Wynnewood's head, I made small talk with the bartender, whose named turned out to be Toni, and ordered my second jalapeño martini, which I soon learned was called the J-Tini for short.

Meanwhile, a group seated at a round table near Arlen provided diversion. I recognized a humor columnist whose picture appears every other day in the *Austin American-Statesman*. He's about forty, balding, and looks like a lonesome turtle with brown, amphibious eyes. And his long neck with a prominent Adam's apple protrudes whenever he talks.

He kept straining to see what was going on at Arlen Wynnewood's table. After one such peering, Turtle said loudly enough to be heard by Merry Mayfield, girl spy, "Yes, once again, our humble watering hole has been honored with the presence of Austin's theatrical prince."

Aha! Was Turtle ridiculing Arlen, or was Turtle merely jealous?

Suddenly, Turtle got up and went to Arlen Wynnewood's table, where Turtle stood unacknowledged until Arlen greeted him begrudgingly, although I couldn't see Arlen's face from where I sat. I had to imagine this part of that scene.

As Arlen and Turtle shook hands and mumbled pleasantries, I couldn't hear much, except Arlen eventually said, "I'd ask you to join us, Carter, but we're in the middle of a rather important meeting."

"No problem, Arlen. I'll catch you at the theater."

When Turtle went back to his table, I decided to get my body in Arlen's line of sight. So, I decided to flirt with Turtle. Poor man. I caught his eye and gazed at him alluringly. The shy soul took my bait. Within minutes, he stood beside me, shouting an urgent drink order to Toni.

I said something like, "So you're a J-Tini aficionado too."

He answered, "Toni makes the best."

Toni helped things along. "Got room at your table for a new regular?"

I didn't wait for Turtle to show me where to sit. I gathered my J-Tini, slid off my barstool, and sat where Turtle had been sitting—one fucking table away from Arlen Wynnewood. We were catty-corner to each other now, five feet away.

Turtle nervously slid across to his newly inherited side of the table. He mumbled introductions to the other men, all reporters at the *Austin American-Statesman*.

I pretended to be pleased to meet them. I also pretended I couldn't wait for our relationship to begin—Turtle's and mine. Yes, I used him.

"I don't think I've seen you here before, Merry."

"I'm new in town." I took my first breathless glance at Arlen Wynnewood's face—beautiful, Roland—olive, tan, lined only where dimples have deepened and smiles have etched their joyous pathways. He must have felt my eyes on him because he turned his to mine. Electricity! We are talking lightning bolts of mega power. He held my gaze. My face flushed. I lowered my eyes and took another sip, then looked up again.

Ever so sensuously, he telegraphed a hello, his eyes verdant pools. We are talking orgasmic zings. Then he raised his glass in a toast.

"Hello," I whispered in a voice so breathless it didn't achieve a whisper.

Turtle thought I was talking to him. "Well, hello again. You seem kind of ... how long have you been here?"

"So, what do you do for a living, Merry?" another reporter asked.

Shit. I was forced to redirect. "I'm a screenwriter."

I hadn't planned to say that.

"A screenwriter?" Turtle repeated, much more loudly than I wanted.

I glanced to see if Arlen had heard, but by that time, he had stood to shake hands with a fat, mustached man who had dropped by his table.

"That's Arlen Wynnewood of Pecan Street Theater," Turtle said. Then he began an annoying attempt to get Arlen's attention, but thank Godot, Arlen did not notice because, oh shit, Turtle was hell-bent on introducing me as a *screenwriter* for heaven's sake.

Stark, raving embarrassment. I panicked! I fucking panicked—your fault, Roland, you with your damn lectures about not defining yourself as a writer until after making $100,000 being one.

"Well, actually, my day job is in real estate."

"Real estate," Turtle said with dismay.

"Yes, until I win an Oscar."

Turtle and his cynical reporter friends were not amused.

I decided to escape to the ladies' room, but right then, my Greek prince of love was walking out with the pudgy mustached guy. Arlen was leaving! And when he got to the door, he did it again. The same thing he had done at Jeffrey's. He paused, turned as if he knew I was watching, and shot me a smile. Then he raised two fingers and walked out.

I smiled back, but it was a Mona Lisa version that indicated, "I am not easy. I haven't spent hours stalking you only to be screwed, then tossed aside. I'm cool. I'll stay with this Turtle and act like I'm having a grand time. And next time you see me, you had better make a move."

I held that smile until even I couldn't stand myself anymore.

After Arlen left, I waited five minutes, then decided to hightail it. I pleaded problems with the kids.

Turtle sort of nodded. He was probably glad I was leaving.

With no bill to pay, I tipped Toni with a five and rushed out, of course scanning the lot for the red 450 SL. But no.

That's okay. Confidence springs eternal. I now know where Arlen Wynnewood goes for a drink. I can hang out at that little bar, which I found out was called The Cypress Door. And it will be my new Raven until fate brings Arlen Wynnewood and me to our destinies.

Godot is coming. Good little heroine that I am, and you have taught me to be, I shall await my fate at The Cypress Door. It won't be unpleasant. Toni makes the world's best J-Tini.

Can you tell I'm in better spirits? (pun intended)

Love,
Merry

SCENE 18

EXT. GLENN'S TRAILER — 1989 — NIGHT

Glenn drives his car into the lot with Nora
in the passenger seat. He pulls up and parks
beside Nora's van.

INSIDE GLENN'S CAR

He leans, kisses Nora gently, then more
passionately, but abruptly pulls back,
remembering his dog.

> GLENN
> I need to let Natasha out. You can
> wait inside.

> NORA
> I'd better not.

Glenn pulls Nora closer. Kisses her deeply.
She's breathless, full of virgin teen passion.

> GLENN
> Come inside. I promise to be good.

> NORA
> That's what I'm afraid of.

The two laugh, then get out of the car.

Natasha BARKS and SCRATCHES from inside, so Glenn bounds in to get the dog.

Nora hesitates, but doesn't follow. Instead, she gets in her van. Starts ENGINE.

Glenn comes out with dog. Sees Nora in van.

Nora rolls down her window.

> GLENN
> Where are you going?

> NORA
> Mom will ground me if I'm late.

> GLENN
> I thought you were eighteen and could do whatever you want.

> NORA
> I'm just not ready for sex.

Nora blushes, embarrassed, and starts to back out, but Glenn and his dog suddenly move in back of the van and block her way.

Nora quickly angles her car past Glenn.

He glares as she drives away.

She gives him a wave but no smile. In fact, she looks quite worried.

Letter Eighteen
March 17, 1989

Dear Roland,

I was dismayed to receive a number of rejections from Hollywood film agents that I queried, so instead of going the agent route, I have given hard copies of my script to a few independent producers I met at Austin Film Society events. Can you believe I'm actually doing what screenwriters do? Networking and giving a script to producers?

I called Sigrid to tell her. She was thrilled. "I always knew you could do it. You have so much talent. Just stick with it, like Roland said."

"Speaking of which, how is he these days?"

"He's fine, I guess. Might be drinking too much, but then, I should talk. We four never do much other than hash over the same dead screenwriters and drink the same too many beers. You know Roland. Genet and Sartre and Pinter. Same old Nothingness."

I laughed. "Raven conversations always did have a pattern."

Abruptly, Sigrid changed the subject. "I guess I'd better tell you before I change my mind, but Frank and I have decided to get married."

"Oh no!" I wanted to say. But if Sigrid is in love with a lousy actor who'll never make it to Broadway or rise higher than part-time lecturer at Columbia, then it's Sigrid's worry, not mine. I tried to be as encouraging as she has been to me. "That's wonderful news. I'll fly up for the wedding." Then it dawned on me that I would see you. "Maybe we five can do a Raven night at least once while I'm there."

"I may have mentioned this before, but things haven't been the same since you left. Something about the chemistry between you and Roland ... I realize Jillian was jealous, but you two kept me laughing all night. Shall I let him know about your screenplay?"

"Not yet. I don't want to jinx myself by saying something is going to happen when it might not. If I do find a producer, you can be sure I will let everyone know."

Sigrid signed off with a promise to send invitations to her nuptials.

Part of me hopes she will go ahead and tell you that I'm shopping my script—that I might really become a screenwriter—maybe not worth $100,000 but at least defined as screenwriter by someone other than myself. That's Genet, isn't it? To the existential core.

I won't call you until I know it is true.

$$\boxtimes \quad \boxtimes \quad \boxtimes$$

You can bet that Dear Pluppy Brandon is another person who won't hear a word until my screenplay is produced. In fact, DPB won't hear from me for a while. That's because the fucker bought a house from somebody else.

In my last account, I told you he had called and said he wanted to surprise Deanna with the new house. Well, I scheduled an appointment to show them properties I had gleaned from the confusing MLS computer system, but Brandon called at the last minute and shouted, "Merry, guess what! We just bought a house!"

Can you believe this? Turns out Brandon couldn't keep a secret from Deanna. After he spilled the beans, the two went looking in a development near Austin Country Club. Within hours, they had signed a contract on a new build for $525,000, without considering that if I were their agent, I could've made one and a half percent on the sale.

"That's $7,875.00 I really could have used right now."

"Having you there would make the house cost more," Brandon said.

"It wouldn't cost you a dime. And I could have had my broker guide you through the process and probably save you a lot of cash. But you just had to show off to Deanna and screw your sister out of a fat commission."

Then I hung up. I haven't spoken to him since. The old me would've felt alienated losing touch, but I have a few friends now—Pamela, Victor, Phillip, Toni, and Turtle at The Cypress Door. (I'll tell you more about Toni and Turtle later.) A motley group, and a bit tenuous, but even if I didn't have a friend in the world, would I need Brandon?

I did talk to Deanna, however. She came to see me last Sunday, fresh from her service, still in her fucking white-satin robes. I had just returned from an afternoon stint inside a B. J. Hathaway booth at the mall, which I must say reminded me of my days selling auto insurance.

Picture me in my red-and-yellow striped polyester knit blazer and red-polyester skirt seated in a red-and-yellow-striped booth in front of a huge picture of B. J. Hathaway, while his slogan "The Search Is Over!" blares from loud speakers, and his TV ad runs in endless loops on the VCR. It had been my role all afternoon to tell the souls who chanced by what a wonderful man B. J. Hathaway is, and how, if they'll buy a house from me, I will make sure B. J. visits them at closing.

After hours of that, I was ready for home, so I was in my kitchen when I heard, "Hellooooooo. Anybody here?"

Deanna had walked right in my front door.

Well, darn if I was going to let her see me in my red-and-yellow striped blazer, so I peeled off my outfit and threw it in the freezer. Then I tiptoed in my bra and panties to my bedroom and pulled out my black-and-gold silk kimono, the one Merry's One Iron brought me from Tokyo when he made the cut in the Japanese Open (Doug was good for a few things). I cinched on the gold obi, fluffed my Victor-styled Demi Moore hair, and walked out as if I had no idea that Deanna was standing in my living room in her shining white-satin robes.

"Why, Deanna. I didn't know you were here. What a nice surprise."

"Didn't you see me drive up, Merry? I could see you in your kitchen."

"My goodness. My mind must have been on real estate. And now, after a hard day at the office, I am in the mood for a J-Tini. Have you ever had one of those? I just found the neatest bar down by Town Lake, and that's their special concoction. Why don't you join me?"

"I don't wish to be rude, but you are well aware—"

"Oh yes," I said sarcastically. "I forgot."

I seated Deanna at my dinette while I bustled about, making a martini. I didn't have a fresh jalapeño, so I had to use a pickled one; I was out of limes but used a lemon; and the olives were Kalamata, so the effect was just not the same. But J-Tini in hand, I toasted Deanna.

Reluctantly, she nodded back, although I knew this confined setting was near the edge of hell for her. First, there was alcohol present. Secondly,

Deanna likes distance, like the time she ran down the hall to avoid the stripper at my birthday party. And thirdly, like her husband, Deanna likes to control—the control she would have if I wouldn't drink.

That's why I had to drink, see?

She sat stiffly, her priestess robes gathered in her lap to keep from touching the floor. In the midday light, her strawberry hair was fluffy enough to give the illusion of having a halo. "Merry, I am a bit bewildered. Brandon is quite upset—has been for weeks. He loves you very much."

"You needn't bother conveying Brandon's feelings. I am thoroughly pissed at him for buying a house from a builder, especially since Brandon asked me to find a house for you, and even more especially, since it was Brandon who got me involved in real estate in the first place."

Now, why in the hell can't I say something like that to Brandon?

Deanna stared out a window. I couldn't tell whether she was praying or gathering her wits. "Merry, you may not believe me or understand, but Brandon and I are having marital difficulties. So, after he said he was going to buy us a new house, that meant he was recommitted to our marriage. I was so excited, we jumped in the car and went looking for areas we might want to live. As we drove around, I felt an urge to stop. I got out in the middle of the road and I felt the Spirit pull me up a steep hill, where I climbed through cedar, live oak, and cactus. I didn't mind the brush because I felt the Spirit's hand on my shoulder. And suddenly there was a house in front of me—just the foundation and wood frame. It didn't have a 'For Sale' sign yet. But I knew the Spirit wanted me to buy that house. So we got the builder's name off the permit, called him from a payphone, and we signed a contract that afternoon."

"Yes, Brandon told me you bought it from a builder."

"No real estate agent was involved, Merry."

"Do you realize that if I had shown it to you, I would make over $7,000 on the deal?"

"It was the will of the Lord, Merry."

"The will of the Lord? The Lord didn't want me to make $7,000?"

"I don't understand why you're angry, Merry."

"Of course, Deanna. You couldn't possibly understand. Neither could Brandon. It's a difference that separates us and always will." I stood up. "Be a good priestess. Let me enjoy what's left of this afternoon."

I went back to my bedroom and shut the door. A few minutes later, I heard Deanna's Cadillac roar off, powered by the fumes of the Lord.

Dear Roland, would you please tell me why I can vocally eviscerate Deanna but cannot give Brandon the same hell? Is it that, deep down, I feel sorry for Brandon, knowing in my heart he was the winner of the least-favorite child award?

✉   ✉   ✉

Ah, but Brandon has had his victories, usually when our parents were not around. I'm suddenly remembering the last physical battle we two had. We were teens. He was a high-school senior; I was a freshman. I was playing records on the den stereo, and Brandon was in the kitchen.

All of a sudden, he announced in a father-like boom, "Come clean up this kitchen. Mother and Father will be home from the club soon."

I didn't move.

"Do what I say. I'm the man of the house when Father is away."

"I'm the man of the house," I mimicked. "Make me."

He sprang from the kitchen; his puffy cheeks flushed. And his thinning hair levitated like Sylvester the Cat's when he gets pissed at Tweety. Knuckles on hips, he repeated his command, "Do what I say."

"Make me."

As siblings do, we repeated this exchange—voice louder, angrier—until Brandon yanked me within an inch of his face. "I'm gonna teach you a lesson."

I bit him on his nose.

When he jumped back, I ran toward the stairs, but damn him, he ran after and clamped his sweaty paws on me. Then he dragged me by my waist across the den linoleum into the kitchen. "The dishes, Merry. Do the damn dishes."

I struggled until a Tweety-like bulb of an idea popped on. "I'll do the dishes, but only if you go away."

He held on to me a few seconds longer.

I smiled sweetly.

"Is that a promise?"

I smiled sweetly again.

He dropped his arms. "Well?"

"Well, what?"

"Well, do the dishes, Merry."

"You do them, Brandon." I stuck out my tongue and bolted toward the stairs. I thought I had enough of a jump, but Brandon snagged the tail of my blouse and pulled me back.

"You little brat. I'm gonna tell Father."

"Gonna tell Father," I mimicked ten times, buying time. I needed a weapon. Then I spied a plastic pitcher of lemonade on the counter. I yanked an arm free and grabbed the pitcher, whirling, smacking Brandon across his fat forehead. Gosh, I loved it. I hammered the stinker.

The lemonade flopped out in liquid chunks, sloshing me, Brandon, the counter, and linoleum floor.

"Look what you've done!"

I started toward the stairs again, but the floor was slick, and I slipped. I slipped. That has boiled in my brain ever since. I slipped and fell.

Brandon pounced on me. He pinned my arms above my head and feverishly ground his horrid, pluppy body into me, his eyes about to pop with rage, mouth in my face screaming, "Give, Merry. Do you give?"

I could feel his genitalia pressing my thigh. That made me furious. I fought and screamed so hard I thought I might throw up. "Get your horrid dick and balls off me." I screamed until my throat was raw and my face flushed with pounding blood.

Brandon must have gotten scared I would tell Mom and Dad. So, he lifted up a bit. "Calm down." But when I didn't calm down, he shouted louder, "Calm down. Please. Calm down."

Eventually, I did calm down, but only because it takes too much energy to rage like I was raging. I lay stiff, glaring into Brandon's eyes. "Get your balls off me."

I summoned my remaining adrenaline and tried to catapult him upward, but I wasn't strong enough. So I stiffened and screamed bloody murder again—probably could have gone on for another hour—except (thank Godot!) the doorbell rang.

Brandon shot upright like a kid caught playing doctor. He desperately tugged at his lemonade-wet shorts.

"Look at what you've done. I've got sticky stuff all over my pants."

Then I saw it! Dear Pluppy Brandon had an elongated weenie in his shorts—that pervert—an erection from grinding on his sister.

"You weirdo! You have a hard-on!"

Brandon shot me a desperate look that was a combination of shock, fear, anguish, and dismay. He pinched at his shorts in an effort to make the bulge less apparent, then went to answer the insistent doorbell.

I bolted upstairs, locked my door, and cried on my bed until I fell asleep. When I awoke, Brandon was gone. He had done the dishes and cleaned up the lemonade. I suppose that was his penance and a bribe.

I never told our parents about that fight. And I never told anybody about Brandon getting a hard-on. That was too disgusting to reveal.

✉ ✉ ✉

Okay, so I got off track with that story, but I'm going to put it in a screenplay someday, primarily to embarrass Brandon. I'll put Deanna in there too. Call it *My Pluppy Brother and the Redheaded Evangelist*.

To finish this, Brandon called as soon as Deanna got home. Claire answered the phone. I waved my finger for Claire to tell Brandon I wasn't home. He called three more times, and I made Claire lie three more times.

I am an awful mother.

As for tonight's missive, I had intended to tell you more about Victor, Toni, and Turtle, but as usual, this has gone on too long.

Love,
Merry

SCENE 19

INT. CLAIRE'S ROOM — 1989 — NIGHT

Claire is in bed, reading JUDY BLUME's *Are You There God? It's Me, Margaret.*

Claire is surprised when her sister Nora walks in, smiling hesitantly.

> NORA
> Can I talk to you?

> CLAIRE
> Me? I thought you hated me.

Nora sits on the end of Claire's bed. Gives her sister a rehearsed smile.

> NORA
> I don't hate you. You're my sister.

> CLAIRE
> You must want something.

> NORA
> Just advice. I'm dating an older guy. Mom doesn't know.

                    CLAIRE
          How much older?

                    NORA
          A lot older. Like thirteen years.

                    CLAIRE
          That means he's thirty-one!

Nora points to a HAN SOLO STAR WARS POSTER
inside Claire's open closet door.

                    NORA
          Harrison Ford is in his forties.

                    CLAIRE
          He wasn't then, and he's still cute.
          For an old guy, anyway.

                    NORA
          My guy is a friend of Mom's. They
          met at some bar, but he thought she
          was too old for him.

                    CLAIRE
          That guy who came to the door? He's
          too old for you!

                    NORA
          He wants to do it. You know. Sex.

                    CLAIRE
          I don't want to hear this stuff.

                    NORA
          I don't have anybody to talk to.

                    CLAIRE
Talk to Mom. She knows about sex.
I mean, she had three kids, so she
must have done it at least three
times, anyway.

                    NORA
She'd tell me to stop.

                    CLAIRE
You might get pregnant!

                    NORA
He said he'd use protection. He's
not like high school boys. Glenn
talks to me. Listens to me.

                    CLAIRE
And then he wants sex.

                    NORA
I'm scared. I don't know how to do
it.

                    CLAIRE
Then you should talk to Mom.

                    NORA
She just wants us to disappear, so
she won't have to make a living.

                    CLAIRE
I know.

Nora gets up to leave. She gives Claire a hug.

                    CLAIRE
Maybe if you tell Mom, she'd pay
more attention.

                    NORA
I don't want to tell Mom. And you'd
better not, or I'll kill you.

Letter Nineteen
March 19, 1989

Dear Roland,

As I mentioned two days ago, I went to see Victor for a haircut. While he wildly cut my hair, I blabbered about trying to get my screenplay produced. I also told him about my latest obsession with a nameless Greek god with dark, curly hair.

As usual, Victor took off on one of his tangents: "Dark, curly-haired men! Oh, how I love them! Phillip had dark, curly hair before he went bald. Didn't you, Phillip?" Victor shouted toward Phillip at the front. "In fact, one of my favorite lovers before Phillip had dark, curly hair. You ought to put him in one of your plays. His name was Bongo." Victor stopped short, came around, then peered at me with his huge green eyes. "You can imagine why his name was Bongo. I get horny thinking about him. He was a stylist and absolutely adored hair. He showed me what hair meant to one's identity. And, even though we broke up, Bongo left me with his passion. I especially love your hair. It's so thick and full of possibilities. What about curls? Next time, let's give you a permanent. It'd be like a huge mass of pubic hair. Wouldn't that be great?"

I'm sure you're wondering why I'm going on about Victor, but you see, a momentous thing occurred while he raved on.

Up front, Phillip suddenly shouted, "Mrs. Wynnewood is here!"

Victor almost speared me with his scissors as we each turned to view a tall brunette with an up-do, stylishly dressed, striding elegantly toward the shampoo sinks. She waved at Victor. He shouted back, "Let's get wild today, Mrs. Wynnewood! I'll be with you as soon as I finish my dear Merry here." Then Victor leaned and whispered, "That's Arlen Wynnewood's wife. He's the creative director of—"

"Pecan Street Theater," I said.

"You know him? But of course. You're a writer! Mrs. Wynnewood!" Victor started to walk toward the back.

"No!" I grabbed his arm and shushed him.

He whispered, "Maybe she could get her husband to produce your play!"

I pulled Victor's mustache within a breath's distance of my face. "I will kill you if you bring that woman over. Arlen Wynnewood is the Greek god I've been following."

"Oh no! Why, they've been married for years. She's loaded—old Austin money. He'd never divorce her."

Shit. Raving dog dung. "He sure as hell doesn't act married."

Victor jumped back and put his hands on his hips. "Well, I don't blame him. You're much prettier. If I weren't in love with Phillip, I'd make love to you myself."

"Oh hush. I'm in agony."

Victor looked confused. He couldn't understand how I have passively/ compulsively-obsessively/irrationally lived my life in wait. Should I quit this now? Or continue chasing Arlen/life the same way I chased you? What if Arlen also has a Jillian? What if he wants *me* to be his Jillian? Am I rushing into another one of these things that Merry does, only to find history repeat?

"Money, honey," Victor sang out loud. Then he leaned close and whispered, "How in the hell do you think Arlen Wynnewood got enough money to start Pecan Street Theater?"

Shit.

✉   ✉   ✉

After Victor finished my hair, I stubbornly zoomed to The Cypress Door and checked out the lot. Yes, a red 450 SL was there with its ARLEN plate. And Merry Mayfield's obsessive pea brain forgot all that she had just realized and was as full of silly excitement as her days in the Raven's lot when she spied your car and knew she was going to see you.

So, she feverishly gazed at her reflection in the rear-view mirror. She touched up her lipstick and mascara. She practiced her smile and alluring glance, the one she would give Arlen the moment she walked in. And during the three minutes it took her to go through these vain preparations, as her loins tingled in almost-orgasmic anticipation, Arlen Wynnewood walked out, got into his Mercedes, and drove off.

Zoom.

He didn't even see me. And I didn't notice him until I heard his 450 SL blaze out of the lot and head west on First Street.

Aaaaarrrrrgh!

Disappointed, I needed a drink and went inside.

Toni raised her silver shaker and smiled when I walked in. "Hi, Merry! J-Tini?"

That simple act made me feel like I belonged somewhere in this damn town. Like Norm on *Cheers*, I sat on a stool and watched Toni go through her well-practiced but elaborate, artistic performance.

"They should rename this after you. The Toni-Tini," I said.

I was just about to take a sip when a thin male voice to my right said, "Toni, your martini is the most wicked potion a bar wench can serve."

It was Turtle again, the humor columnist. I hadn't noticed—that's the kind of guy he is. I had sat right next to him.

He didn't look my way but kept his eyes straight ahead to Toni.

"Say, Carter, meet Merry. Merry, meet Carter Abrams."

Turtle blushed, flustered. He turned my way far enough to nod.

"We met some time ago. My name's Merry Mayfield."

He didn't reply. Just blushed and nodded.

"Good, now you've been properly introduced."

Poor Carter Abrams cleared his throat to speak, but nothing came out. So, I asked him something inane like, "How goes the column?"

"Humorlessly."

I laughed. He didn't. After all, Toni had put him in the horrid position of having to entertain a woman who was obsessed with somebody Turtle seemed to dislike. Eventually, he silently slid off his barstool and shuffled to a table where some guys were gathered.

Toni leaned close and whispered, "Carter's a sweet guy. It just takes him a while." Then she flitted off to fix some other drunk a J-Tini.

So, with Turtle gone, I was by myself. Again, eh? I immediately got high. One J-Tini will do it, not to mention the ache of having missed

Arlen Wynnewood, even if he has a wife. What to do? Order another. But then I broke my rule and ordered a third.

By 9:00 p.m., when the after-dinner crowds packed the place, I was roasted. Also, by that time, my bladder had started screaming. So I slid off my stool and attempted a move toward the john, but—I am horrified to tell you this—I fell straight on my ass. Thump. Bumble. Thud.

Toni came around the end of the bar. "Are you all right?"

"My mind's working okay, but my body—"

"I'll get some coffee." She went behind the bar and poured me a cup.

I drank one, then two—before Toni escorted me to the restroom, where I must have tee-tee'd for five minutes. Then, well you know how time flies when you're blackout drunk, Toni was ushering me outside, down the steps, and into a car—Turtle's car, a beat-up white Volvo.

He magically (it seemed to my addled mind) had reappeared and was driving me home.

I kept objecting, apologizing.

He kept apologizing back. "I'm sorry Uncle Ed isn't in adequate shape for company."

Uncle Ed was his car, full of a tennis bag, shoes, papers, a Sunday golf bag, books, you name it. Junk. There was so much junk there wasn't room for me, so I had to sit with my legs wrapped around the tennis racket as though I were riding it home.

On the way up MoPac, the freeway lights dizzied by in swirls of electrifying green fantasy.

Turtle pulled out a six-pack of Big Red soda from the back seat and offered me one.

"Oh no! The thought of more liquids makes we want to puke."

Turtle was silent.

I sighed loudly and said, "So, can't you talk to girls?"

He didn't respond.

I looked over. Bless his heart, Roland, he had blushed absolutely blood red. "I'm sorry. Toni said you were shy. I just wanted to make conversation. If I don't talk, I might get sick."

He looked panicked. "You want me to stop?"

I laughed. "Just talk to me. Do you know anything about querying film producers? How long I should wait for one to decide on my screenplay. Both Big State and Live Oak are looking at my script. So is Lyle Davis. Should I pester them or wait? They've each had the script for about a month."

"I thought you said you were in real estate."

"Well, I'm also trying to be a screenwriter."

"What's your film about?"

"A divorcée is trying to overcome heartache to succeed and find love."

"Talk to Arlen Wynnewood. He backs film projects. He's the creative director of—"

"Pecan Street Theater," I said. It's amazing how many times I finish others' sentences with that very phrase.

"Maybe he'd take a look at it. But beware, the man's an asshole."

"I remember your saying that before."

Turtle got quiet after that. Maybe he was thinking I couldn't write worth a shit. You know how that is. The minute you tell somebody you're a writer, they ask what you've written, and if you don't have some blockbuster to your credit, they get really quiet, and you can tell they're thinking, "Oh, another writer who's not really a writer."

Somehow, Turtle got me home before I could throw up. When we pulled in my driveway, I thanked him and got ready to stagger to my door. But the sidewalk was uneven in a spot. I couldn't negotiate that much of a diversion, so I fell sideways into the bushes outside my duplex. The branches poked my arms, but something—maybe a bag of leaves— saved me from falling through the bush and hitting the brick wall.

Bless his heart, Turtle got out and escorted me to the door. I kept insisting I could make it on my own, but we made so much noise, Pamela rushed out to see what the hell was going on.

"Merry, you need a keeper." Then to Turtle, "Who the hell are you?"

"Carter Abrams," Turtle said sheepishly.

"Well, Mr. Abrams, you don't look like you're in such hot shape either. I'd suggest hot coffee. Come into Aunt Pamela's parlor, or I'll call the cops and report two drunks having a domestic disturbance."

Like a pair of sheepish teenagers, Turtle and I went inside Pamela's and slugged down coffee while she scolded me like a Jewish mother.

"I thought you had decided to limit yourself. The new Merry Mayfield and all that. You have children at home. They're in there now, poor neglected things. What are they supposed to do if you die on MoPac? Do you want them to live with Brandon and Deanna?"

Yatta, yatta, yatta.

After about thirty minutes of this, Turtle worked up enough courage to leave, mumbling, "Thank you very much for this sobering moment." Then he said to me, "You might go ahead and contact Arlen. Like I said, he's an asshole, but he does back indie films."

This is a thought, isn't it, Roland? Although he is married, this might be my chance to become the writer you taught me to be.

⊠ ⊠ ⊠

More on Turtle later.

I must change subjects and tell you about my first real estate deal. I have saved it for last because that's where it is in my mind's order of importance.

I took a bald, stocky judge from La Grange out condo shopping in Austin last week, and the fucker bought one for $225,000. Signed on the dotted line and wrote an earnest money check. I will get $3,375 after the deal closes. Not $7,000, but something. That will show Brandon, or that will show me, that I can indeed be a success in real estate.

"And screenwriter?" you ask.

My dearest Roland, at this time, I wait for definition from Arlen Wynnewood and various indie producers.

Love,
Merry

SCENE 20

EXT. MERRY'S DUPLEX — 1989 — NIGHT

Glenn is hiding inside the bushes, silently
watching as

Merry gets out of Carter Abrams's VOLVO and
drunkenly makes her way to her duplex.

Merry trips and falls into the bush where
Glenn is hiding.

He instinctively pushes her back with his
shoulder. Then cringes, fearing discovery.

Merry rebounds upright, but she is so drunk
she doesn't realize someone pushed her.

Carter rushes up the walk to help.

> CARTER
> Are you all right?

> MERRY
> (mumbling drunkenly)
> I tripped on something. But ...

Merry glances in confusion at the bushes.

INSIDE THE BUSH

Glenn sees Pamela watching out her door. He
silently curls, making himself small.

                    PAMELA
          Merry, you need a keeper.

As Merry and Carter go inside Pamela's house,
Glenn waits for the door to close.

                    GLENN
               (whispering)
          And I know just where I'm going to
          keep her.

Letter Twenty
April 1, 1989

Dear Roland,

Appropriately or not, today is April Fucking Fool's Day, and I closed my first real estate deal this morning. Yes, Merry Mayfield, star REALTOR®, will make $3,375, and I earned every sweet penny.

You see, the pudgy judge from La Grange tried to back out. I only found out about it a week ago, when the seller's agent, Teresa Miller from West End Properties, called and asked me to drop by to "discuss problems with the closing." So off I went, wearing my horrifying red-and-yellow-striped blazer.

To my mortification, Teresa turned out to be a gorgeous brunette in a smoky-blue Ellen Tracy silk suit with matching hosiery and floral accent scarf. She all but sneered at my polyester. "Your client is not performing."

"What do you mean, not performing?"

"The title company says he's hasn't applied to assume the loan. I should think that you as his agent would have known this, if you stayed on top of things. Now you'll need to take him the loan app and get him to fill it out. Closing will be delayed, and my clients inconvenienced."

Needless to say, I was pissed beyond belief, but good little B. J. Hathaway agent that I am trying to be, I drove ninety miles through rolling countryside, dotted with fields of bluebonnets and bright-red Indian paintbrush, to the Fayette County Courthouse in La Grange.

You should see this building—a Gothic structure straight out of Ghostbusters. Up four steep flights of stairs, I found the judge's office, but his secretary said he was too busy to see me. So, I sat on a brown bench in a dimly lit foyer until his secretary went to the bathroom. That's when I barged in and stood in front of the judge's desk.

"You need to fill out this application to assume the loan."

The judge sighed. "Merry, $225,000 was too much to pay."

"As I recall, you thought you were getting a great deal."

"A great deal in Austin doesn't look like a great deal in La Grange. In fact, I don't have the financial muscle to handle this extra payment."

"Then lease it to somebody. You can write off any negative."

"I don't need more write-offs."

We argued for an hour, but the stinker refused to fill out the app.

So, after I got back to Austin, I called Teresa Miller. "I'm sorry, but he refuses to fill out the application. I really don't know what to do."

"I'll tell you what to do. You tell B. J. Hathaway that your client owes mine $2,250 in earnest money. We'll expect that release form by the end of the week."

Release form? Sounds simple, but in Texas, the law says in order for a seller to receive earnest money from a defaulting buyer, the buyer must agree to the release of the escrowed funds.

So, the next morning I naively asked my manager Erica Cooke, "Where can I find an earnest money release form?"

"Earnest money release form? What have you done? Goodness. I'd better call B. J. You come in my office. I'll put us on speaker."

Erica fumbled around, trying to do a conference call. Typical dysfunction. After dial tones and wrong numbers, she finally got us connected to the Godot of Austin real estate.

Yes, I spoke to B. J. Hathaway! At least he said he was B. J., although he could have been pretending to be B. J., while the real B. J. is preaching real estate development to the indigenous people of Brazil.

Erica shouted into the speaker. "If I've told Merry once, I've told her a thousand times: control your transaction from showing to closing—"

I interrupted before she could blame me for this mess. "B. J., we haven't met, but I'd like to respond to Erica's remarks. First off, I really have no control whether a judge in La Grange refuses to take over a loan he now says he cannot afford."

B. J.'s voice boomed like it does on the radio commercials he subjects Austin to each day. "Girls, I hold you both accountable, but if you want B. J. Hathaway to hold your license, Ms. Mayfield, you'd better put your rumpus in gear to La Grange. Get that judge to fill out those loan papers and deliver them to Teresa Miller by the end of today. Otherwise, you can find yourself a different broker, but I'll put out a warning on ya'."

Yikes. So, guess who drove back to La Grange. Even the fields of bluebonnets and Indian paintbrush did not make this a pleasant ride.

After I got to the courthouse, I tried to get past the judge's secretary, but I had to wait outside his office until he finally came out at 6:00 p.m. He was surprised as hell. Being a judge, he knew that his earnest money could sit in escrow until it forfeited to the state's unclaimed money fund, and then he could file for it later.

"Merry, why can't you help me with this? I spent the entire day negotiating with the Lower Colorado River Authority about how I want Austin to stop mucking up our water supply—and I won, dammit—so why can't I get anywhere with you?"

"I am here representing B. J. Hathaway, who, by the way, is pissed that his name is connected with this deal. But not as pissed as I am. You are trying to cost me $3,375, not to mention my having to deal with tedious bullshit that is so far outside my realm of intellectual concern, I can hardly stand to continue, except I must do it to fool a pluppy brother named Brandon, all to make him think he's wrong about me."

The judge's eyes narrowed in confusion. "I don't know about your brother, but you know damn well, that with a little time I can get my earnest money back."

I decided to change tactics. "Let's talk hypothetically. Say you go ahead with the condo. You can resell it for more than you paid. I'll make it my number one priority to find a buyer. How does that strike you?"

"It strikes me that you're trying to screw me."

"Well, how about this: put down numbers on the loan app that make you look like a financial dud."

"I'm a judge. I can't lie on a legal document."

We went on until 8:00 p.m. I kept presenting hypothetical options, and he kept refusing. So eventually, I gave up and did one of the two things a woman can do to get a man to do what she wants. I started to cry. It really wasn't hard. I was emotionally exhausted. So, I let the tears roll. I didn't sob. I cried with dignity.

At first, the judge blustered how the law was on his side. Then, as my tears rolled nobly down my cheeks, he fetched Kleenex, for which

I thanked him quietly. "This was my first sale, and I was so excited," I quivered. Then I gently dabbed my tears.

He exhaled a defeated man's sigh. "You really think I could flip it?"

I said, with a hint of pleading, "We'll have to wait a few requisite months, but you'll make money on the deal because I won't take my agent's percentage, just B. J.'s." Before he could bluster again, I gathered the papers. "Let's fill these out." I was praying he wouldn't balk. If he did, I'd have to resort to a blow job, and I truly wasn't up to it.

If B. J. were there, he would have said, "Now that's what I would call closing the sale."

Long story short, the judge filled out the app, and I gratefully shook his hand before I left for Austin at 10:30 p.m. I got home at about midnight, exhausted. I once again felt guilty for missing dinner with my kids, but at least I called them earlier. Nora wasn't home yet, Claire told me, and Scottie was pouting in his room, as usual.

"I made some Mexican pizzas," Claire told me.

"Thank heavens for tortillas, cheese, Pace, and a microwave."

"You don't need to be so dramatic about it, Mom."

The next morning, I got up early and delivered the loan-assumption application to the title office. Teresa Miller was so snide to me by phone, I shall not glorify her with another line.

When I got to my office a bit later, Erica Cooke scolded, "B. J. told you to get that app to Teresa by end of day yesterday."

"I got back from La Grange at midnight."

Erica frowned. "Sometimes I wonder if you want to be in real estate."

That's one of the few intelligent things Erica has ever said.

Oh, but it wasn't over. Sometime during this entire mess, Jack Carleton—that slick sales manager Brandon introduced me to—heard about my recalcitrant judge and called Brandon.

And, not long after, Brandon called me. In his father-like voice, he said, "Merry, I had a disturbing call from Jack. He said you messed up a sale and got fired."

"I was not fired. I closed a sale and made $3,375."

"I put my reputation on the line for you."

"You've got the wrong information, Brandon. I had a difficult client who tried to back out on a deal. My manager got hysterical and called

B. J. I explained the situation and did what he told me to. I got the client to close. Everybody's happy. Why aren't you?"

Click! That asshole hung up on me.

Then he must have called Deanna, because she zoomed over not long after and rang my doorbell. (What a day I'm having!) I greeted her with a fake smile but told her I was about to leave for an important meeting.

She brushed past me and sat in the living room. "Brandon is concerned that your problems in real estate are alcohol related."

"Alcohol related! If it weren't for alcohol, I wouldn't have made it this far. I only went into real estate to keep Brandon happy. And I'm a success, Deanna. I just sold a house."

"Brandon is determined to help. So am I." She touched my knee.

"Do me a favor. Tell Brandon what I am very soberly telling you—yes, smell my breath—I am what Brandon so desperately wanted me to be. Successful in real estate. And, while you're here, I might as well tell you that my spirit requires more than financial success. I need a life with meaning. Guts. Feeling. I must have those things, Deanna, because I am a screenwriter, no matter how much Brandon does not want me to try."

"Well ..." she said, doubting the way everybody doubts when you announce what you have chosen to be, "Brandon is concerned that, well, with Doug not sending child support, you'll run through your inheritance. Then we'd have to—" She caught herself and patted my knee once more, her eyes wet with sincerity for a cause. "He's very worried about your future."

"Brandon will drive himself insane trying to control everybody else."

"How can you say such things? He's your brother."

"What kind of brother? An interested, supportive brother? Do you realize that Brandon has never read one damn thing I've written? Does he even know that I have revised my screenplay and I'm trying to get it produced? No. That's because you both pretend my writing doesn't exist. You diminish my efforts and refuse to define me as a writer—therefore I am not one."

She shook her head in confusion.

"Not into existential philosophy? Did they make you study anything other than religion before they let you act as a counselor and spiritual leader of the masses?"

"The Eternal Spirit is the source of all truth."

"And whoever started your bullshit Eternal Spirit faith probably had a brother named Brandon who told them to get into real estate."

Then I went to my office and slammed the door. Eventually, I heard Deanna roar off, likely hell-bent on telling Brandon that Merry is in serious trouble.

So that is why I toast you with a Diet Coke on this April Fool's Day, proving to myself and Brandon that I am a sober and responsible person.

Love,
Merry

SCENE 21

INT. GLENN'S TRAILER — 1989 — DAY

Nora nurses a BEER on Glenn's sofa. Beside her, he gently touches her thigh.

> GLENN
> I'm glad you came back. I missed you.

Glenn kisses her, and she responds, but Natasha suddenly jumps between them.

Glenn jerks, hits the dog with a hard smack.

> GLENN (CONT'D)
> Natasha! Down.

Natasha squeals and jumps off the sofa.

> NORA
> Don't hurt her, you jerk.

> GLENN
> Sorry. I think she's jealous of you.

> NORA
> Maybe she just needs to go out.

                    GLENN
          Okay, I'll take her out. C'mon,
          Natasha. You big pest.

Glenn leashes Natasha and takes the dog out.
He closes the door behind him.

EXT. GLENN'S TRAILER — DAY

Glenn leads Natasha to the grass. He paces
while the dog sniffs and circles to go poop.

INT. GLENN'S TRAILER — DAY

While Glenn is outside, Nora heads for the
back office to see what's in there. She tries
the door, but it's locked.

Just then, Glenn and the dog come back inside.
He sees Nora trying the office door.

                    GLENN
          What are you doing?

                    NORA
               (nervously)
          Just looking for a bathroom.

                    GLENN
          It's by the bedroom. You know that.

                    NORA
          That one is kind of dirty. I thought
          maybe there was another ... you got
          another beer?

                    GLENN
In the fridge. You know that.

                    NORA
I'm sorry. I'm just nervous again.

Glenn unleashes Natasha, then approaches Nora.

                    GLENN
Everybody has a first time.

                    NORA
I know, but—

                    GLENN
Look, you came back to see me. That
means you want to be here, with me.

                    NORA
I don't know what I want. But I feel
like you're pressuring me again.

Nora shakes her head and heads for the door.

Glenn scowls.

EXT. GLENN'S TRAILER — DAY

Nervously, Nora opens her van door, just as
Glenn comes outside with Natasha off-leash.

                    GLENN
Goddamn teenage cock tease, that's
what you are.

Nora gets in her van, closes door, starts
engine. She rolls down her window.

                    NORA
        Shouting at me does not make me want
        to have sex with you. Especially not
        my first time.

As Nora drives away, Glenn glowers.

INT. GLENN'S TRAILER — DAY

IN BACK OFFICE

Glenn sits at his desk and gazes menacingly at
Nora's photos.

                    GLENN
        One way or another, I'm gonna get
        your cherry.

Letter Twenty-One
April 4, 1989

Dear Roland,

To celebrate closing on the judge's condo, I called Pamela and invited her to Jeffrey's. Of course, my underlying rationale was to see if Arlen Wynnewood was there. I've seen him enough at The Cypress Door that I could casually approach him about my screenplay, offer him a look, ask if he thinks it would be better as a stage play. Who knows? Maybe the stage is where it belongs. And you would be so pleased.

Pamela was reluctant at first, primarily because of the expense. "I'll go this time, but don't come begging when you and your kids have to live on the streets because you spent your commissions at Jeffrey's."

We got dressed up—I did, anyway. Pamela doesn't spiff up well. And with her blond Dutch-boy haircut, well, let's just say Pamela might someday work up to being cute, but that's it.

Meanwhile, I overdressed in an off-white-satin shirtdress, slit to mid-thigh and belted with a wide, blazing-red sequin band. Red-patent high heels. Huge red-enamel earrings. Jet-black hair in Victor's latest Connie Chung-style bob—I'm growing it out a bit.

Pleased with my image, I was high on my looks and anticipation.

When we got to Jeffrey's, the *maître d'* sat us next to the same table Arlen Wynnewood occupied when I first saw him. Was this coincidence or Godot?

Our waiter, Bruce, poured by-the-glass wine, which we drank quickly, requiring Bruce to retrieve more. Pamela is no teetotaler, either. We got high. Giggly. After Bruce returned with our second glasses, Pamela and I responded to his recitation of the specials with corny one-liners like, "What's a great piece of meat doing with a saucy bitch named Béarnaise?"

Bruce tried to ignore us. "We also have lamb chops with oyster-stuffed pockets—"

"I didn't know lambs had pockets," Pamela snorted.

Shriek, giggle. We were disgusting. Eventually, she and I both ordered the redfish Newport, "swimming in a puddle of lemon, butter, cream, and shallots, alongside poached oysters, dotted with capers on request."

"Please, no capers. They make me caper to the can," Pamela said.

Bruce chuckled as he headed to the kitchen. "Tell Chef to can the capers."

Enough of this silly dialogue. What I'm getting to is that while we awaited dinner, I noticed two well-dressed older men accompanied by two flashy younger ladies with stacked bob haircuts revealing super-long gold loop earrings. Each was dressed in a thigh-high black skirt, topped by some sort of low-cut camisole, and a brightly colored jacket with gigantic shoulder pads. Clearly, this was a business arrangement. The two older guys would lay out megabucks for dinner in the hope that the younger ladies would allow them to play with their pussies afterward.

But all of a sudden, one of the older guys, a plump fellow with a gray beard, nodded and smiled at Pamela. She blushed and got flustered.

I raised my glass and toasted a silent hello. "He's kinda cute. Looks like Santa. And I think he likes you."

"You seem to be on the big bald guy's radar."

"Even though they've got dates, we might get a drink sent our way."

Pamela and I started flirting. Madly. Smiling, toasting hello, and adding ridiculously coy glances.

Santa Claus smiled and waved back whenever his date wasn't looking.

The other guy, a husky fellow, kept turning to catch a glimpse. He wasn't bad looking. Sure, he was bald and over fifty but with a cherubic twinkle, especially in his flushed cheeks and hazel eyes.

Long story short, after a half hour of furtive flirting, the older guys and their dates stood to leave.

Pamela didn't notice because she was entrenched in an argument with Bruce, the waiter. "There's one. A caper. You don't want to know what these bee-bees do to my intestines"

I stomped on her foot. "Hush. They're leaving," but she wouldn't stop complaining. So, I waved a flirtatious goodbye to the big bald guy, and he smiled back, even as he and his clueless date headed to the door. But to my surprise, the big bald guy came back inside, as if to leave more tip, but instead he aimed toward us and slipped me his business card.

"I'm Jerry Manning. Drop by my gallery sometime." Then he winked, smiled, and left.

I glanced at his card. Manning Fine Art.

Meanwhile, Joan Rivers, i.e., Pamela, was still arguing with Bruce. "Jeffrey's doesn't require people to have diarrhea after one of their overpriced dinners, does it?"

"All I can do is talk to Chef. I asked him to leave them out." Bruce left for the kitchen.

"I really can't believe—"

"Hush." I showed her Jerry Manning's card.

"So, the beautiful one gets a guy, and I get the shits?"

"Perhaps Jerry Manning of Manning Fine Art will fix you up with his obviously wealthy Santa Claus pal."

"Just don't tell him what I do for a living. Guys want me to do things while we are riding in elevators ... do things you wouldn't believe."

Moments later, the *maître d'* interrupted. "Ladies, your checks have been taken care of by the gentleman who just left."

"Which one?" we said in unison.

"The baldish gentleman who just left."

The older fellow, Jerry Manning. Wasn't that a hoot?

Do you suppose he's my Prince?

Love,
Merry

SCENE 22

INT. AUSTIN RESTAURANT — 1989 — DAY

Merry and her sales manager ERICA COOKE are at a table for lunch. They're both in B. J. Hathaway red and yellow striped blazers and red skirts.

As Merry looks for a waiter, she sees Brandon across the way, chatting MOS with Luna.

Merry recognizes Luna as the woman Merry had seen in a car with Brandon.

From Brandon's flirtatious demeanor, Merry is shocked to see that there might be more going on with Brandon and Luna than lunch.

Merry gets up and goes to Brandon's table.

                    MERRY
          Well, hello, dear brother. And who
          are we lunching with?

Brandon gets jittery and drops a fork to floor.

                    BRANDON
          I had no idea you would be here.

When Brandon gets up to retrieve his fork,
Merry sits in his place beside Luna.

                    MERRY
        I'm Merry Mayfield, Brandon's sister.

Luna smiles hesitantly.

                    LUNA
        Luna Alvarez, community-relations
        director for Austin Search for
        Knowledge. Brandon is my boss.

The women shake hands while Brandon retrieves
his fork.

                    LUNA
        Brandon and I are going over my
        plans for the annual report.

                    MERRY
        Were you now?

Brandon holds his fork high, and gets ready to
sit, but sees Merry in his chair.

                    BRANDON
        Merry ...

                    MERRY
        Will Deanna be joining you today?

                    BRANDON
        Merry ...

                         LUNA
                      (faking)
            Is Deanna coming? I know Brandon
            tried to call her.

                         MERRY
            I'm sure. Well, I should get back to
            my table. I don't want to intrude.

                         LUNA
            Oh, you're not intruding.

Merry reaches in her pocket and pulls out a
BUSINESS CARD.

                         MERRY
            I'm with B. J. Hathaway. If you're
            looking for a house, let me know.
            Unless you want to screw me out of a
            commission like Brandon did.

Merry glares disapprovingly at Brandon, then
marches to her table.

                         LUNA
                      (whispering)
            What was that about?

                        BRANDON
            I'll tell you later.

AT MERRY'S TABLE

Merry rejoins Erica and pretends to be
interested in the menu, but she looks
disturbed by Brandon's apparent affair.

SCENE 23

INT. BRANDON'S OFFICE — 1989 — DAY

As Brandon works at his messy desk, he checks a WALL CLOCK. It says 5:30 p.m.

Luna peeks in the open office door.

> LUNA
> I waited until everybody left.

Brandon reluctantly waves her in.

> BRANDON
> What's up? I'm trying to get home.

Luna smiles hesitantly.

> LUNA
> Shouldn't we talk about your sister?
> What happened today at lunch?

> BRANDON
> Close the door.

> LUNA
> Nobody else is here.

                    BRANDON
         Close it anyway.

Luna closes the door, then sits in a chair in
front of Brandon's desk.

                     LUNA
         Your sister seemed suspicious.

                    BRANDON
         Merry has a fertile imagination.
         She's a 'screenwriter,' you know.

                     LUNA
         She might say something to Deanna.

                    BRANDON
         Deanna thinks Merry is a lunatic.

                     LUNA
         But if Merry says anything, that
         forces the issue, and you'll have to
         tell Deanna the truth about us.

Brandon scowls and gets pissy.

                 LUNA (CONT'D)
         Brandon, we've talked about this. I
         cannot go on this way.

Luna gets up and leaves in a teary huff.

Brandon shakes his head in dismay.

                    BRANDON
         Oh, what a tangled web ...

His DESK PHONE catches his eye.

> BRANDON
> Maybe a little sister schmoozing is
> in order. I certainly don't need
> Merry telling Deanna I'm having an
> affair. My God, I'd lose my job, my
> home, my children, and half of my
> bank account!

Letter Twenty-Two
April 14, 1989

Dear Roland,

DPB called me about noon this morning. "I just wanted to know if you're okay," he began in a deep, soothing voice I hadn't heard before.

I remained cautious, since the call came out of the blue. Last he and I spoke, things didn't go well. "I'm doing fine. Closed one house sale and I've got several producers taking a look at my screenplay."

Oddly, instead of his usual minimizing criticisms, Brandon expressed interest. Even chatted inquisitively for about ten minutes, saying things like, "That sounds promising. What are the next steps?"

There was a hint of yearning in his voice, but I do not trust him enough to open up. When we said goodbye, I got the feeling there was more to his call than he wanted me to know.

I sat at my kitchen table and drank Diet Cokes until I was so wired on caffeine, I thought I might have to have a martini to calm down. But I resisted the urge. The kids were off to school, bless their hearts, so they didn't have to endure my agitation.

Besides, I did not want to thicken the walls that already have risen between us. Nora has become secretive lately, and Claire has been distant. Scottie, being the only male in this three-female nest, wallows in his room when not at school, and I don't blame him.

What to do with my free afternoon? I called Sigrid, hoping to catch her between classes.

"Why, Merry, we hoped we'd hear from you soon."

"I take it that you and Frank are for sure 'we'?"

"Seems so. We plan to marry July tenth. I was going to call, but I've been too busy with school. Teaching two sections and taking nine hours toward my doctorate have got me running. I don't know how I'm going to plan a wedding too. Frank doesn't want anything formal, but my mother would have a breakdown if we didn't have a church ceremony! You're coming, I hope. Please come. July tenth," she gushed.

"Of course. That is, if I have enough to buy a plane ticket."

"Doug still not sending child support? Why don't you sue him?"

"How am I supposed to sue a man who owes his lawyers hundreds of thousands of dollars?"

"Sue him for spite."

"I divorced him for spite. I'd rather kill him with my recently inherited Glock 27 than spend money on lawyers."

"Tell me you don't really have a gun. That sounds so Texan."

"My dad left it to Brandon, but his redheaded evangelist wife wouldn't let him have it. So, I took it. I must say having a gun gives me a sense of power. Tell you what, if Frank ever treats you as badly as Doug treated me and my kids, I'll take care of Frank for you."

"Goodness. You sound so angry."

"I'm sorry. I've had too many Diet Cokes."

She giggled. Then I told her how Brandon was trying to make amends after accusing me of being fired. "But I'm not buying it. Brandon wouldn't believe the truth of my success if it stared him in the face."

"No wonder you're angry. You're still trying to prove your worth to Brandon."

"You'd think I'd know better, with Roland teaching us to define ourselves, choose our zone, and—"

"Oh dear, I can't bear that existentialist nothingness now. Frank's up to his eyebrows in a production of Pinter's *Dumb Waiter*. He's playing the paranoid character, and I think he's taking on too many of the traits. I don't know how you existentialists can tolerate daily life—what with your bleak philosophies. Frank won't even talk to me at dinner for fear of losing hold of his character's fears."

"Now who's angry?"

"Seems like we both are. Quite often, I wonder if I'm doing the right thing. Frank is not likely to be a Tony Award winner. And he won't make much teaching. Then again, Mom and Dad set up a trust fund for me, and that's nice, not having to make money. I don't know what I'd do if I had to make a real living. I admire you for that, Merry. I never told you, but I'm proud of the way you've managed to make it so far. Your parents dying, the divorce, the trip, three kids, two dogs, gads. You're my hero."

"I don't think I'm trying as hard as I could."

"Have you heard anything about your screenplay yet?"

"I'm still waiting. I do not move."

"There you go again." She giggled.

As we chatted on, our conversation became more like old times. I hate to lose friends. Sure, time and distance make it difficult to talk often and see each other in person, but I never had so many friends I could forget one in favor of the next.

After I got off the phone, the kids came home, but as teens do, all three were headed to friends' houses to study. I issued a mom-like warning. "Be home by 8:00 p.m., no later. And I mean it this time, or you're grounded."

That was met by the usual, "Oh, Mom."

After they left in Nora's van, I was still in a social mood, so I decided to head to The Cypress Door for some adult conversation. Although it wasn't yet happy hour, the seats were filling up fast. Immediately, my eyes scanned for Arlen, but he was probably home with his chic, wealthy wife. Regardless, after a day full of caffeine, a J-Tini was my immediate desire.

Toni nodded hello and shook me a drink without even asking.

As I took a sip, I noticed Turtle at that same back round table with a bunch of guys who were probably reporters. Since I am now a regular, I bravely steered toward Turtle's table, putting my hand on his shoulder.

"Hey, Carter. Thank you again for driving me home the other night."

I cannot tell you how shy this poor soul is. He jolted at my touch and turned claret, unable to find enough breath to power words. Finally, he found the courage to mumble, "Oh, don't worry about it." He didn't look at me or say more.

I stood beside him for a century, until a bearded guy, who turned out to be a reporter for the newspaper's "Neighbor" section, said, "Won't you join us?"

I sat and we stared silently at each other. Turtle appeared too shaken to speak until the bearded fellow resumed a conversation about how the new managing editor had messed up everything.

I nodded, as if I knew what they were talking about. But—and this is an important "but"—one of the fellows at Turtle's table, a decent-looking blond named Nick Asher, was not a reporter, but instead a set designer for, you guessed it, Pecan Street Theater.

"Are all bosses screw ups? The other day Arlen Wynnewood—"

Turtle surprised me by spouting, "Arlen is an asshole." Then Turtle stared at his glass and enjoyed the shocked silence.

Nick snickered. "Let's just say Arlen is quite imperative about what he wants."

"My editor has made me aware of what Mr. Wynnewood wants— rather, doesn't want."

"Carter, your reviews can make or break a local production, so you need to consider the financial impact of what you write," Nick said.

"Look, I'm a humor columnist, so if they're going to make me do arts reviews, I'll call 'em like I see 'em. That production of *Our Town* was the worst I've ever seen. But your set designs were grand."

"Hey, I just create the sets and collect paychecks." Then Nick got up and left, apparently pissed.

I didn't blame him. Turtle's resentful funk was a side I had not seen.

Things got quiet, and I figured I should go sit at the bar and talk to Toni. I scooted my chair back so Turtle got the point I was about to leave. But Roland, he did something so un-Turtle-like it touched me. He reached and grasped my hand urgently, yet so tenderly. "Merry, I'm sorry. I've been rude. I'm not used to having a lovely lady sit at my table. Don't let me scare you off."

His eyes were deep puddles of need. And for some inexplicable reason, I decided to stay. Call it a hunch. Call it my own need for companionship. Whatever. But I stayed.

"I know how you feel. I've grown angry today at people who want to define my fate."

He smiled. For a Turtle, he had a fine set of teeth.

"Beckett?" he asked.

"Jean Genet."

"One to another, thanks for being irrational enough to stay."

We laughed. I won't bore you with the rest of our dialogue. Basically, we got to know one another. He went to J-School at the University of

Missouri in Columbia, but he grew up in Texas. He's been married once and has two kids in their teens. They live with their mother in Dallas. From the wistfulness and pride in his voice, I could tell he had the depth of caring to be a good dad.

I hope he *is* a good dad, even if he has to do it long distance.

We chatted more about raising teenagers until I realized I needed to get home before 8:00 p.m. I said good night and left feeling as if I had made a friend.

Love,
Merry

SCENE 24

INT. LUNA'S APARTMENT — 1989 — DAY

IN THE BEDROOM

Brandon and Luna sprawl in her unmade bed
after rewarding sex.

                    LUNA
          You make me feel like sunshine.

                    BRANDON
          I don't know how to answer that.

                    LUNA
          Do I make you feel like sunshine?

                    BRANDON
               (laughing)
          You make me feel like I need to pee.

He gets out of bed and heads to the bathroom.

Luna grimaces at the sound of Brandon
URINATING.

                    LUNA
          Tu está tan romantico.

                    BRANDON (O.S.)
          You know I don't speak Spanish.

Brandon comes back, puzzled because Luna is
pouting. He gets in bed and cups her chin.

                      BRANDON
          I'm not good with romantic stuff. But
          I do love you.

                       LUNA
          I don't know how to answer that.

                      BRANDON
          Touché.

                       LUNA
          You know I don't speak French.

The two exchange smiles. She's feeling happier
now. Brandon looks deeply into Luna's eyes.

                      BRANDON
          I'm at the end of my rope with
          Deanna. Her phony ministry disgusts
          me. She only got this 'calling'
          after my mother died.

                       LUNA
          Maybe Deanna finally felt free to be
          what she wanted to be, instead of a
          Catholic like your mother demanded.
          I come from a Catholic family and
          know the pressures.

                    BRANDON
Maybe so, but Deanna didn't bother
telling me about her 'ministry'
before we got married. Now she's
got my daughters in the Eternal
Spirit school. All they study is
manufactured doctrine ... a bunch
of hooey. I want them to get a real
education. That's why I'm paying a
fortune in taxes to live in West
Lake Hills ... for the schools.

                    LUNA
If you divorce, Deanna will get the
house. So, you'll still be paying.
And you won't get to decide where
the girls go to school.

Brandon turns and stares at the ceiling,
considering what Luna just said.

She shakes her head, gets out of bed, and
walks into the bathroom in dismay.

IN BATHROOM MIRROR

                    LUNA
             (whispering to self)
I need to keep my mouth shut.

Letter Twenty-Three
May 1, 1989

Dear Roland,

So many amazing things to report! Number one, I got an option! Can you believe it? Merry Mayfield, girl screenwriter, has an option contract on *Those Who Try*. I got a whopping $1,500 for a twelve-month development deal.

An option means I truly am a writer, right?

"No, Merry—only after you've made $100,000."

Oh, screw you. I am orgasmic with delight. Now I can say, "My producer, Lyle Davis."

He's a guy I met though Austin Film Society listings. I queried him a month ago, and he just called and told me, "I really like your screenplay, despite its too-much muchness."

Not exactly inspirational. But hopeful? Lyle won't be the one who makes the film. He puts together deals between studios, investors, screenwriters, directors, actors, and any others needed to make a film. Although he is based in Austin, he told me, "I know how to get a film made in Hollywood."

I called you earlier today to tell you about it. One of your daughters answered. I asked for you, then listened while she shouted, "Daddy! Phone!" A TV was blaring the theme from *Gilligan's Island*. I stifled a laugh. How could a noted scholar let his kids watch *Gilligan's Island*? Then a boy's voice shouted, "Turn down the TV," and I heard voices mumbling, until someone eventually shouted, "He's out back." Then I heard feet shuffle across hard floors, a sliding door open, and a shout—your wife Marianne's voice. "Roland! Telephone."

"Who is it?"

That was you! Your voice from afar.

"I don't know," Marianne said.

Then your footsteps came inside. A vision flashed: you rearranging your hair over the bald spot, you pushing up your wire rims, you saying, "Hello? This is Roland Holmes."

I inhaled, but my throat tightened. Suddenly, I couldn't bring myself to say a word.

You said, "Hello?" again, this time with irritation, but my heart pounded as I tried to gather courage.

Then slam. You cut the connection.

What a ninny I was. Too fearful to speak. I was mortified by my shyness. But I decided to mail you a cutesy note with no hint of how much I care. And I actually stuck it in the mailbox to be picked up.

Dear Roland,

Remember your long-lost Guinness-drinking student? Well, you may brag to your class tomorrow that my screenplay for Those Who Try *has been optioned by Lyle Davis Film Productions of Austin.*

Hope you are doing well,

Merry Mayfield (formerly Merry Garner)

Formal. Distant. Masked.

To redeem myself, I called Dear Pluppy Brandon. After all, the man did sound a bit more interested the last time we spoke.

"I have good news you might enjoy hearing."

(No response from Brandon.)

"A producer optioned my screenplay."

(No response from Brandon.)

"This means a producer wants to make a film using my screenplay."

"How much did you get for it?" Brandon asked cynically.

"Option fees are not that much. The point is someone may make a film out of my work."

(Skeptical pause.) "Oh."

"Indie producers pay an option fee and then put together deals with a film studio."

"But you don't have any money coming in."

"Not yet. But I've made it through the first step."

(Pause while gathering guilt-rendering remark.) "Do you think it is wise to hinge your children's futures on some tiny possibility that a producer will make a film from your script?"

"Brandon, I am trying to become a screenwriter."

"Merry, I really think you should focus on your real estate career."

(No pause, but there should have been a pause, because if I had paused, I wouldn't have lost it.) "Dammit, Brandon! You called a few weeks ago to see how I'm doing. Something wonderful has happened, and I wanted to share the news. But I should have known that you, in your infinite solipsism, would find a way to tell me to live life as you see it. You are a jerk, Brandon. And please tell your evangelical wife not to fly over to tell me how much I have hurt your feelings."

Slam! Brandon and his goddamn guilt.

After I hung up, I was desperate to talk with someone who cared, so I called Sigrid. But the moment I said hello, she started blabbering about her love life and wouldn't let me get in a word. So much for the July wedding. She and Frank have (thank heavens) gone separate ways.

"Screw me once, shame on you. Screw me twice, shame on me. I ran into Frank one night with one of his leading ladies. He confessed that it was L O V E. Right in front of this other woman, he actually said, 'It's bigger than both of us.' Corny damn line. This was two weeks ago. Actually, I have not missed him. Now I'm dating a sixty-year-old Jewish lawyer with a penis that won't work."

"Sigrid?"

"It's one of those trade-offs Roland used to preach. We must settle for less than we dreamed." She added that she was drowning in research for her doctoral thesis. "No more sliding by like we did through our masters, conducting research at the Raven with Roland and Jillian."

Shit. Did I want to hear all this? But Sigrid eventually hushed and redeemed herself after I told her my news.

"Oh, Merry! I knew you could do it!"

That's what I needed.

And her next words were, "Did you call Roland?"

I lied carefully. "I didn't want to disturb him at home."

"He'd be thrilled."

"Hopefully."

"Call him. I really think you should."

"I'll write to him," I said, which wasn't a lie.

"I did run into Roland and Jillian several weeks ago. It was the first time we've had a beer together since Frank and I went kaput."

"How is the dynamic duo?" I asked, trying to sound nonchalant.

"Roland is writing a biography of Jean Genet. He's a hot topic lately. And of course, Jillian is madly typing Roland's manuscripts. But he seems moody. I don't know whether it's the effort about the book, too much Guinness, or, well, maybe a lovers' spat."

One could hope there was a rift in your zone. Call me petty, but I'd rather you stay with your wife than with Jillian.

⊠   ⊠   ⊠

On the real estate front, I have not been to the office for a while. After the chaotic deal with the judge from La Grange, I decided I'm not cut out for selling houses, especially since I now have an option for *Those Who Try*. Given that, I must develop another project and hopefully get an agent. Maybe I'll write a *Psycho*-style thriller about a desperate woman who kills her Dear Pluppy Brother (accidentally-on-purpose) and gets away with it.

Finally, I have another great news item to report. Saved a treat for last! The older fellow who paid for dinner weeks ago, Jerry Manning, called and asked me for a date. No, I didn't drop by his gallery. Seems he got my name from the reservation sheet at Jeffrey's. Clever fellow.

He may not be you or Arlen, but he's a date. Perhaps even a prince? One must try.

Love,
Merry

SCENE 25

INT. RAVEN BAR — 1989 — NIGHT

Sigrid, Roland, and Jillian are in their booth, sipping Guinness.

                    ROLAND
          You and Frank still kaput?

                    JILLIAN
          Roland, don't be so nosy.

                    SIGRID
          It's okay. As you both know, some
          relationships are not meant to be.

Jillian makes an angry CAT SOUND.

                    ROLAND
          Gosh, you two make me miss Frank.

                    SIGRID
          Sorry. Guess I was a bit defensive.

                    JILLIAN
               (meowing like kitten)
          Remember, dear, I'm a Persian
          feline, not some alley cat.

                    ROLAND
Well, this alley cat needs a change
of subject and a trip to the loo.

Roland starts to get up, but Sigrid puts up a
hand to stop him.

                    SIGRID
Wait, I forgot some big news.
A producer optioned Merry's
screenplay!

                    JILLIAN
Did she get a studio contract?

                    SIGRID
A producer named Lyle somebody was
putting a deal together.

                    ROLAND
Well, that's wonderful news!

                    JILLIAN
Hell, anybody can get an option.

                    ROLAND
Oh not so, my dear.

                    JILLIAN
Well, I guess I've been told.

                    ROLAND
Yes, several times. Merry has
talent. It needs honing, but that's
what directors and producers do.

                         SIGRID
            She seemed very excited.

                         ROLAND
            I might have to give her a call.

                         JILLIAN
                      (sarcastically)
            Oh, gee, if you two giddy fans will
            please excuse me, I've got papers to
            grade.

Jillian gathers her purse, dons her BLACK
CAPE, and strides out in a dramatic huff.

                         SIGRID
            Did I say something wrong?

                         ROLAND
            Jillian gets dismayed by my
            admiration for Merry.

                         SIGRID
            Oh dear. Now, I miss Frank too.

Letter Twenty-Four
May 5, 1989

Dear Roland,

Last Friday, Jerry Manning picked me up in a midnight blue Cadillac Allante, one of the two he owns that are exactly alike. Why two Allantes?

"Because I don't like loaners."

A high roller.

He was as bald as I remembered, but sharply dressed in a warm-brown silk suit, light-tan silk dress shirt, and a beige-blue-and-brown-striped silk tie—the king of silk.

I wore a black jersey number, sort of a rejuvenated mini. I figured that an older guy would like a tight dress over my round derriere. And he did. ("You look beautiful, darlin'.") I smiled back with one of those smiles that comes from nature, I suppose.

As we headed down MoPac, we had a surprisingly enjoyable conversation, revealing that Jerry High Roller is educated (MA in Art History), as well as witty, and charming. But definitely a Texan. His calling me darlin' felt patronizing—primarily because I spent two decades in the Northeast, where you overeducated me into being so freaking aware. Despite his darlin's, High Roller was so pleasant to be with I decided to simply enjoy his company while keeping an eye out for Arlen Wynnewood at dinner. And I almost saw him!

As Jerry and I waited for a table, I overheard the *maître d'* murmur to a waiter, "Did you take care of Mr. Wynnewood's check?"

"Arlen Wynnewood," I gasped.

Jerry was quick. "You know Arlen?"

"I'd like to know him. He is a well-known film backer."

"There's backers and there's assholes. He's the latter."

Goodness, evidently Jerry High Roller is another Austin man who doesn't like Arlen Wynnewood. Red flag number two.

I decided to excuse myself to the ladies' room, which of course was just beyond where Arlen customarily sat. As I rounded the corner, I scanned the room but saw no sign of him. I must've looked lost, because one of the waiters asked if I needed help.

I whispered, "I was looking for Arlen Wynnewood."

Crushing response: "Oh, he just left."

I was dismayed but did my best to smile when I rejoined High Roller, who politely stood holding my chair.

He turned out to be one of those old-fashioned dates that dotes on you. He ordered caviar, duck-liver pâté, sorbet, and Dom Pérignon, followed by roasted quail and redfish Newport (again with the redfish) and more wine, wine, wine. I was a quite tipsy by that time. We both finished with chocolate intemperance for dessert.

Everything was perfect and the conversation energetic, but then things got sticky. After dinner, we drove away in Jerry's Allante, and he took me to his place. Similar to Zoran, he didn't present an option, although I was so high on champagne and wine, I didn't protest. Besides, I was having fun for a change.

Jerry High Roller lives in a soaring waterfront condo on Lake Austin. The living room has two-story-high vaulted walls that display elaborately framed paintings. I mentally counted over thirty—big ones, little ones—each an original worth thousands. I was in awe.

One huge painting above High Roller's sofa especially caught my eye. It was a large still life of roses, of all things. I've never been one for florals, but these were velvety, alluring roses in a dark-green vase, filtered by impressionistic strokes. I was astounded by their ethereal power. The lush, deep-red roses, surrounded by verdant leaves, seemed to lean toward me, as if to say, "Don't worry. You will find your way."

"You really like those roses, don't you?"

"It's amazing. Compelling. And so big. Who painted it?"

"A. D. Greer. He's ninety years old. It'll be worth about $15,000 after he goes, but right now, it's the cheapest damn thing on my wall. How does that make you feel, darlin', choosin' the cheapest painting?"

"Absolutely tacky. But how much is it worth right now?"

"Oh, about $10,000."

"$10,000."

"I might let you have it for $9,500, darlin'."

"Oh, just $9,500." I kept staring at the roses, especially the largest rose on the right. It had a dusky tinge that was alluring.

"Well, maybe we could take a little more off ..." he began.

Now, Roland. This was definitely a proposition. And you know what? With that much champagne and wine in me, I fell for it. I wanted those roses enough to have sex with this man.

As High Roller kissed me, I felt his immediately erect dick press against my inebriated *mons pubis*. "How much did you say for those roses?" I whispered.

His voice shot breathlessly, "I suppose I could let you have them for $9,000 even."

"Only $9,000," I murmured, as though I could afford that. As he kissed me again, I kept staring at those roses. In my mind's eye, they appeared three dimensional, seemingly bowing to a gentle breeze.

"Deal?" He mumbled, lips on mine, tongue firmly probing. He was good, this old fart.

"Deal," I whispered between kisses. And so, the deal with the devil was done.

Wine flooding my veins, plus the euphoric horror of having promised $9,000 and what virtue I have left for a huge painting of a green vase, full of dusky red roses, I pulled High Roller down to the sofa and angled my body into a position where I could keep an eye on what would become my painting.

From above, my roses watched High Roller undress me.

Fortunately, I didn't have to wait long to pay my sexual obligation. Jerry had barely fiddled with my whatever, then inserted his prominent appendage, and stroked vehemently while I held on for dear life. My salvation was to concentrate on the roses, my roses—their color deepening to a claret, complemented by the shadowy green of the leaves. Within moments, my roses seemed to bob in rhythm with the antics going on beneath.

As Jerry whammed away, I meditated on the floral until I suddenly began to feel High Roller inside me, something I had not expected to do. This surge of passion caught me by surprise, and I became excited quickly. "Ohhhhhh," I heard myself moan in an echo that stunned me because I was responding so freely to this man I'd only just met.

Now, Roland. I probably could have had a fantastic sexual reaction to my painting's surrogate named Jerry, but before I knew it, he hollered, "God, it's so hot in there," then gnashed, groaned, and collapsed with the weight of a man who had eaten too many dinners at Jeffrey's.

With that, my unexpected euphoria ended as suddenly as it began.

"I thought you were about to come," High Roller said.

"You didn't give me a chance."

"I'll give you a rain check on that part of the deal."

Then it hit me, Roland. I had promised to pay this man $9,000 for my painting. Me, who only has $20,000 of inheritance left, not to mention no real job or real paycheck.

As he rose off me, Jerry's dick swayed thigh to thigh beneath his round belly, and I noticed wrinkles in his fanny as he reached for the gigantic picture frame above me. When he lifted my roses off the wall, he grinned. "That'll be $9,000, darlin'."

I felt as if I were in an altered state as I wrote my check.

Still naked, High Roller padded and wrapped my roses in brown paper. "This is the best investment you've ever made. A.D. is on his last legs, and you'll be able to turn that around for $15,000 within a year."

When I gave him the check, I tried to act as if I did this all the time, but when I went to the bathroom to clean up and dress, I stood in front of the mirror and shook my head at the preposterous nature of this deal. Was this my irrational, gratuitous act? I felt wicked. And full of glee! I couldn't wait to tell Sigrid. She'd be one friend who would understand. You would too.

When I came out, High Roller was asleep naked on the sofa. "Jerry," I whispered. "Jerry," I shouted. But his snores were deep and heavy.

What to do? Spend the night, then endure another round of wham-bam the next morning? Shudder. I decided to take one of High Roller's midnight blue Allantes and ride home in style.

In Jerry's garage, I struggled to load the enormous painting in the trunk. It was too long, so I went inside to find string to tie the trunk lid down. Once it was secure, I backed out, using Jerry's remote to close the garage door. Then I drove home with the package hanging two feet out the back. I was scared to death a cop would stop me.

Luckily, the kids were asleep when I pulled in. To avoid their prying eyes, I stayed up until 4:00 a.m., wrestling with toggle bolts, frame wire, and picture hooks. But before I went to sleep, I lay at the foot of my waterbed, put a vibrator to good use, and watched my roses rise and fall with the undulations.

The next afternoon, Scottie wandered in after school and noticed the painting. "Gosh, Mom. Where'd you get that?"

"It was a fabulous investment. Will almost double in value within a few years," I lied.

Would Jean Genet feel the same appalling guilt?

Love,
Merry

SCENE 26

INT. ANCHORAGE POLICE STATION — 1987 — NIGHT

Glenn angrily submits to being fingerprinted by
BOOKING OFFICER.

Next, BOOKING OFFICER takes a COTTON SWAB and
holds it in front of Glenn's mouth.

> BOOKING OFFICER
> Open wide.

> GLENN
> What the fuck for?

> BOOKING OFFICER
> DNA.

> GLENN
> What's DNA?

> BOOKING OFFICER
> 'Do Not Ask.'

Booking Officer laughs at his own joke.

At first, Glenn balks, but reluctantly lets
Booking Officer swab inside his mouth.

                    GLENN
What's DNA, anyway?

                BOOKING OFFICER
Some new test the Lower 49 dreamed
up. Our new lady D.A. wants it for
all sex crimes. You can say no, but
if you do, she'll get a subpoena,
then I'll get it another way. This
way is easier for everybody.

                    GLENN
I didn't commit a sex crime. I was
screwing a little cunt who lied
about her age. For no reason, she
started hollering.

                BOOKING OFFICER
Not for me to say. I'm just doing my
job.

                    GLENN
Can't be legal to take spit from a
guy's mouth. I'll have my lawyer
look into this.

                BOOKING OFFICER
Lawyer, you got one?

                    GLENN
Just as soon as I get my free call.

Letter Twenty-Five
May 15, 1989

Dear Roland,

I found out something awful. Frightening, in fact. Nora is on the verge of having sex with a guy who's way too old for her. I found this out yesterday afternoon, when Claire confided in me after school. Nora was at rehearsal for the senior play—she's the lead—and Scottie was at baseball practice.

Claire's sweet, wide eyes welled with tears of concern and fear. "I need to tell you something, Mom, but don't tell Nora I said anything."

"Claire, if Nora is having problems, I need to know."

"If she finds out, she will kill me."

"No, she won't, because I will kill her, and she knows it."

Claire's golden eyes nervously fluttered.

"Sorry, dear. Just joking."

"But I promised I wouldn't tell you."

"Promises don't matter when something might endanger your sister."

"He's pressuring her to have sex!"

"Who's pressuring her to have sex?"

"I don't know his name. He's a man Nora met. He's in college."

"College! What's the matter with dating high school boys?"

"I don't know. Nora said she and this guy have been going out, and now he wants to have sex. Nora says she likes him a lot, but she doesn't want to have sex yet."

"That's a relief. I'll talk to her after school tomorrow."

"She has rehearsal again."

"Then I'll talk to her when she gets home. Claire, I promise Nora will not kill you. You were only trying to protect her."

Part of me wanted to drive to Nora's school and take her out of rehearsal, but she has been so sullen of late. My showing up might cause an angry response, especially since she landed the starring role. A diva!

I decided to wait. To soothe my maternal nerves, I went in for an afternoon appointment at Victor's. Nora wouldn't be home for several hours, so I took a thermos of J-Tinis and plastic martini glasses with me, just for fun.

As usual, Victor bounced around my chair, jabbering as he snipped and we both sipped.

Phillip was there too. "You're Victor's favorite. He really loves you. I do too." Then Phillip added, "You're his last appointment for today. Why don't we three do drinks after Victor finishes your hair?"

Victor got frenetic. "Yes! Let's do Jeffrey's! I adore happy hours there … cheap eats!" He whirled in glee, snipping his scissors like castanets.

Given the situation with Nora, I thought I should beg off, but then wondered if this might be Godot interceding. My chance to bump into Arlen. After all, Jeffrey's happy hour started at 4:00 p.m., so I could be home fairly early. And I was getting my hair done too.

"You'll be the most fashionable woman there!" Victor shouted as he drank a third J-Tini and smeared some sort of curling cream into my normally straight hair. Then he twisted a few strands, then more strands, and this went on and on. I thought he was going to brush this all out, but he curled, ooohed, twisted, and aaahed in a frenzy that eventually resulted in a mess I can only describe as a mons pubis atop my head. And to make a bad thing worse, he kept adding hairspray so that my now very curly hair was like steel wool.

"Victor, what in the world are you doing to me?"

His face fell. "You don't like it?"

Phillip got defensive. "Jheri curls are very in, and not only for African Americans. Jheri Redding invented them. Spelled J-H-E-R-I. He's a world-famous stylist. If you were clubbing in L.A., you'd look like the top socialite there."

"Jheri curls? My hair looks like a Brillo pad."

From the anguish on Victor's face and disappointment in Phillip's eyes, I realized this must have been a hair-stylist "major moment" that Victor had tried. Trouble was, I hated it.

"I thought you would love it," Victor said as he went to change.

"Why would I love looking like a Brillo pad?" I murmured under my breath, as I finished my J-Tini and worried about perhaps seeing Arlen at Jeffrey's. Would the man even recognize me? My hair looked like a mons pubis, to mix my metaphors, although the mons-pubic version is more true. Oh, dear.

After I dressed, Phillip extended an elbow. "Ready for the ball?"

Victor took my other arm. "I get to be the handsome prince."

I laughed forcibly and reminded myself that this, too, can be washed out. Or at least I hoped it could.

Because I still needed to talk with Nora later, I insisted that the guys drive in their own car. So, I parked mine in Jeffrey's lot and smeared on as much makeup as my face could hold. Then I slammed a gigantic pair of red sunglasses on top of my head in an attempt to hide the curls.

In spite of my nerves over the hairdo, I felt like a Jeffrey's regular when I walked inside. Even the lady *maître d'* recognized me, although she did give my hair a rather curious glance. When the boys arrived, I asked her for a corner table, but darn it, she said she had nothing but the center, where at least twenty diners were in view of my black bush hairdo.

As we settled in, our waiter approached. Wouldn't you know it, but he turned out to be very gay. "Hi. My name is Fabian," he said eagerly and with a slight lisp.

Victor smiled flirtatiously and ordered a bottle of Dom Pérignon.

Fabian winked. "Half-price during happy hour. Excellent choice."

Phillip glared. "Just get the champagne, stud. And the happy hour menu. We're not paying full price for a thing."

Oh, dear. As we awaited the bubbly, Victor chomped on a basket of breadsticks. He was clearly in the bag after three J-Tinis at the salon. He also popped a couple of blue pills, and washed them down with the champagne that Fabian artistically had opened and poured.

Victor leaned near me and whispered, "I've got some terrific X for you to try."

I shook my head no. "I have enough trouble with booze."

Irritated by Victor's drunken drug use, Phillip shook his head and tried to change the subject. "Merry, forgive Victor. He's a bit over-served, but don't worry, I'm driving. Let's change the subject and talk about the future. Did you know I always wanted to move to the Pacific Northwest? Seattle. Victor and I have talked for years about setting up shop there, but our salon is doing so well here, we can't figure out how to leave."

Boom! Victor slammed the table and shouted, "If I hear one more frigging word about Seattle, I'll shit in your shoes. You can darn well move there alone, that is, if you can make any money without my talents."

Our server Fabian seemed concerned at the rising voices. He patted Victor on the shoulder. "Now, boys. Smiles, everyone, smiles."

Victor cracked up laughing. "At least one of us has a sense of humor."

"Victor, if you weren't so busy flirting with the waiter, maybe we could talk this over. Let's get Merry's input."

Before I could chime in, not that I had a clue what to say about Seattle, Victor stood up without a word, took Fabian by the hand, and the two skipped toward the front door, leaving me and Phillip stunned.

Red with anger, Phillip shouted after them, "Well, if you want him, you can forget about me!" Then, Phillip also jumped up and ran out, knocking his chair to the floor.

I was mortified. All around our table, diners issued a collective gasp, and I felt very alone at center stage. Me, with pubic hair on my head.

Guess who had to pay for the Dom Pérignon? At least it was half-priced.

Not only was I pissed at Victor and Phillip, but part of me worried about what they might be doing with the Fabian fellow. My hairdresser Morgan often told me wild tales about his various lovers, and now there is this terrible AIDS disease.

After such a downer happy hour, one might think I had enough sense to go home, tend to my dysfunctional daughter, and not pursue my quest to find a backer for my screenplay. But no. I did not go home. Instead, I drove to the parking lot in front of Pecan Street Theater, whereupon I sat in my car, played Neil Diamond's "Be," and scanned for signs of Arlen Wynnewood—with a foolish plan to follow him to The Cypress Door, where I now could approach him about my screenplay option and see if he might want to contact Lyle Davis. But the parking lot was dark and without cars from the beginning to the end of my mission, which suddenly ended when a City of Austin Police patrol car pulled up behind my LeSabre, and an officer of the law got out.

He tapped on my window. When I rolled it down, the aroma of champagne probably surged into his face like a tropical storm, as did the very loud Neil Diamond.

"Wow! May I see some identification?"

I turned down the music and fumbled for my license, feeling quite like a fool.

The policeman took my license and did the usual walking-back-to-his-car bit, where he waited while his partner checked to see if I had murdered anybody. After about five minutes, the officer came back and shined the flashlight in my face again. "Ma'am, have you been drinking?"

"I don't have to answer that question."

"Ah. She knows her rights. However, I smell the aroma of alcohol, and that makes me wonder what you are doing here? The address on your license says you live northwest."

"Is it against the law to park here?"

"No, ma'am. Between performances, this is a public lot for the hike and bike trail, but the theater security guard got nervous and called."

Roland, this is when I treasure the gifts you have given me—the ability to take a germ of truth and expand it into a world of my creation. I became a storyteller on parked wheels.

"Officer, to tell you the truth, I have been drinking. I was at a party with my boyfriend. But people were doing drugs like ecstasy and then some of them started an orgy in the upstairs bedroom. My boyfriend wanted me to come up with him, but I just couldn't do something like that. Drugs and a sexual orgy. I'm really not the type, and I can't believe my boyfriend would do that sort of stuff either, but he's there with them right now. Probably doing things ..." About then, I got the tears to roll, and I stammered, "Officer, I only stopped here to sober up, so I could drive home safely."

Did the police officer buy it? Sort of.

"Ma'am, I'm sorry you've had such a bad experience. Tell you what I'll do. My partner and I are going off shift in thirty minutes, so why don't I drive you home in our squad car, and my partner will follow us in your car. That'll end our shift, and you will be home safe."

"Oh, I don't want to inconvenience you. Just let me stay here a while. I'll sober up and drive myself."

"Ma'am. I've got three choices. One, I can impound your car, take you to the station and book you for public intoxication. Two, you can let us drive you home. Or three, we can go find your boyfriend at that party, and my partner and I can bust some drug users and perverts."

He wasn't as stupid as I had hoped.

I let him drive me home. Yes, Merry Mayfield, girl sleuth, arrived at her duplex in a squad car. And true to the luck of the evening, my heavenly sister-in-law Deanna had decided to drop by after work, probably to give me guilt about yelling at Brandon. So her Cadillac was parked in my driveway when I arrived home in a squad car—accompanied by two officers of the law.

Is Godot on my side?

When I walked in, Scottie and Claire were in the living room with Deanna. Luckily, or perhaps not so luckily, Nora was not home yet.

Since I had sobered up quite a bit, I decided to play it for laughs. "Deanna. Gosh, it's great to see you."

"Was that a police car in the driveway?"

"Yes, I was out earlier with a pair of hair stylists who made my hair look like a bush, so I drank a bit too much champagne to soothe my nerves."

Deanna glared at me, aghast.

Scottie started laughing. "Gosh, Mom, you look like you got stuck inside a tornado."

"Awful, isn't it? And I paid for this, not to mention a bottle of expensive champagne. If you and Claire would please go finish your homework and do whatever you need to before bed, I will tell you all about it, after Deanna leaves."

"Did they let you post bail?"

Gosh that woman was persistent. "I wasn't arrested, Deanna. I was assisted home. Be sure to tell Brandon that truth."

"I'll also tell him about that A. D. Greer still life hanging above your waterbed."

Whoops. Before I arrived home, the kids had shown Deanna my roses. Unfortunately, she has an affection for a few things beyond religion, expensive things like houses in West Lake Hills, Cadillacs, and timeshare condos. Deanna also can spot art. Art she knows I cannot afford. So, other than my being escorted home in a squad car, not to mention my hair being a monument to deranged hairstyling, I now had to deal with Deanna about my painting.

"It was a gift from a friend."

"Scottie said you got a good deal on it. What kind of a deal?"

"I got a discount from a friend in the business. The artist, A. D. Greer, is not dead yet, but after he ascends to artist heaven within a year, I'm told the painting will be worth $15,000."

"Regardless, how could you spend thousands for a painting? What about your children? As the *Bible* says, 'Any man who takes not the care of his family cannot call himself a Christian.'"

"Although the kids are not living in the style to which they were accustomed, they are well-fed and seem contented, while I manage to enjoy atrocious hairdos and delicious bubbly. Now, will you tell me why you are still here?"

"Merry, did you trade sexual favors for that painting?"

She was nearer the truth than I cared to admit. "Deanna, I do not have to explain how or from whom I purchased that painting. So please, get into your sanctimonious Cadillac and fly back to West Lake Hills. After all, you don't want my sins to tarnish your eternal spirit."

Roland, that last dig sent Deanna into a spiritual fever. She got up, spread her arms, and began to moan, saying, "Praise the Spirits, save this woman. She is infested with a devil who has possessed her house, possessed her mind. All is perversion. Strike it dead. Come, spirits. Let me be thine instrument. Wash her in the blood of your salvation."

Then, like lightning, she zoomed to my bedroom. I tried to keep up, but Deanna was fueled by fire, brimstone, and the passion to save my spirit. By the time I got to the bedroom, she had grabbed a pair of scissors from the bathroom drawer and jumped on my waterbed. Then, in spite of being wildly off-balance from the wave action, Deanna lunged the scissors at my roses ... my roses, my roses! Slash, slash, slash—the canvas wrinkled like the High Roller's fanny, leaving my painting in frayed flaps, even my favorite claret rose on the right. As Deanna steadied herself with one hand on the wall, the other hand drew back to strike another blow.

I had to stop her. I dove on the bed and clambered over the rocking waves until I got hold of her left calf and yanked her down. After she fell, she kept trying to stand, which was impossible, what with two of us on the rolling bed. Although she is much taller and stronger than I, managed to get on top of her. Fueled by too much champagne, I held on with all the vengeance I could muster, perhaps leftover from losing childhood battles with Brandon.

This went on for a while, until she eventually succumbed in babbling tears. "Dear heavenly spirits, I cannot fight this woman's perversion alone. Come to my side and bring the sword of your eternal passion."

On and on she beseeched, her howls alerting Claire and Scottie, who ran in to see what the tussle was about.

"Auntie Dee, what's the matter?"

"Your mother is possessed by a devil ..." Deanna began.

As Claire and Scottie fearfully hovered and gawked, I figured the only way to stop Deanna's fervor was to douse it. So I wiggled off her, then slid off the bed to the bathroom, where I rummaged under the sink until I found my ancient douche bag. I filled it with cold water to the point it became a pink globe about to burst. Then I drew back and aimed the neck of the bag at Deanna's face. When that torrent of water hit, the look in Deanna's eyes went beyond incredulity. They sank deeper, blacker, into a vision only Deanna could see.

Gosh, I loved the power.

Shocked to silence, her hair soaked and makeup running, she stoically slid off the bed and walked dripping down the hall.

Moments later, I heard her drive away in her Cadillac.

"Mom, have you been drinking?" Claire asked, hands authoritatively on her hips.

"I might resume soon. Unfortunately, Auntie Dee went a little overboard spiritually and slashed my new painting because she thinks I am in cahoots with the devil. I figured cold water would do the trick."

"But she'll tell Uncle Brandon, and he'll come over too," Scottie said.

"I'm sorry, kids. Truly, I am embarrassed by all this. Sometimes adults behave like children, but that doesn't make it right. I apologize if I have frightened you. Now, let's get a snack before bed. I bet you're hungry. In fact, I am too."

Claire didn't buy my bullshit. "Mom, I think you need to see a counselor or somebody about all this."

"Claire, I promise you, things are fine."

"I wouldn't call what you did to Auntie Deanna 'fine.' And you better not forget to have that talk with Nora."

My youngest daughter sounded very much like my mother.

✉ ✉ ✉

A half hour later, Nora got home, so I had to deal with that. But I was sober by then. She wouldn't tell me much about her new beau, only that he was "a few years older," very cute, and she liked him. She also said she was going to kill Claire, who was now hiding in her room.

"Claire was afraid for your safety."

"I am eighteen. That's the legal age of consent in Texas."

"Just because you are of legal age does not mean you should do something as momentous as having sex. It makes babies, for one thing. This is your first time, isn't it?"

"That's none of your business."

But the earnestness in her eyes gave her away. "Nora, I don't want you to make the same mistake I made."

"Thanks for reminding me why you had to marry Dad."

"That's not what I meant. And I didn't have to marry him. I could have aborted you."

"Gosh, thanks again."

"I didn't mean it that way. I had options, but we chose to marry and have our first baby girl. And I'm glad to this day that we did." Part of that was a lie, but oh, well.

"He said he'd use protection."

"That can fail too. Just remember, no boy or man should pressure you. When the time is right, you will know and be able to plan for it. I'll be happy to make a doctor's appointment for you."

"I can make my own appointment, Mother."

I sighed. "Claire also told me you were concerned about this guy being older. Please wait until you are sure. Perhaps he is not the best partner for your first time."

"I don't want to talk about this anymore. And I'm going to kill Claire." Then Nora marched to Claire's bedroom, but the door was locked. So

Nora went into her own bedroom and slammed that door hard.

So much for our little talk. Parenting is not easy. If Pamela were home, I would've gone over for emotional support, but she's out inspecting elevators in Oklahoma, last I heard.

All of this was last night. Early this morning, Nora left for early play rehearsal, so I don't know if my talk did any good. But something else did. A bit later, the doorbell rang. When I answered, a delivery man handed me a brown envelope. Inside was a check for $10,000, paid by the Eternal Spirit Center. No accompanying explanation. No apology.

I guess Deanna contacted Jerry's gallery to get a price. His is the only gallery in town that sells A.D. Greer, so I've made $1,000 profit already, But even $1,000 extra in my coffers cannot dull the pain of seeing my beautiful roses slashed into huge flaps.

I called Jerry to see who might repair the painting. He said he would see what could be done. "We've got a guy who fixes things. But that'll cost another two or three thousand, darlin', or better yet, how about dinner and a hot tub next Thursday?"

Oh dear, another deal with the art devil. But to my relief, I am $1,000 up on the cash spent for an amazing painting. Hopefully I can make an even larger profit on it soon, that is, if I ignore the sexual thrashings Jerry will require to get a bargain price on repairs.

And here I am, lecturing my daughter not to have sex.

Love,
Merry

SCENE 27

EXT. NORA'S VAN — 1989 — DAY

Nora is driving her van to Glenn's trailer.

INT. NORA'S VAN — 1989 — DAY

Nora rehearses aloud to herself while she's
driving.

> NORA
> Glenn, we need to take another
> break. Maybe if you were younger ...

She slams the steering wheel. The horn BEEPS.

> NORA (CONT'D)
> He won't like that. Insulting.

She dreams up another good excuse.

> NORA (CONT'D)
> When you pressure me for sex, I feel
> like you're making me do something I
> don't want to do.

She slams the steering wheel again, and the
horn BEEPS.

                    NORA (CONT'D)
          Shit. Too much like the teenager who
          accused him of rape. But maybe she
          was right.

Nora's shakes her head and drives on.

EXT. GLENN'S TRAILER — 1989 — DAY

IN THE LOT

Nora pulls in.

Glenn and Natasha come out.

Nora gets out, pets an excited Natasha, and
lightly hugs Glenn. All go inside.

INT. GLENN'S TRAILER — 1989 — DAY

Nora sits on the sofa with Glenn beside her.

He fondles her hair, but she lightly pushes
his hand away.

                    GLENN
          I'm glad you wanted to see me again,
          but what is so important? I had to
          miss my afternoon geology lab.

                    NORA
          Glenn, I like you so much. I really
          do. But I think ... well, this is
          hard for me, but I wanted to tell
          you in person ...

GLENN
What, I missed lab so you can come
do this prick-tease act again?

NORA
I think we need to break up.

GLENN
Is this your idea or Mommy's?

NORA
Mine.

GLENN
This kind of tease gets little girls
what they're due.

NORA
Please don't be angry. Even though I
like you, sex is just something I'm
not ready for yet.

GLENN
Your mommy sure was ready.

Nora looks confused.

NORA
My mommy. What do you mean?

GLENN
Your mommy's been here. Been in my
car. Been in my bed. We fucked and
sucked all kinds of ways.

                              NORA
           What are you saying? You and my mom?

                              GLENN
           She dug it too.

                              NORA
           You're lying. I know you're mad at
           me, but you don't have to be mean.

                              GLENN
           I'm not lying. Just ask your hot
           little mommy.

                              NORA
           I'm going to leave now.

Nora gets up, grabs her purse, and rushes to
the door.

                              GLENN
           Sic her, Natasha.

Natasha alerts, confused.

                              NORA
           Don't you dare. I thought you cared
           about me. Now I see you don't.

In tears, Nora runs out.

EXT. GLENN'S TRAILER — 1989 — DAY

As Nora rushes to her van, Glenn lets Natasha
out. From the doorway, he watches, grins.

                         GLENN
          Get her good, Natasha.

Nora sees Natasha coming, freezes for a
moment, but opens her van door. She gets
inside, nick of time, then slams and locks it.

Natasha BARKS, jumps up, and claws the van's
door and Nora's window.

Nora frantically starts her engine and puts
the van in gear. Her tires grind on gravel.

Natasha runs after the van, BARKING, as Glenn
hollers at the dog from behind.

                         GLENN
          Dammit, Natasha. You piece of shit.
          You missed her. Come back here!
          We've got planning to do.

Letter Twenty-Six
June 22, 1989

Dear Roland,

This afternoon, as I waltzed to my mailbox, not feeling one bit more futile than any other day, I found a note from Lyle Davis. Also enclosed, was a copy of a rejection letter addressed to him from Gwendolyn Gaines, acquisition producer for United Artists. Went like this:

Dear Lyle,

Thanks for the opportunity to read Those Who Try. *I'm afraid, however, it's not right for UA. Although the main character is sympathetic, and I empathized with her plight, the ending is a bit preposterous, even in today's enlightened age—she's going to marry her gay hairdresser who has AIDS? I think the audience might leave laughing (or screaming).*

Let me know if you have anything more believable. And especially, if you find any intelligent thrillers. We're always on the lookout!

Sincerely, GG
Gwendolyn Gaines

⊠　⊠　⊠

"Anything more believable." What does Gwendolyn Gaines know? She probably didn't read it herself. And whoever covered the script for her is likely to be a recent grad from UCLA film school, who has never lived one true moment.

Tell me, Professor Brilliance, will there be an endless series of similar rejections?

⊠ ⊠ ⊠

I'm back with a J-Tini. Would you expect me to plod through sober? Pamela is back in town but working late in a downtown high-rise. Sigrid is not home (I've called her four times). So, I just had to tell somebody about this rejection. That done, I'll slog onward with the latest news, for your eyes only, *Dear Diary*.

In spite of frequent trips to The Cypress Door and Jeffrey's, I have not seen a trace of Arlen Wynnewood. I was beginning to think I had made him up, except I have called the Pecan Street Theater office weekly, using a vast repertoire of pseudonyms and fake voices, pretending I am a Hollywood agent.

His secretary replies, "I'm sorry, but Mr. Wynnewood is out of state."

Apparently, my obsessive brain has finally given up on him as a romantic paramour. At least I learned something from you—other than how to write a screenplay no one wants to produce.

Let's see, what else. How could I forget? Dear Pluppy Brandon came over one Saturday morning after his heavenly wife slashed my beautiful roses. DPB didn't even call first. He simply rang the bell and waltzed in. It was 9:00 a.m. I was still in my PJ's, staring out the kitchen window, wondering if I should give up writing entirely. I faintly remember hearing the kids shout, "Mom! It's Uncle Brandon," but I didn't budge until I heard DPB pull back a chair and sit at my table.

His wide brown eyes made only the slightest squint of revulsion at my offer of a Saturday-morning mimosa.

I did not have one, mind you. I was just trying to piss Brandon off.

He cleared his throat. "Deanna was in tears the other night. She refused to say what happened. I figured you two had another run-in, so I thought I'd ask you face to face, so you can't hang up on me." He paused and gave me a manufactured smile.

I did not say a word. I merely beckoned for Brandon to follow.

In my bedroom, his eyes followed my pointed finger to my slashed roses, still hanging on the wall awaiting Jerry High Roller's pick up for surgical repair. Brandon glared at me aghast. "Why would you do something like that?"

"Your lovely wife did that in one of her spiritual fits."

"That's not what I meant. Why would you buy an expensive painting when you're broke?"

"You liar! You knew about this."

Brandon's face flushed mauve.

"As I told Deanna, the painting will be worth $15,000 within a year."

Okay, so I omitted the fact that I'd paid $9,000 for it. When I'm dealing with Brandon, lies are my only leverage. And when I lie, a wonderful switch catapults me into a land wherein lies become their own truths, so fucking more exciting than reality. However, lies are also like characters in a drama. You think you can control them, but you can't.

As Brandon glared at my painting, his mustache twisted into a Hitler-like contortion. "How in the world did you pay for it?" he asked, with heavy emphasis on *pay*.

"Cease your insinuations. I traded the boat for it. You and Dad always wanted me to get rid of that boat."

More lies.

"Your boat wasn't worth $5,000."

"Regardless, your celestial wife wrote me a check for $10,000 after she slashed the hell out of my beautiful roses."

Brandon stopped dead and squinted while his cerebral wheels turned. He clearly did not know Deanna had paid me $10,000. In avoidance, he turned a slow one-eighty, feigning interest out my bedroom window. I must say, DPB faked it pretty well. By the time he turned back to me, his moon-pie eyeballs squinted into mine.

"Merry, I remain concerned about your irresponsible attitude. Alcohol is the cause, you know. You've been drinking already today. I can smell it on your breath."

"I have not been drinking, Brandon." (That was not a lie.)

"Just like Father's breath. Didn't you learn from him how alcohol fuels impulses but takes away your initiative? Wasn't Dad's life proof? Do you want to end up like him, with your testicles the size of grapefruits?"

"I don't have testicles—as Dad and you kept reminding me throughout my childhood."

In a fit of teary-eyed sincerity, Brandon reached his hands for mine, but I refused to meet his grasp. So he grabbed my forearms instead.

"Merry, I want to help. Please. Let me take you to the Faulkner Center downtown. They're doing wonderful things for alcoholics these days."

Shit. It doesn't matter to Brandon that his script and my reality do not mesh. That I had not been drinking that morning. That the real and, admittedly irrational, reason I paid too much for that painting was an obsessive quest for the unattainable. Yes, I was drunk when I made the deal. But I wanted those damn roses enough to spend too much on them, because doing so was my sincere attempt at a fuck-you-world, blood-rushing statement that, yes, I truly exist.

"Brandon, I'll take my foolishness, financial stupidity, and occasional tendency toward drinking too much in comparison with your inability to see, feel, or say one true thing."

"You are lashing out at the one person who's trying to help."

He did look hurt, and I felt a bit sad as he left in a huff—eyes oozing a narcissist's tears.

✉ ✉ ✉

Oh, Roland, but the entire world cannot be as enlightened as you and our little theater-and-film gang, with our urgently intellectual conversations about life, love, art, and philosophy. You, Sigrid, Frank, Jillian, and I—lifting dark beers in a dark bar, laughing, shouting, discussing. How pleasant life would be, were it only that. The great writers and scholars of yesteryear lived like that. They wrote and exchanged letters, met each other on holiday, and discussed literature, politics, and life. They were not so encumbered with real estate careers, weekend trips to K-Mart, boats, and paying rent on a duplex.

As for these mental masturbations, which I vehemently type to you, if you'll recall, I said I might try to craft a screenplay out of them. I've reread a few lately, alongside my revised script. Plot-wise, both tell the same story about a writer's efforts to become a writer. Needless to say, that's been done too many times. I must figure how to take my story beyond the truth of myself. Add a few thrilling plot twists—maybe even a murder by a nefarious character.

"Intelligent thriller," Gwendolyn Gaines requested.

Can I turn my sad, sorry life into an intelligent thriller?

⋈   ⋈   ⋈

Gin poured over ice, shaken slowly, strained into a frosted glass, rimmed with jalapeño juice, garnished with lime, olive, and a jalapeño slice on a toothpick equals a J-Tini.

I needed fuel.

To end this, I shall tell you something that is at least uplifting. Since I hang out at The Cypress Door so often, I have developed a closer friendship with the shy Turtle. One night last week, I confessed to him that I have only a few months of money left and need to get a full-time job. After all, real estate is not something I excel at, or even try to do.

He said, "Did you contact Pecan Street? I heard they're hiring a script editor."

I won't bother describing the lightning bolts that flashed through my mind. I was so uplifted by the thought of being a script editor, with my lord and master being none other than Arlen Wynnewood, I hugged Turtle and gave him a kiss on the cheek, which turned a deep mahogany.

I think Turtle may have a bit of a crush on me.

Despite being rejected by Gwendolyn Gaines of United Artists, there is hope. The role of script editor has an honorable ring. Not as exciting as Academy Award-winning screenwriter, but I'm willing to take one step at a time.

Love,
Merry

SCENE 28

INT. LUNA'S APARTMENT — 1989 — DAY

IN THE LIVING ROOM

Brandon and Luna sip WINE. He fiddles with the
TV REMOTE and changes channels.

                    BRANDON
          Damn cable. Hundreds of channels but
          nothing to watch.

                    LUNA
          Stop evading. Have you told Deanna?

                    BRANDON
          Told her what?

                    LUNA
          You said you would tell her.

                    BRANDON
          I have to get Deanna settled in the
          new house. I owe her that much.
          She's the mother of my children.

                    LUNA
          But she left you long ago for Jesus.

                    BRANDON
          Jesus can't get it up like I can.

                     LUNA
                 (sarcastically)
          Wouldn't you rather have a lover who
          calls out your name?

                    BRANDON
          Ask yourself that same question.

Luna frowns at Brandon's zinger, remembering
when he had shouted Deanna's name.

                     LUNA
          Thank heavens you didn't holler,
          'Jesus.'

                    BRANDON
          That's right. I said, 'Deanna.'

He gets up to leave.

                     LUNA
          So, now you're staying with her?

                    BRANDON
          Look, I've already got too much
          pressure.

Letter Twenty-Seven
July 7, 1989

Dear Roland,

You answered my letter. Y-O-U. You cannot imagine my joy. I looked in my mailbox, and the envelope was right on top. "Film and Theater Program, Columbia University, New York, NY," with "Holmes" scribbled across the return address. No, I did not rip it open. I wanted to treasure it, so I held it close and walked methodically into the house, then down the hall to my bedroom where I closed and locked the door.

I stretched out on my waterbed, toes pointed at my roses, which Jerry High Roller had repaired at the cost of only $2,500 and my virtue (more later about that). I held your letter over my heart and caressed the paper, imagining you hunched over your ancient typewriter, tapping this to me. I envisioned you signing and folding it, slipping it into an envelope, licking the glue, pressing your fingers to seal it, then, hurriedly scribbling your surname and placing it in the outgoing box at the office.

Do you have any idea what it meant for me to know that you were thinking about me? To know that I existed in your mind, to know that some concern and possibly even desire filtered through your brainwaves as you wrote and mailed this letter to me?

Finally, I elaborately opened it, listening to the paper rustle and caressing the page as though I were touching you.

Merry,

Congratulations. I knew you could do it. And, if you'll remember, my dear, I was the one who first said that to you. I shall look forward to your premiere.

News about your non-writing life was skimpy: tell me, dear, about the men with whom you've been keeping company? Of course, I am curious. Matter of fact, I did, whilst in San Antonio to speak at a conference, consider driving north to see you. But I didn't. Probably better for both of us.

I would love to describe some exciting news about my life, except things are merely the same, whatever they were and are. I'll write more later when I have time and more to say.

Fondly,
Roland

P.S. Okay, a juicy letter later, when I am feeling juicy.

Damn you. So elusive, but I loved it anyway. I read and reread it, must have been twenty times, searching between the lines. To think you were in San Antonio for a conference! Only ninety miles away. Damn you. Why didn't you come see me? Or call me to come see you? We could have laughed the way we used to. We could have, might have, even made love.

That was probably why you said, "Better for both of us that I didn't." What else could you have meant? Did you mean that you and I should never be?

"Better for both of us that I didn't."

And the other line, "Tell me, dear, about the men with whom you've been keeping company?" That was the first thing you asked. Are you curious out of friendly, natural curiosity or curious out of jealousy?

Regardless, I wrote you back and actually mailed it, not this entry but a note, starting with these lines:

Dearest Roland,

Thanks for your letter, such as it was. Short, sweet, obtuse. You always were an elusive charmer, never quite my friend and never quite my lover.

⊠   ⊠   ⊠

Such talk of our being lovers will scare the hell out of you. Too direct. But I tempered it with updates about the option, my opportunity to get a job as script editor, etc.

Although your note did cheer me, I have a startling change of subject. I followed up with Nora to see how things were going with her older guy. She was in the bathroom, styling her hair, so I sat on the toilet seat and tried being a cool friend-style mother. That was my approach anyway.

However, in response to my questions, Nora revealed that her older guy is Glenn, that UT engineering student I had one wild night of sex with. Needless to say, I was horrified, since our hot encounter was a far stretch beyond beginner sexual relations. I certainly don't want my daughter engaged in similar activities, not for her first time. I want that to be sweet and tender—more an exploration, not a detonation.

Nora promised me that she and Glenn have not done the deed.

"He's gotten real pushy, so we are taking a break."

"Nora, I'm saying this as sincerely as a mother can. Glenn is eleven years older than you, he is far more experienced sexually, and he is not the right person for your first time. For all I know, he may have been stalking you, since I rejected him as being too young for me."

"We bumped into each other accidentally."

"It may have been accidental to you, but how do you know he didn't follow you? I know Glenn is cute. And he is bright and charming. But I also know other things about him that make me concerned."

"Mother, I know a lot more than you think I do. And I am eighteen. This is my life!" Then she rushed to her bedroom and slammed the door.

That's what I get for trying to be a good mother. I thought about calling Glenn and telling him to leave Nora alone, but that would probably add more fuel to her fire, or his. Besides, it's a contradiction for me to tell my daughter not to have sex when I am now having sex regularly with Jerry Manning.

A scene that happens all too regularly: High Roller's place, the back deck high above Lake Austin. Naked, I step into the foaming Jacuzzi hot tub and stare over the tops of cedar and juniper trees toward the city lights beyond. Austin is so pretty at night. In the distance the huge pink capitol dome glows like a monument should. And downtown, there are all manner of cranes and new buildings with twinkling lights that sparkle clearly in this non-industrial air.

Wearing nothing, Jerry appears proudly with two dishes of H-E-B guajillo-honey and vanilla bean ice cream, topped with a shot of B&B poured over. He hands both bowls to me. I smile as his fat tummy and wrinkled fanny sink in the water beside me. Knowing sex with me is also on his menu, I try to concentrate on his face. He is not bad looking for his age. I take a bite of the ice cream. He gobbles his in three spoonfuls then waits impatiently until I finish mine. As soon as I do—floooosh!— we are awash in a thrashing hot tub sea as High Roller kisses me furiously, mounts me, inserts his humongous appendage into my lonely flap, which is lubricated only by Jacuzzi water, and one, two, three, four, sometimes five or six, mighty strokes later, Jerry calls out, "You got me, Darlin'!" Physically exhausted, he heaves himself upon me and falls dead asleep.

Each time this happens, I summon enough adrenaline to slip out from under him and haul his ass out. First, I pull his arms over the edge. Next, I get in the tub and push his legs up, using the water for buoyancy, until the trunk of his body slides just far enough for me to gain leverage. Then I get out and pull the rest of him onto a bath towel.

But not this last time. The water level wasn't high enough to float Jerry's body over an edge, so I had to drain the fucking tub and leave him in it, like an elephant in a dried-up water hole. I draped him with towels before I dressed and drove home in one of Jerry's Allantes. Perhaps this is why he has two of them.

Why do I continue to screw this man? He has money. He shows me a wonderful time, and then I pay my dues. It's socially accepted prostitution. (Maybe not acceptable to Brandon or Deanna.)

⊠   ⊠   ⊠

To end this on a more positive note, we have Merry's career. I sent in my résumé, cover letter, and a sample from my screenplay to Pecan Street Theater, letting them know my work had been optioned by Lyle Davis Film Productions.

Turtle was kind enough to write a recommendation letter as well.

"Arlen hasn't liked some reviews I've given his productions, but he knows to keep me on his good side until the paper hires a full-time reviewer instead of abusing their humor columnist."

Wish me luck. Perhaps I will soon be defined as script editor. That would be a tolerable existence? I can almost be a writer.

Love,
Merry

SCENE 29

INT. ANCHORAGE, ALASKA AIRPORT — 1989 — DAY

AT CAR RENTAL COUNTER

It's July. Glenn is in a t-shirt and jeans as
he pulls out his wallet and shows his ID.

INSERT: GLENN'S ALASKA DRIVER'S LICENSE

EXT. ANCHORAGE AIRPORT — 1989 — DAY

Glenn drives a 1988 SUV out of the car rental
parking lot.

EXT. ALASKA GUN SHOP — 1989 — DAY

Glenn parks at a gun store, gets out, goes
inside, but he's always checking his back to
see if anybody's watching.

INT. GUN SHOP — 1989 — DAY

SALES CLERK shows Glenn several semi-automatic
PISTOLS.

Glenn takes pretend aim with one, then nods
his head to indicate approval.

SALES CLERK
Need ammo?

GLENN
Something that'll stop a bitch dead
in her tracks.

Sales Clerk gives him a curious look.

GLENN
Just jokin', man. Can't even laugh
about shit anymore. Goddamn liberals
have us all watching our backs.

EXT. ALASKA HARDWARE STORE — 1989 — DAY

Glenn heads inside.

INT. ALASKA HARDWARE STORE — 1989 — DAY

Glenn buys wire, two wooden lawnmower starter
handles, a black tarp, and a shovel.

INT. ANCHORAGE MOTEL ROOM — 1989 — DAY

Watching CNN on TV, Glenn fashions a garrote
from the wire and starter handles. He pretends
to wrap it around a neck and then twists.

He grins, puts the garrote down, picks up his
new pistol, then aims it at a woman on TV.

GLENN
Hope I won't need this.

EXT. ANCHORAGE MOTEL — 1989 — DAY

Glenn comes out with the shovel, tarp, and garrote in hand.

INT. GLENN'S RENTAL CAR — 1989 — DAY

Glenn puts the tarp in the trunk and the shovel beside it. He closes the trunk, gets inside, and tosses the garrote on the passenger seat.

Under his shirt we see the outline of a gun tucked in his waist.

EXT. SMALL LAKE, ANCHORAGE — 1989 — DAY

Across the lake, the sun is setting. Glenn parks near a house and watches. Waits.

Teen Girl comes out in jogging gear. She dons Sony headphones and plugs them in a Walkman DD9. She jogs slowly down the road.

Glenn waits for a while, then starts his car and drives slowly by Teen Girl, watching in his rear-view mirror. He drives to a secluded, woodsy area beyond the houses, where he parks.

When Teen Girl jogs by, Glenn silently gets out with his garrote, then grabs her from behind. He tries to strangle her, but the garrote wire tangles in her earphones.

She struggles as Glenn yanks off her earphones. Even in fear, she recognizes him.

                    TEEN GIRL
        Glenn! You motherfucker. I'm going
        to call police. Help! Help!

She bolts toward her house, but Glenn chases
after. Grabs her. As he strangles her, she
kicks and fights until Teen Girl succumbs.

With her body now at his feet, Glenn glances
to see if anybody noticed, but all is quiet.

                     GLENN
        Fucking Walkman screwed that up.

He drags limp Teen Girl to rental car, plops
her on the tarp, then closes trunk door. He
gets in car and drives off slowly.

INT. ANCHORAGE BURGER SHOP — 1989 — NIGHT

Glenn sits alone and munches a double burger
with fries. Out the window, he keeps an eye on
his car. Checks his watch. Gets up for more
soda. Sits and waits.

INT. ANCHORAGE MOTEL ROOM — 1989 — NIGHT

Lying on the bed, Glenn watches a movie on TV.
Picks up his pistol. Aims it at an ACTRESS.

                     GLENN
        One bitch down, two more to go.
        Heck, maybe I'll go for three.

He checks a CLOCK. It says 1:00 a.m.

EXT. ANCHORAGE MOTEL — 1989 — NIGHT

Glenn walks out with his backpack, gets in the
rental car, and drives off.

EXT. SMALL LAKE, ANCHORAGE — 1989 — NIGHT

Glenn parks near the wooded area, far from
the houses. He gets out, takes the shovel out
of the trunk, goes into the woods and starts
digging.

Glenn returns to his car, wraps Teen Girl
in the tarp, then carries the bundle to the
grave. He places Teen Girl's body in the hole.
Fills it.

                    GLENN
          All you had to do was keep your
          mouth shut and let me fuck you.

Letter Twenty-Eight
August 4, 1989

Dear Roland,

I got the job at Pecan Street! I was shocked. The interview was not what I would call cordial. Tall, haughty, young, but with a saggy rear inside baggy olive linen cargo pants, Rachelle Proctor gave me a cold-fish handshake when she met me two weeks ago. I watched her fanny jiggle as she led me into her office. She leaned back in her chair. Not a smile. Not a preface. Just a confronting monotone, "Why do you want to work for Pecan Street Theater?"

What a question. How should I have answered?

"I desperately need a job because my ex-husband lost all our money gambling, and my Dear Pluppy Brother is not about to help me because he thinks I am a drunk." Better not. I went with, "I've always wanted to work in live theater, and Pecan Street is the best in Austin."

"You submitted a screenplay sample, but you must understand that you will be editing established stage plays—each completely different—and you will not be writing original work. Arlen Wynnewood is an innovative creative director who needs an editor with the ability to take great works and craft them into his vision."

"I can edit anything," I said, hoping she would buy the line. She didn't reply, so I decided to pretend I was interested in her. "How did you get started at Pecan Street?"

"I majored in theater at NYU."

Aha! A common background. "Did you ever venture up Broadway for a beer at the Raven? That's where all the Columbia majors hang out."

"Why would I bother doing that?"

"It's a fun spot for conversations about the meaning of life."

She sat like a stick.

"Have you ever written for the stage or screen?" I asked.

"In college, but I've moved on. I feel as if I've conquered writing."

"Oh, so you've conquered writing," I wanted to scoff, appalled by her haughtiness in an interview that meant so much to me—I mean, here I was, almost forty, nervous, trying to land a job as a writer, hoping for an occupation—a definition that meant sustenance for my family.

⊠   ⊠   ⊠

INT. RACHELLE PROCTOR'S OFFICE — DAY

Merry catapults across Rachelle's desk and chokes her, watching Rachelle's eyes bulge from shock to fear as she tries to scream, but only gasps.

Rachelle passes out and collapses limply across her chair.

Merry smiles.

> MERRY
> That's what you get for saying,
> "I've conquered writing."

⊠   ⊠   ⊠

No, that's only what I wish happened. Instead, I sat stupidly, passively.

Rachelle Proctor replied, "Now, if you'll excuse me, I have another interview."

Chagrined, I drove home in misery and knocked on Pamela's door, hoping she would commiserate. But she wasn't there. Again. She's been spending a lot of time away, and I understand she has her own life, but I need an available girlfriend too. Women rely on one another for talk therapy. Otherwise, we'd have to run to a shrink weekly.

Dejected, I thought I had grim news to tell my children, but when I walked in, the three of them greeted me with a group hug.

"Great job. We knew you could do it," Claire and Scottie crowed.

"This will be a job you can stay with," Nora said with a bit of an edge.

I didn't understand what the kids were talking about until they played the message. "Merry, Rachelle Proctor here. You've got the job. Please report for work on Monday, September 4. Our office opens at 9:00 a.m. We are delighted to have you on board."

"Delighted to have me on board? The woman behaved as if I had leprosy."

The kids laughed with me, then we headed to celebrate with doubles at Wendy's.

✉ ✉ ✉

After we got home, I went back to Pamela's and was so happy to find her there. She was as excited for me as the kids had been. We did a silly jig in her kitchen to Pamela's vocal version of "Happy Days Are Here Again." Then we had a few drinks and talked.

As she got her second Crown and Coke, her tone became confidential. "I'd better confess. I've been dating Jerry's friend."

"The Santa Claus? When do you have time? You're never in town."

"I'm in Austin more than you know, but I've been at Timothy's. That's his name."

"So, how is Santa Claus in the sack, and I don't mean the sack with the gifts?"

"Merry, you are a funny girl, but I refuse to get graphic. His last name, by the way, is Le Mans. You know, like the car race."

"Is he French?"

"His grandfather emigrated before World War II."

"So ... how are things going? Maybe we should plan a double date?"

"Merry, quit prying. I've heard so much about your escapades in the hot tub with Jerry, I'm afraid that if I see him again, I'd blush red remembering your tales."

We laughed. Girly giggles. And I told her another silly story about Jerry.

⊠   ⊠   ⊠

In other good news, Nora is speaking to me again—although she is likely chagrined at her mother's morals. A week or two ago, she came into my office to tell me she had stopped seeing Glenn for sure. Needless to say, I was relieved. I've always felt uncomfortable about Glenn's rape charge in Alaska. And, after my insane night with him, I could see how someone younger and far-less drunk might think she'd been raped.

"He was pissed when I broke it off. Said mean things," Nora whined.

"Uh-oh, more red flags."

Nora paused and took a deep breath. "He said something about you. Said you two had sex. Was that a lie?"

Oh dear, Roland. What was a mother to do? Given the circumstances that Nora was unlikely to see Glenn again, I could have lied. But then, I wouldn't want my daughter to lie to me, so I decided I must fess up. "I made a mistake when I first met him. I'd had too much to drink, but I didn't want to tell you because I was embarrassed."

Nora took a chair beside my desk. "Oh, Mom. That makes me want to vomit."

"It makes me sick too. I was immediately sorry about the whole thing, but I was at a low point. And Glenn was, well, very persuasive."

Nora thought for a minute. "First you, then me. Maybe the guy really is a stalker. And there was all that stuff about a girl in Alaska, how she lied about her age to him, he kept saying. Now I wonder if maybe he should actually be in jail."

"I've wondered the same thing. But unlike me, you made the right decision."

"The more he pressured, the more I saw how he got that rape charge."

"My dear, pay attention to life's red flags, and you will avoid much heartache."

She got up, and we hugged each other, a close mother-daughter hug. Teenagers have so much hormonal rage, it is difficult to see the young girl Nora probably remains inside. But then, she endured Doug's and my tempestuous marriage for years. Hopefully, that taught her about recognizing a good mate from a lousy choice.

⊠   ⊠   ⊠

On the bad news front, I'm getting used to rejection. Lyle Davis sent me another negative—this time from Metro-Goldwin-Mayer's Harriet Morris. She said, "The author has a deep identification with her heroine; but the work would require a full rewrite to give it some sizzle. This writer shows promise, but she must remember, 'No plot, my dear, no story.'"

"No plot, my dear, no story?"

This is your fucking fault. In class, you absolutely stood stock-still at the mention of the word plot. Then, you would give us each a daring glare from those sky-blue orbs and begin your patented dramatic tirade: "Plot! Plot! Plot! There are only seven possible plots. Pick one. As Hemingway said, 'Every story is about the good and the bad, the ecstasy, the remorse and sorrow, the people and the places, and how the weather was.'"

That might be conceptually true, but as far as selling a film script goes, you were wrong. And I, a victim of your esoteric propaganda for so many years, cannot get a screenplay to the silver screen because my script does not have enough sizzle, a freaking plot—even though you, oh mighty academician, would insist it does.

Girl meets boy, falls in love, changes, leaves him, finds new love. Metro-Goldwin-Mayer says that isn't enough.

Shit. Rejected again. My guts on the page. My character. A knife in my heart. One failure to another, you know how awful that feels.

Love,
Merry

SCENE 30

INT. COLUMBIA FILM DEPT. — 1989 — DAY

Roland sits at a messy desk that has a
TYPEWRITER and TELEPHONE. He rummages through
several drawers but can't find something.

                    ROLAND
          Phooey. I put it somewhere.

He eventually finds Merry's business CARD.

INSERT CARD TEXT:
          Meredith Mayfield, Screenwriter
          5134 Festival Street
          Austin, TX 78731
          (512) 555-1234

                    ROLAND
          And now for the call I should have
          made so many months before.

He dials Merry's number. Listens as it rings.

                    MERRY'S VOICEMAIL (O.S.)
          You've reached the Mayfields. Please
          leave a message. We'll call you back
          as soon as possible.

Roland inhales nervously, then begins.

                    ROLAND
        Hello, this message is for—

Abruptly, Jillian barges in.

                    JILLIAN
        We've got to get things straightened
        out. Everybody's gossiping about us.

Roland reluctantly hangs up, although he
worries about the partial message he just left
on Merry's machine.

                JILLIAN (CONT'D)
        Oh, I'm sorry. I didn't realize you
        were on the phone. But—

                    ROLAND
        Now that I'm off, what needs
        straightening or gossiping? I
        thought we agreed that our being
        together was impossible, and you
        needed to explore a new zone.

Jillian closes the door for privacy and sits
in a chair beside Roland's desk.

                    JILLIAN
        Cut the Tarkovsky crap, Roland.

Roland scratches the back of his head and
frowns. He's between a rock and a hard place.

                         ROLAND
          I confess to shoveling the
          existential bullshit now and then,
          as Sigrid calls my philosophical
          insights. But you and I agreed
          it was time to end our affair. I
          cannot afford to leave Elizabeth or
          our children. So that keeps you in
          the role of mistress. You said you
          would not continue. I respect that.
          And perhaps it *is* time for us to
          explore—

                         JILLIAN
          Bullshit. Are you going to be
          emotionally constipated all your
          life, or unload your baggage and
          love me, hell, anybody? And by the
          way, you only get to love *one* woman.

Jillian holds up her index finger.

                         ROLAND
              Jillian ...

His answer says it for him. Jillian leaves in
a huff and SLAMS the office door.

Roland digests the scene. He takes Merry's
note and starts dialing her number again. But
he stops.

                         ROLAND
              If you only get one, which one do
              you choose?

Dear Roland,

I must tell you about my disastrous party. An anniversary party. I stupidly surmised that since I've lived in Austin one whole year and have gotten a real job as a writer, I should celebrate. However, my guest list was a bit limited: Pamela, a female elevator inspector; Victor, a gay hairstylist; Phillip, a gay receptionist; Jerry High Roller, a rich playboy; his buddy Santa Claus, a.k.a. Timothy Le Mans, who is now Pamela's squeeze; Turtle, a.k.a. Carter Abrams, a shy humor columnist and sometimes arts reviewer; my Dear Pluppy Brother Brandon; and his evangelical wife, Deanna. A bizarre mélange. I would not have invited DPB and Deanna, but she had sent me a letter of humble apology, likely at Brandon's insistence, so I felt I should and must.

Luckily, I was able to arrange for my teens to spend the night with school chums, so they missed this mistaken affair.

With Paula Abdul's "Straight Up" in the background, Pamela and Timothy had delved heavily into the frozen margaritas by the time Brandon and Deanna arrived.

Stupidly, Brandon had thought he and Deanna were the only two invited. She came straight from Saturday-eve service in her glistening white-satin robes, while Brandon was in his weekend seersucker shorts and white-polyester Polo, still a bit sweaty from yard work. He noticed a huge spread of hors d'oeuvres on the coffee table. "All this for us?" Then he saw Pamela and Timothy.

"It's a party! You've met my duplex-mate Pamela, haven't you? And this is her friend, Timothy. As I said in my invitation, this is my first anniversary of moving to Austin. I thought we should celebrate."

Carrying a margarita pitcher, Pamela offered Brandon and Deanna a drink, which was met with heads shaking in horror.

Deanna smoothed the folds of her robes. "Merry, I am not allowed to attend an event in spiritual raiment if alcohol is being served."

"Do you expect us to stop drinking because you're in robes? If you'd like to change, I can loan you my black kimono."

Pamela tried to save me by patting Deanna on the shoulder. "Even the Big Guy would understand. Remember that bit about changing water to wine?"

Brandon interrupted. "Merry, may I speak to you privately?"

"Yes. I think we three need to have a talk," Deanna murmured.

Thank heavens, the doorbell saved me from Deanna's sanctimony about defiling raiment. I bolted for the door as Jerry High Roller walked in, bearing a dozen symbolic red roses. I kissed him lightly on the cheek and introduced him to everybody.

High Roller did a little bow that only older men do. A nice touch.

DPB hissed to remind me, "Merry ..."

"Brandon, I have to take care of these roses." I escaped to the kitchen where I took a major slug of my margarita, praying as I swallowed that High Roller, Santa Claus, and Pamela could somehow converse with Brandon and Deanna, except my gut knew differently. In avoidance, I slowly put the roses in a vase with water and refilled my margarita from one of several margarita slush buckets in the freezer. Then I took three breaths for courage and walked back into the living room.

High Roller whispered, "Merry, do not leave me alone with your brother again."

"Well, let's all have some guacamole," I answered.

High Roller's eyes rolled heavenward as he poured another drink.

Pamela handed Deanna a paper plate. "Why don't you try Merry's guacamole? It'll spice up your halo for sure."

I fake-smiled at Brandon and Deanna. "Well now, isn't it nice to celebrate together?"

Brandon scowled. "How much have you had to drink?"

I began to appreciate the full weight of my mistake in inviting these two, when Deanna stepped so close, I could smell her halitosis. "We cannot stay. My robes ..."

Deanna and her fucking robes. You might say I was forcing an impossible situation.

Luckily, the doorbell rang again, so I shot from the sofa and greeted Turtle, Victor, and Phillip, who unfortunately had arrived at the same time. Turtle's eyebrows were arched in terror, not only because he is so shy, but also because he had just met Victor and Phillip, the gay blades. And they were really performing in style.

"We dressed to party," Victor shouted as he and Phillip twirled in matching pink-satin punk shirts and bright purple David Lee Roth latex rocker britches.

Phillip's genital package bunched so hugely, it appeared he had a hard-on. And Victor, well, Victor looked like a damn girl in his purple pants, with only a slight bulge in front, and wide, curvy hips from the rear. Clearly, he was the feminine half of this pairing.

"Victor! Phillip! Carter! I'm so glad you three could make it." I hugged each as though they were my dearest friends.

Turtle gave me a wild look. "I'm not with them."

From there, things deteriorated. High Roller and Santa Claus got drunk quickly. In one corner of my living room, the two men and Pamela had commandeered one of my frozen margarita buckets from the freezer and were serving themselves amply. They didn't talk or eat my *hors d'oeuvres*; they just drank.

Like me, they must have felt alcohol was the only solution.

Turtle stood paralyzed in an opposite corner. When I asked if I could get him a drink, he murmured, "Everything is delicious, Merry."

As for Brandon and Deanna, they resolved to sit silently on the sofa, hands folded.

Mortified, I served myself guacamole and chips from a large glass bowl on the coffee table. Then I gazed blankly at the atrocity I had created.

Victor and Phillip, bless them, were the only guests who at least tried to have fun. Victor piled a plate with food and complimented me loudly. "Please give me your recipes, won't you?"

Phillip and his purple-latex bulge went from guest to guest and attempted small talk, to little avail. After he'd made the rounds, he shrugged at Victor, who hesitated, then held up a finger as if he'd found the solution to this debacle.

Victor put fists on hips and shouted, "I know what this party needs. Dance music! And I will be your deejay!" He scampered to the stereo and changed my party background music CD to Michael Jackson's *Thriller* album, which at least made the atmosphere boogie. But eventually, oh dear, "The Lady in My Life" came on, a lovers' dance tune, and Victor forgot the lie I had silently hoped he and Phillip would carry through the evening: to act straight.

"Honey, I need a dance," Victor said.

Shit.

Victor put his arms around Phillip's waist, and Phillip put his around Victor's neck. The two began to sway, but soon started grinding their purple pelvic regions, propelling the pair around the room like a couple in heat. If only they had simply danced, that would have been okay from my perspective, but this wasn't a dance. This was vertical foreplay.

Brandon's jaw dropped, while Deanna shook her head so severely, her white satin robes quivered. Even Pamela, Jerry, and Timothy gawked— although Turtle in the opposite corner seemed somewhat amused.

Mortified, I bolted for the kitchen, hung my head over the sink, and dared to pray: "Godot, if you're there—please, have Victor and Phillip not still be doing that by the time I get back in the living room."

But no such blessing.

Even worse, by the time I got enough guts to return to my party, Deanna had totally lost it and mounted the coffee table, feet spread wide to avoid various food bowls, arms raised heavenward as she beseeched, "End this debacle of sin, oh Eternal Spirit. Strike those who pervert the holy gifts of a man and woman's love. Evil is in this house. Protect us from the perils strewn into our paths. Oh true spirits, smite the evils of these perverse males and cleanse rid their loins of ..."

On and on—you can imagine the rest.

Either angry or embarrassed, Brandon's face was as red as testicles after a hot bath. He ineptly tried to pull Deanna from the coffee table, but she was in such a frenzy she yanked out of his reach and expertly continued her righteous hat dance around the guacamole.

So, while Victor and Phillip circled the room, Brandon marched over to me, seething avocado breath. "Merry, how could you do this to me?"

Another of his egocentric observations.

Then Brandon grunted that he was getting the car and stomped out the door, probably trying to escape the shame of having a wife like Deanna and a sister like me.

Meanwhile, Turtle, Pamela, Santa Claus, and High Roller silently gawked at Deanna as she preached in Victor and Phillip's direction.

I wanted the nightmare to end, so I turned off the music.

In the silence, Victor and Phillip kept up the charade of dancing, but with Deanna shouting louder than ever, they eventually backed away. Without looking at me or anybody, the guys walked out the door, hands tucked on each other's purple rear ends.

Back at the coffee table, Deanna was in such a tizzy she hadn't noticed Victor and Phillip were now gone. Her eyes glazed heavenward, her arms pumped in glory, and her strawberry curls flopped with frenzy. I prayed she would trip and splat on a deadly piece of furniture, relieving me and my poor brother of further such moments. But Godot did not intervene. Deanna kept it up, while Pamela, Santa Claus, and High Roller downed more margaritas and giggled behind their hands. Eventually, Turtle had enough guts to murmur excuses about a deadline.

Pamela looked at me in desperation. "Gee kid, I would stay for more fun, but I'm drunk as hell. Timothy wants to leave, and Jerry says he'll come with us until your sister-in-law shuts up. That's the best I can do."

As she hugged me and left with Timothy and High Roller, Jerry murmured, "I'll be back when the coast is clear."

Just then, Brandon blustered back in. He didn't even mumble an excuse as he reached and grabbed Deanna's hand, then yanked her off the coffee table. Only then did she realize that everybody had left. "My prayers have been answered. The demons are gone!"

Brandon didn't look my way as he escorted Deanna out.

When Jerry High Roller came back, he murmured, "Darlin', that was not what you would call a good social mix."

I started crying, burying my head in Jerry's furry chest. Assuming sex makes all things right, he escorted me to my bedroom and made love like a battering ram on my wildly rocking waterbed, my head at the foot so I could stare at the painting. Happily, the ramming didn't last long. Afterward, he brought me a margarita, then another—until the fluid seared my esophagus, and I ran to the john to throw up.

⊠   ⊠   ⊠

One dismal note I have avoided—I am running out of money. Fast. All things considered, I have only three months of funds left. Three fucking months.

Do you know what Brandon will say if I run out of money? He'll say, "Merry, I can't help you anymore. I have tried to help you. I have tried." Then he'll go read another chapter in his self-help novel, *How to Say No Without Feeling Guilty*.

My children's future rests on my new job at Pecan Street. My first day is September 4.

Love and Guacamole,
Merry

SCENE 31

EXT. MERRY'S DUPLEX — 1989 — NIGHT

IN THE BUSHES

Glenn peers in Nora's window. The garrote is
in his pocket, and the pistol is tucked in the
waist of his jeans. He hears a car door SLAM.

He peers between branches and sees Pamela with
her PURSE, walking toward the duplex front
doors.

He crouches low and stays still.

ON THE DRIVEWAY

Pamela hears Glenn move in the bushes.

> PAMELA
> Hey, you. What are you doing?

Glenn jumps out and startles Pamela, who drops
her purse.

Before she can escape, Glenn wraps his garrote
around her neck, twisting.

Pamela struggles mightily to get away,
but can't escape. In a last ditch effort,
she scratches Glenn's arms severely, but
eventually, she succumbs.

Arms bleeding, Glenn drags Pamela's limp
body to his car, opens the trunk, then slams
her body inside. He quickly tiptoes back to
retrieve her purse.

He returns to his car and talks to the trunk.

                    GLENN
          You're buying the gas, bitch. Thanks
          for fucking up my plans.

EXT. WEST TEXAS GAS STATION — 1989 — NIGHT

At a country gas station a SIGN says, "Fried
Chicken, Gas, Ammo."

AT THE PUMP

Glenn uses Pamela's credit card to pay. As he
pumps gas, he glances around furtively.

EXT. WEST TEXAS HWY 118 — 1989 — NIGHT

Driving down a desert highway, Glenn sees
shadowy mountains in the distance as he passes
by a HIGHWAY SIGN that says, "TX 118."

Further down the way, a large EXIT SIGN says,
"Highway 170, Lajitas."

Glenn takes the exit toward Lajitas.

EXT. LAJITAS GOLF COURSE — 1989 — NIGHT

IN A SAND TRAP

Glenn uses a sand-trap rake to dig a trench.
He lays Pamela's body in. Her mouth is frozen
in a gasp as Glenn fills it with sand.

> GLENN
> Fucking cunt messed up everything.

Letter Thirty
September 9, 1989

Dear Roland,

I was a nervous wreck when I arrived for work on Monday morning. First thing on the schedule was a production meeting with the Greek Godot of Austin theater, Arlen Wynnewood.

Unaware of our prior interactions, Rachelle introduced me to Arlen and the others at the table, which included Nick Asher, that set designer I had met at The Cypress Door. He gave me a subtle wink.

Arlen's green eyes flashed surprise and delight when they connected with mine, but since he was now my boss, I merely nodded and smiled hello, as if I had never seen him before—or blatantly flirted with the man, or followed him all over Austin.

He began the meeting welcoming me. "Merry, you've joined us at the perfect time. We are going to produce Jean Genet's *The Balcony*. It's risky to do it in a town like Austin, so I think we must give it a very Austin twist. Instead of setting the play in a brothel during a revolutionary uprising, we will set *The Balcony* inside the Texas Capitol. That's why I need you, Merry. You will take my concepts, Genet's text, and create a blistering satire of the Texas Legislature."

Murmurs of excitement and approval circled the room, but my murmur was not among them. In fact, I was horrified. I was supposed to take a work by Jean Genet and convert it into a modern-day statement about Texas politics? Although I did my best to nod and smile, my heart had sunk to my intestines.

Arlen rambled on. "In addition to the setting change, I think Genet was a bit off the mark with the depths of his despair. Take the sexual perversion. It was so evil; it wasn't even titillating. Why is it for Genet, and Pinter for that matter, evil lurks in every corner and dooms man's efforts? You and I know many people who actually achieve their dreams, find happiness, love—and wonderful, giving, pleasurable passions."

Aha! This was my chance to convince Arlen and Rachelle that they made the right choice in hiring me. "I don't think Genet thought those things were impossible, just improbable. So few of us have the guts to commit the irrational, intuitive, gratuitous acts that catapult us beyond everyday ennui into the vivid existences we desire."

"Who would cut off his balls in order to exist?" Rachelle scoffed.

"Van Gogh supposedly cut off his ear," Nick Asher said.

Arlen shut him down with a glare. "For today's audiences, Genet would use less barbaric actions to make a point. Actions delivered with humor. Sure, we humans fling ourselves into the unknown for, let's say, a new career, new city, or even a new love affair," Arlen said as his eyes glistened lustfully in my direction.

I avoided the direct hit and came back with, "But Genet would not classify those things as heroic. He'd say those are the ordinary things we do, not something Genet would call real."

Arlen seemed dismayed by my intellectualism. "Well, for this Austin version, we'll have to tone down Genet's angst and pepper it with more palatable humor."

And so, I've spent this past week rewriting Jean Genet into a Texas-twanged satire.

Since you are writing a biography about the man, I thought about calling you to ask how to approach this. Was there anything new you've learned about Genet that could help me temper his work? I mean, that's an actual excuse to call you—not merely my idiotic infatuation.

Sadly, I chickened out because I didn't want to appear needy. After all, I sent you that note. It's your turn, but you've not yet replied.

Love,
Merry

SCENE 32

INT. MERRY'S DUPLEX — 1989 — DAY

Merry, dressed in office wear, walks in, puts down her purse, and checks the answering machine. The message light BLINKS. Merry pushes the button and hears Roland's voice.

> ROLAND (O.S.)
> This message is for—

Next, Merry hears Jillian's voice.

> JILLIAN (O.S.)
> We've got to get things straightened out. Everybody's gossiping about us.

Merry's eyes light up. She recognizes both voices, rewinds the recorder and plays the message again.

> ROLAND (O.S.)
> This message is for—

> JILLIAN (O.S.)
> We've got to get things straightened out. Everybody's gossiping about us.

Merry shakes her head, puzzled.

                    MERRY
              (to herself)
        What in the hell was that about? Why
        was he calling? Maybe I should call
        him back.

Letter Thirty-One
October 24, 1989

Dear Roland,

I'm going to summarize this entry because it would go on forever if I detailed everything. Over the past six weeks, I did as Arlen requested. In spite of my misgivings, I rewrote a renowned existential drama and turned it into an absurd satire set inside the Texas Capitol. I sent drafts of every scene to Arlen and Rachelle for review. Arlen returned each draft with notes of praise, along with a few remarks. Rachelle actually offered some solid input. A true collaboration, I thought.

Who needed you?

One afternoon at The Cypress Door, I confided in Turtle about my dilemma. "Either I bastardize a visionary, or I find another job."

"Now you know why Arlen never made it to New York. He has a hokeyness about him. Like the annual production of the Christmas Carol. Each year, he turns it into a rock opera with the latest tunes. It's funny, packs the house with local-yokels, and makes megabucks, but it's nowhere as poignant or powerful as the original."

Looking back, maybe I shouldn't have confided in Turtle. After all, he is the newspaper's interim arts critic.

Over the next weeks, the cast rehearsed. The marketing department promoted the event as "Genet Does Austin." I blushed when Rachelle and Arlen cheered loudly when my name was announced at dress rehearsal.

And opening night—this past Saturday, which also happened to be my fucking fortieth birthday—there was a packed house, including Turtle to review the play and Jerry High Roller as my escort. I did not invite Pamela, Victor, Phillip, or my kids for fear they simply would not get it. This stuff is not for the uninitiated.

At first, I thought the performance went well. The audience chuckled in the right places and gasped appropriately during other scenes. By the play's end, there was applause, but I would not call it thundering—I would call it hesitantly polite, bordering on dismissive.

At the cast party afterward, Arlen patted me on the back and said, "I think they were receptive. Probably not aware of Genet's importance in theater. Next performance, I'm going to introduce the play and give them a bit more background, so they'll understand our concept."

That was Saturday night, but on Sunday morning, Turtle's review was on the front page of the paper's lifestyle section. It was a scorcher. "Genet Would Not Be Amused" was his headline. Then he proceeded to blister Arlen for taking "one of the most originally written gems of the existential absurdist movement and turning it into a corny Texas hoedown."

Oh dear. My heart sank and my stomach rumbled as I worried all weekend about facing Arlen on Monday morning.

When I walked in at 9:00 a.m., the regular opening hour, a full-company meeting was already in session. Through the conference room glass doors, Rachelle Proctor urgently waved me in.

As I sat at the meeting table, Arlen would not look in my direction. "To say our opening night went well is a lie. I swear, this town will not support innovative art."

Rachelle looked chagrined. "Arlen, what if we revise some of Merry's edits? Perhaps keep it nearer to the original Genet."

"If I wanted the traditional version, I would have done that. I wanted something edgy, funny, and very Austin."

"Carter Abrams wasn't the only reviewer. *The Chronicle*'s review comes out Thursday, and their opinion matters more with the university and theater arts crowd," Rachelle said.

"By that time, we may have to close. If we only had a better script editor ... fuck, I'll have to do it myself," Arlen said with a heavy sigh.

Knife! Knife! Knife! What a cheap shot. I was astonished that the handsome, flirtatious, and enthralling Arlen Wynnewood had turned against me, in spite of his prior approval and exuberant praise of every written line. I couldn't help sounding defensive. "But Arlen, you and Rachelle approved every draft. You both even contributed to the work. Rachelle ...?" I said, hoping she would back me up.

My words fell on turncoat ears.

"No excuses. Not in my theater. Rachelle, meet me in my office. We must make plans." Then off Arlen strode, my Greek Godot—and I now realized why Turtle and High Roller had called him an asshole.

I gingerly got up, went to my office, and wondered if I still had a job.

About an hour later, Rachelle's fanny jiggled in. Haughtily, she announced, "Arlen wants to take a new direction, Merry. We appreciate your efforts, but we feel you're just not ready for theater at this level."

"Look, Rachelle, I didn't think it was a good idea to rewrite *The Balcony* as a Texas political satire, but I did it. And I did a damn good job. Both you and Arlen reviewed every draft. Even wrote a few lines. I received praise from both of you. But because the play did not get accolades, that's my fault?"

"Truth is in the beholder's eye. Arlen wants you gone. It's his house."

✉ ✉ ✉

So that's how I got fired.

Mortified, I didn't want to face my kids, so I went to The Cypress Door. I realize this was not the best idea. But Toni greeted me warmly, served me a J-Tini, fed me lunch, and listened to my woe until Turtle walked in about 3:00 p.m. He avoided my eyes but sat shyly beside me.

"Carter, you can't blame me for that debacle," I seethed.

"Sorry things didn't go as well as you had hoped."

"Maybe I should have included more of the original elements. But Arlen is the Godot of Austin theater, and this was his production. How could I say no? It became my job to edit a very bad idea."

Turtle patted me gently. "I didn't direct my review at you, Merry. The words were fine, but the concept sucked. It was a bomb."

"Well, anyway, I got fired."

Turtle uncharacteristically reached to hug me. His touch was tender. "I'm sorry if my review caused Arlen to fire you, but I had to be honest."

He bought me another J-Tini, then another. The rest of the afternoon was a blur of my angst repeated, until I even bored myself to death.

About 5:30 p.m., I got up to go home, trying to avoid the possibility of running into Arlen.

Turtle walked me outside. "Merry, I think you've had too much to drink. Let me drive you home. You and I can exchange cars tomorrow before I go to work."

With no other option, I let Turtle drive me home. Again. This was becoming a habit, but this time, when he pulled into my driveway, he stopped and parked, as though he wanted to talk.

"Merry, I can tell you have a lot of talent. My review was about Arlen's creative direction and stupid idea. Arlen has his pet issues. Politics is just one of them. He's also big on liberal and gay-lesbian issues, as well as racial stuff. Be glad he didn't ask you to rewrite the *Birdcage* or *Raisin in the Sun*. He skews serious productions to sell his messages. Sadly, you got snared in a play about politics. Those are the ones that don't usually pan out. I will do a follow-up review that includes praise for your efforts."

I was so thrilled by Turtle's promise I reached to hug him, but he seemed to think I was trying to kiss him. His lips met mine in a clumsy bump that turned into a kiss I will describe cornily as sweet and tender— like his sympathetic hug had been earlier at The Cypress Door. As we each explored the kiss further, it took us a while to unwind from one another, but when he pulled away, he was out of breath. We each looked at the other with surprise.

"Gosh, I hope that was okay," Turtle's eyes showed deep concern.

I couldn't speak, so I simply sighed with a smile.

The next morning, he picked me up to exchange cars. On our way back downtown, he apologized again, fearful that he had taken advantage of my inebriation.

I told him I didn't feel that way. And I was pleased we had made the surprising connection. Whatever it was.

Enough for now.

Love,
Merry

SCENE 33

INT. RAVEN BAR — 1989 — NIGHT

In their usual corner booth, only Sigrid
and Roland are there, silently toasting one
another with a dark beer. He's already had too
many. Sigrid keeps looking to the door.

> SIGRID
> Jillian running late?

> ROLAND
> She's not coming at all.

> SIGRID
> So, it's just the two of us?

> ROLAND
> That make you nervous?

> SIGRID
> Intimidated, actually.

> ROLAND
> First Merry, then Frank, now
> Jillian. Our drunken little gang is
> shrinking. Kind of like my penis and
> love life.

                    SIGRID
So, the office gossip is true?

                    ROLAND
She's pressuring again.

                    SIGRID
I guess you mean tricky stuff like
divorce and marriage.

                    ROLAND
Tricky indeed. I have a wife, four
children, and a mistress to boot.

                    SIGRID
You almost had two.

                    ROLAND
Two what?

                    SIGRID
Mistresses. Merry never said, but I
could tell.

                    ROLAND
That obvious? Sometimes a man feels
trapped, even when he has two women,
but if he explores a new zone of
desire, the poor sot can't possibly
leap into a third.

                    SIGRID
Some of that is Tarkovsky, isn't
it? I remember *Stalker* from one of
my film classes. His zone of desire
might be a convenient metaphor, but

males invented marriage. Why can't
they commit to one woman?

                    ROLAND
Oh, Sigrid. That would take years.
So, how is she doing. Any news?

                    SIGRID
She's waiting to hear. Why don't you
give her call?

                    ROLAND
I did, but I was interrupted.
Besides, I think it could be
dangerous.

                    SIGRID
I swear, I will never understand the
male point of view.

                    ROLAND
You should see it from this zone.

Dear Roland,

I'm on a roll. In my mailbox today was another darn rejection letter, this one from Kyle FitzGerald (with a fancy capital G, no less), a producer for Paramount Pictures who said, "Lyle, don't you have something more marketable? We're really not into abject grief."

Abject grief! That's what he thought of my film, my life?

You're scoffing, aren't you?

"That's what you get for doing as I did, not as I said."

That reminds me of Jean-Paul Sartre's *The Flies*. According to him, I must not blame you for my lack of success. But as you and Genet taught me, I must find the way to *act*, some irrational, intuitive, gratuitous act to prove myself, although I have no idea what that action might be.

"Those who can't do, teach. Those who try are the true existential heroes."

And so I'm still trying, although I have received two other rejections since I last wrote to you.

Columbia Pictures: "We already have a project in the works by a pro baseball player's wife, so I don't think this would be for us."

Twentieth Century Fox: "I'm not convinced we could successfully promote a screenplay about the woes of a professional golfer's wife. Sorry."

Why in the hell didn't I write an entwined thriller with a shocking ending? That's what the world wants, even though you, my mentor, expounded that plot did not matter.

Screw you and your lofty idealism. You failed writer.

Those who can't do, preach Sartre.

⊠   ⊠   ⊠

On the topic of money, after paying the rent, I have one thousand dollars to pay one month's worth of bills. I have been so dismayed about this, I went back to the B. J. Hathaway office and signed up to staff other agents' open houses on weekends—perhaps snag a percentage of a sale. I also sit at the front desk and take calls. I have not yet sold a house, but I'm trying (again). At least my sales manager Erica Cooke seems to like me again. She's been asking about my education and computer skills. Not sure what's up with that, but at least she's not glaring at me anymore.

⊠   ⊠   ⊠

This all sounds terribly grim, but I recently had the opportunity to never have to get a fucking job.

High Roller asked me to marry him.

Noooooooooo!

Yes.

For my birthday celebration, Jerry took me to Jeffrey's like any civilized male other than Dear Pluppy Brandon would do, since Brandon doesn't even know where Jeffrey's is—although every time I tell him I went there, he says, "Jeffrey's? Now where is Jeffrey's?" Then I tell him where it is. And the next time I mention that I've been there, he says, "Jeffrey's? Now where is Jeffrey's?"

(Maddening tangent. I remain angry with Brandon over the party.)

At a quiet side table, High Roller and I chatted over our redfish, duck, sautéed spinach, chocolate intemperance, and walnut mousse. Then we went back to his place, as they say in the movies, and yes, we did it, only I didn't feel much except him whamming and bamming, hunk that he is. Even when he lasts longer than thirty seconds, why should I abandon my emotions? This relationship is going nowhere. He's fifty-two. I am forty. But our problem is more than age. Jerry is surface fun, surface conversation, surface sex—a business deal for each of us. He takes a fading beauty (me) to dinner and dancing, teases me, chatters, and shows me a fun time. Then we have sex, rather he has sex. It was never more than that for me.

But after he was done with his wham-bamming, I felt the need for human touch, so I snuggled close. He misinterpreted that as my expression of satisfied love.

He breathed hoarsely in my ear, "Darlin', maybe you and I should make this more permanent. How about you move in with me? Even walk down the aisle, if that's what you want. I'll take care of you and your kids, darlin'. I'll take care of everything."

Whoa baby! I pulled back and blurted, "Oh no, Jerry. No, no."

He sighed and heaved to one side, rejected.

I began elaborate lies. "It was a lovely proposal, but I'm not ready for a committed relationship. I'm too shell-shocked from all that's gone on."

Even to me, my excuse rang hollow. I am fond of High Roller. If I didn't need to love someone who at least understood who I'm trying to be, Jerry might have made a fine husband. He absolutely dotes on me. Why in the hell do I require more?

He didn't say anything, but lay curled with his creased fanny to me.

I felt sad for him, so I rubbed his thick, furry back. "I appreciate the proposal. It was very generous." He didn't respond to my appeasements, so eventually it seemed easier to tell him the truth. "Jerry, I have a wonderful time with you. Lovely dinners. Dancing. You fix us ice cream. We take a hot tub. You screw me. You have orgasms. I don't, but being with you is fun, dammit. Still, we're not in love. And I want to be in love. I don't want to settle for something that is merely entertaining."

"Entertaining ain't bad, Darlin'; I've been in love once, and it turned out pretty bad."

"I still need to dream."

"You got somebody else in your dream?"

"You could say that." Whether I was thinking of my passion for you, or my surprising response to Turtle's clumsy kiss, I couldn't say.

Jerry was quiet for a long time. Then he rolled over and reached for me. We hugged for a good five minutes. A sweet goodbye. In fact, it was the sincerest emotion either of us had expressed during the past months of our relationship.

"Well, he's one lucky son of a bitch," Jerry whispered huskily as he got out of bed and went into the bathroom.

I put my ear to the door. The shower was running. Time for my exit.

A cab met me outside. Yes, I felt guilty for leaving without a formal goodbye. But marrying High Roller was impossible for an idealist like me. Even though my financial problems would have been resolved, Jerry's and my shared emotions did not rise to the sunshine I felt for you. Or the curious excitement I felt when Turtle kissed me.

⊠   ⊠   ⊠

No, I did not make a J-Tini tonight. I remain boringly sober. In fact, during my non-journal-writing time, I don't drink as much as I write about drinking. Even then, I seem to describe only the times when there's been too much.

As my pal Pamela often says, "God put booze here for a purpose."

She's so funny. I wish she would come home.

⊠   ⊠   ⊠

One more note that is actually of major importance. Just as I wrapped up this entry to you, I realized that I need to revise my screenplay—*again*. Yes. Genet is right. I must add an action, a P-L-O-T, which means I must invent something thrilling or scary or bizarre for my heroine to endure or escape.

To that end, I might take some events from *My Dear Diary* entries to you, add imaginary plot twists, and massage the mess into a nail-biting "intelligent thriller" with a shocker ending.

I know that would disappoint you ... my stooping to contrive a plot after the fact. But if I dream up some amazingly evil guy who's out to kill my heroine, Hope, I might actually have a salable project.

After all, "No plot, my dear, no story."

Love,
Merry

SCENE 34

INT. NORA'S ROOM — 1989 — NIGHT

Nora wears an "Austin Community College" T-shirt and reads an *American History* BOOK.

Claire shyly peeks in.

> CLAIRE
> You asleep?

> NORA
> Studying. My first American history test is tomorrow.

> CLAIRE
> They make you study American history all over again in college?

> NORA
> High school courses leave out a bunch of stuff.

> CLAIRE
> I can't wait until I get to college.

Claire sits on Nora's bed, hesitates.

                    CLAIRE
I need to tell you ... I saw Glenn.

                    NORA
Oh no! Where?

                    CLAIRE
Near the running track. They made us
run four laps in gym, so on my third
time around, I saw Glenn standing in
the woods, you know, down by that
little creek.

                    NORA
You should tell your gym teacher.
Glenn's should not be on campus.

                    CLAIRE
He wasn't on campus. Just next to
it.

                    NORA
He's stalking someone. Maybe you,
for all we know.

                    CLAIRE
Oh no! Think I should tell Mom?

                    NORA
That's a sticky subject. Just tell
your gym teacher. Glenn has a thing
for young girls. He had a rape
charge in Alaska.

                    CLAIRE
He did?

                            NORA
            Yes. I was too dumb to see what he
            was about. Mom was too.

                           CLAIRE
            What do you mean, 'Mom was too'?

Nora makes a finger-in-hole sign.

                            NORA
            Mom dated him too.

                           CLAIRE
            Oh no. You mean he and Mom had sex?

                            NORA
            Yeah, gross, isn't it?

                           CLAIRE
            I think I'm gonna puke.

Claire shakes her head and stands to leave.

                            NORA
            Don't tell Mom I told you. Or
            Scottie!

                           CLAIRE
            I won't. It's too disgusting anyway.

Claire nods and leaves.

Nora returns to reading. But she looks up and
shudders as she recalls Glenn's touch.

Letter Thirty-Three
November 15, 1989

Dear Roland,

I am employed! Saved from financial despair! I am assistant advertising director for B. J. Hathaway Real Estate. Turns out Erica Cooke was promoted to VP of advertising, a job for which she is so totally unqualified, even she realized she needed an assistant who could do the job. That's what her questions to me had been about.

My duties will be to manage the Sunday classified ads and write print brochures. I will also do an annual report that I have to design, although my only design skills were gained at your insistence in Journalism II. Remember? You encouraged film majors to take two semesters of journalism in case we decided to become theater critics.

"Those who can't do, criticize," you once said.

During my post-grad work, you charmed me into keying in your reviews of Broadway plays for the university newspaper, which had begun using computers, although you had tech phobia. So I leapt at the chance to type in each piece. We'd go over the drafts together in your office.

You were such a flirt—playing the mad editor as you leaned near enough to touch. "I'll teach that producer to overlook my plays."

I laughed as your eyes twinkled with the infatuation we shared. The hair on my arms rose in anticipation of a brush against yours. With a brief intersection of our hair follicles, we grew quiet, relishing the sensation of our zones connecting. Yet I feared rejection if I made an overt move.

You backed away and quipped, "Maybe I should give the producer a fabulous review, so he'll be more open to my work in the future."

"But you said his production was a 'shrink-wrapped bowl of last week's spaghetti.'"

You started pacing wildly, throwing your hands heavenward. "Thank you for reminding me. How could I have suggested that we suck up to the bastard? That goes against everything I've taught you. There must be honesty in art. Truth in theater. Art is emotion." Then you looked intently at me, gathering your thoughts. "Being a writer is a hard road. Don't say I didn't warn you. You will spend your time alone, fighting the indifference and disinterest of ninety-nine percent of the population."

By that time, you had backed to the office door, where you again centered your eyes on mine. "But Merry, your writing is your declaration of independence. You'll never have to walk another round at Pinehurst, hoping your husband will make the cut. You have the greatest possessions anyone can have. Creativity, originality, and best of all, talent. Cultivate them. Don't merely be an existential heroine. Be a successful one."

I wondered how much of your diatribe was aimed at me and how much toward your own failed self.

As usual after one of your rants, you raised your hand in a wave. "Every time I hear myself go on this way ..." and out the door you went, leaving me to wish you were still there to banter about your review.

⊠   ⊠   ⊠

Yes, I am moving on. With Pamela still away, I have been expanding my social universe. Turtle and I actually had a date, although it wasn't supposed to be a date, as in a guy asks you to dinner with the hope/ expectation that romance will follow. Instead, we two were talking with Toni one early afternoon at The Cypress Door, and she said she had gone to see the film *Dead Poets Society*.

"I actually liked it, even though I'm not a writer like you two."

"I haven't seen it yet, have you?" Turtle asked me.

I blurted, "Let's get out of this dive and grab an early show."

So off we went in Turtle's car, two bar flies high on J-Tinis. At the show, we bought popcorn and Cokes. There were only a few others in the theater. We sat side by side without touching, made quite a bit of noise laughing and talking, and had a grand time.

After the movie, he drove me back to the bar, but instead of going in, we sat in his car and talked about the film—especially how the teacher encouraged his students seize the day: To make their lives extraordinary, as in "not ordinary," as too many people wind up doing.

"If I reviewed the film, I'd say it was a bit sappy, but it was good to see artistic themes presented to a broad audience."

I agreed. "I don't know if the script was too sappy or more likely Robin Williams was too sappy."

"He does overdo dramatic parts. The comic trying to be serious."

Later on, we shared stories about teachers who had inspired us, and I told Turtle about you. Only, I left out my unrequited desire for you.

"He taught me how great stories evolve from character. Characters and emotion."

Turtle's weak chin gulped with sentiment, and he gazed at me with those wide brown eyes. "I'll bet he was happy to have such a bright, fun, and beautiful student like you."

Carter blushed, embarrassed at his too-flattering compliment.

I tried to ease his shyness by leaning to give him a wee kiss, a fond peck. But I must have opened a door that Carter wanted to dive through. He cradled my face in his hands and kissed me tenderly, but with a real man's potent desire. And we kept at this kissing for some time, until our breathing became intense.

I worried that Carter was becoming too aroused, so I pulled back, a bit amazed.

"I'm sorry. I don't know what came over me ..." he began.

"Don't be sorry. I rather enjoyed it."

He grinned, and his reptilian eyes turned dreamy. "*Carpe diem!*"

When he smiled, he even looked kind of cute.

And so, this is my first *Diary* entry with only good news. I'm going to call Sigrid tomorrow, so you will hear that I am making a living writing. And yes, I will continue to revise *Those Who Try* on weekends, freed by the security of being employed.

Love,
Merry

SCENE 35

INT. BRANDON'S OFFICE — 1989 — DAY

Brandon is at his desk working. Luna quietly comes in and closes the door. She carries an ENVELOPE with her resignation LETTER inside.

                    LUNA
          I need to speak with you.

                    BRANDON
          I hope this is about business. I
          don't need any of your personal
          trauma today.

                    LUNA
          Matter of fact, it is all business.

Luna hands him the envelope.

                    BRANDON
          What's this?

                    LUNA
          Open it and you'll see.

Brandon opens the envelope and reads her letter.

                    BRANDON
But you can't quit. We've got the
annual report and newsletter due.

                     LUNA
You see ... just what I thought.
You're more concerned about the work
than about my leaving.

                    BRANDON
I'm concerned about both, but I'm
trying to be professional. Can't we
work this out?

                     LUNA
I cannot come to work each day and
want to go home each night with you.

                    BRANDON
But I told you ... I can't make the
change now. Not yet. We just bought
a new house. I've at least got to
get my family settled there.

                     LUNA
You won't ever leave her. She's got
you wrapped around her financial
finger.

                    BRANDON
We can discuss these issues later.
In the meantime, I need you to stay.

                     LUNA
This is my last day, Brandon.

                        BRANDON
          But what am I going to do?

                         LUNA
          Hire your sister. She's a writer.

Luna storms out and SLAMS the door.

Brandon rereads the resignation letter, then
slaps it in his in-box and SIGHS in dismay.

Letter Thirty-Four
December 24, 1989

Dear Roland,

Thank heavens for a week off during the holidays. I haven't had time to write you since I've been employed. In fact, this morning is the first weekday I've had off. My manager Erica Cooke and I are battling over the annual report. She keeps changing everything, so I constantly rewrite and redo. She's a maniac.

But as Carter reminds me, "You are employed and solvent."

(I am trying not to call him Turtle anymore.)

On the subject of Carter, he and I are dating for real now, but we have not done the sexual deed as yet. We try out restaurants and experiment with cuisines like Ethiopian and Vietnamese. Carter cannot afford Jeffrey's, and that's fine with me, now that I no longer want to see Arlen Wynnewood, unless he's in a casket at his own funeral.

Carter and I also go to plays, films, classical guitar concerts, symphonies, operas, ballets, and Austin City Limits shows, which are awesome. Carter's now-and-then job as an arts reviewer gets us in free to most events. He still writes his humor column three days a week—it's a good one. He has a self-deprecating, satiric wit—especially about the Texas legislature. University of Texas Press even approached him to do a book of his columns, so that might bring in a few dollars.

Our outings sometimes conclude at The Cypress Door where Carter proudly shows me off to his reporter pals. One night last week, to my mortification, he took my hand and waltzed us toward Arlen's table, but I pulled away to the bar, hoping Carter got my hint.

He took a stool beside me and whispered, "Sorry. I forgot your side of things."

Arlen saw us anyway. "Those who can't do, criticize," he muttered as he passed by on his way out.

That stung and reminded me of you.

I was about to retort, but Carter put a finger over his lips to shush me. "Don't waste your efforts on that asshole. Just save them for me."

When he batted those big muddy eyes, I had to grin in amazement. I have spent most of my forty years pining over attractive guys or elusive charmers, while this homely Galápagos inhabitant has been the most supportive friend and comforting romantic interest I've ever met.

Now that I have a partner in Austin who shares my passion for the arts, for quality theater and film, for great music and writing, I find myself letting go of you at last. It happened without my realization—no major decision, no self-disciplined announcement—but I have felt your aura slip away, becoming less about physical desire and more about what I have learned from you. I will never forget your influences that have driven my life, but both of my feet have leapt beyond your zone—hallelujah, at last!

✉ ✉ ✉

This is a terrible cliché, but it has been fun to have a date for the holidays, especially since my kids are off to Greenwich to visit Doug. Carter keeps me company, which is good because I have not seen or heard from Pamela, not in quite a while. Her duplex remains dark, and her car is not in the driveway. I have called her home and work numbers and left messages to say happy holidays, let's have a drink, and so forth, but there have been no replies. I have no clue of a phone number for Timothy Le Mans, or I would call him to see what he knows.

Carter suggested I call our leasing agent, which I did.

"I have not heard from Pamela herself, but her December rent was paid. She gives us post-dated checks because of her business travels," the agent said.

That did not ease my worries. Maybe I should call Jerry High Roller. That's a thought. If Pamela does not resurface by the New Year, I will call him to get Timothy's number.

✉   ✉   ✉

The following news is a scene I should put in *Those Who Try*. After deciding that I never wanted to see Brandon or Deanna again, DPB called me a few weeks ago—not to find out how I am, but to offer me a job! Seems his community-relations manager resigned unexpectedly.

I took great pride in telling Brandon I was already employed.

"I thought B. J. Hathaway fired you," he scoffed.

"Pecan Street Theater fired me. As for B. J. Hathaway, my manager asked me to work in advertising. You see, Brandon, some people think highly of my skills."

Deanna's voice came on the line. "Merry, how can you let your brother down?"

"Deanna, let me handle this," Brandon said quite harshly.

"Merry, your brother has stood by you through thick and thin. You must be inebriated to turn down such a wonderful offer."

"Deanna, I am not drunk—although I might go on a tear if you don't stop harassing me."

"Merry, please at least listen to my proposal—" Brandon began.

Deanna scolded me in the background. "She's too much of a drunk to know what's good for her. I need to exorcise the evils of her addiction. There is an order of service I can lead. It's even in your faith, Brandon."

Brandon's voice hissed. "Deanna, now is not the time."

"Look, you two, I may enjoy too many cocktails on occasion, but I am stone-cold sober now. And it is my thrill to tell you and Brandon to put your job offer and righteous ceremony up your ... well, the light does not shine there except during a colonoscopy."

Carter was beside me at the time and applauded my bravado.

"Is someone clapping?" Brandon asked.

"With all four hands." I hung up and gave Carter a kiss.

Enough for now. It is Christmas Eve morning. Carter is coming over for dinner later, and I might even find out how a turtle makes love.

Love,
Merry

SCENE 36

INT. MERRY'S DUPLEX — 1989 — DAY

IN LIVING ROOM

Wrapping Christmas packages, Merry hears a
KNOCK. She hopes it's Pamela, so she opens the
door without checking to see who it is.

Deanna zooms in, wearing white satin robes.

> MERRY
> What are you doing here?

> DEANNA
> Is that how you greet your sister?
> I am going to save you from the
> damnation of addiction.

> MERRY
> No, you are not.

> DEANNA
> Yes, I am. Now, bow your head. I
> will begin the liturgy.

> MERRY
> No, you won't.

The much-taller Deanna grabs Merry and holds her tightly. Merry struggles but can't get loose.

                        DEANNA
          In the name of Jesus Christ, our
          God and Lord, strengthened by the
          intercession of the Immaculate
          Virgin Mary, Mother of God, of
          blessed Michael the Archangel, of
          the blessed apostles Peter and Paul,
          and all the saints and powerful in
          the holy authority of our ministry,
          we confidently undertake to repulse
          the attacks and deceits of the
          devil.

Merry manages to pull away, but Deanna grabs her again and maneuvers Merry to the sofa, where Deanna pushes Merry down on her back. Deanna then straddles Merry and hollers in her face, spit spewing everywhere.

                        DEANNA
          God arises; his enemies are
          scattered, and those who hate him
          flee before him.

Merry struggles to escape, but Deanna holds her tightly, fueled by religious fervor.

                        MERRY
          Deanna, stop this idiocy! This is a
          Catholic exorcism, isn't it? Get the
          fuck off me, you freaking maniac!

                         DEANNA

As smoke is driven away, so are they
driven; as wax melts before the
fire, so the wicked perish at the
presence of God. Behold the cross
of the Lord. Flee bands of enemies!
The Lion of the tribe of Judah, the
offspring of David. May thy mercy,
Lord—

                         MERRY

Deanna, get off me now! I swear to
God, I will call the police. This is
assault. You are assaulting me!

Deanna squeezes Merry harder with her thighs.

                         DEANNA

May thy mercy, Lord, descend upon
us. As great as our hope in thee.

Just then, Brandon bursts in the front door.
He sees Deanna straddling Merry, His eyes grow
wild.

                         BRANDON

What in the hell are you doing?

                         DEANNA

I am driving the devil out of your
sister, out of our family.

                         MERRY

Brandon, make her stop! She's a
fucking nut job with this exorcism
mumbo-jumbo.

                    DEANNA
We drive you from us, whoever you
may be, unclean spirits, all satanic
powers, all infernal invaders, all
wicked legions, assemblies, and
sects.

                    BRANDON
Deanna, you've gone too far. I
was reared Catholic, studied my
catechism, even wondered if I might
be a priest. I know one thing: those
words are only to be spoken by a
priest.

Brandon yanks Deanna upright.

              BRANDON (CONT'D.)
And you are no priest.

                    DEANNA
I am an ordained minister of the—

                    BRANDON
You are a charlatan. And I've had
enough of your phony Eternal Spirit
Center. I am going to leave you.

                    DEANNA
You can't mean that.

                    BRANDON
Just watch me. And as for you ...

Brandon turns his glare to Merry.

>   BRANDON (CONT'D.)
>   I helped you get a real estate
>   career. I've counseled you to stop
>   drinking. But when I needed your
>   help, even offered you a full-
>   time job with health insurance and
>   a good salary that could support
>   your children, you wouldn't take
>   it because you are delusional.
>   Oh, I know, you're going to be a
>   screenwriter and make movies in
>   Hollywood. Sure.

Released from Deanna, Merry struggles to get
up, but her glare to Brandon can melt steel.

>   MERRY
>   Your narrow-minded negativity cannot
>   stop me. I am a writer, Brandon. And
>   I will be, as long as I keep trying.

Brandon fumes in dismay.

>   BRANDON
>   Mother would be so ashamed.

Brandon heaves a SIGH and exits, slamming the
front door.

Deanna collapses in hysteria on the sofa.

>   MERRY
>   Oh dear. Now I'm stuck with you?
>   Don't you need to go preach
>   something? It's Christmas Eve.

Deanna curls into a ball, shudders, and weeps.

Dismayed, Merry tucks a throw PILLOW under
Deanna's head and covers her with a BLANKET.

>   MERRY
>   Carter will have to help me with
>   this mess as soon as he gets here.
>   So much for my romantic evening.

Letter Thirty-Five
January 25, 1990

Dear Roland,

The happiest of New Year's to you. A new decade, a new era has begun, although I feel somewhat deceitful writing to you because, well, I am now in love with Carter. Yes. I am *in love*. I know this might seem abrupt. After all, it's been only a month since my last *Diary* entry. But Carter's and my relationship has deepened since we became sexually involved. I refuse to provide graphic details, as my desire for Carter grows with each roll in my waterbed. Let's just say, he is well-suited to aquatic adventures.

Beyond sex, our romantic love evolved as naturally as sunshine. We hadn't gone anywhere special or done anything amazing. We were sitting out back in my tiny yard, basking in the light of an unexpectedly warm winter day. But when Carter reached his hand to couple mine, our fingers entwined, and we gazed at one another in the adoring way couples do. I felt a joyous glow arise as this homely man I once called Turtle morphed into the lover I now see as my kindred spirit.

I told him right then. "I've fallen in love with you, Carter."

He didn't blush red, but his eyes filled with tears. "Likewise, Merry. But I guess you could tell that from the way I've been hanging around."

There we were: two forty-something singles who had re-discovered love and relished its surprise.

He doesn't know about these letters and my long-ago quest to have you as my lover. I imagine that my squirminess is the same discomfort that kept you from reaching out to me so long ago. You must have been perplexed at finding yet another woman you might love. Yet another zone of desire to leap into. And then what?

⊠   ⊠   ⊠

Regardless of my dedication to Carter, I decided to write you, because I have wonderful news about *Those Who Try*.

Lyle Davis read my recent revision and told me he thinks Warner Brothers will love it. "If not, I'll re-submit it to Universal. They wanted an intelligent thriller. And now we've got one!"

Among other things in the revision, I added a rather violent and shocking ending that surprised the hell out of me. I didn't know my imagination could go that far dark. In fact, I felt anguished about what I had written. It was too painful, so I deleted it at first, but then I hit Command Z to bring it back.

You once taught us, "Creativity flows from a hidden river."

And as Genet said in *The Balcony*, my ending is "a true image, born of a false spectacle."

Still, I worry that my teens might be upset by it. Brandon would be, that is, if he bothers to see the film, but since we are no longer speaking, that won't matter.

Who knows what zany Deanna might think?

If I do land a studio deal, I refuse to contact you directly but will have Sigrid do the honors. Call me petty, but I want you to hear of my success from someone other than me.

⊠   ⊠   ⊠

With my screenplay and love life going well, I still have one concern. Pamela has been gone so long I can't remember when she left. I called Jerry High Roller to get a number for Pamela's beau Timothy, who told me, "That neighbor of yours comes and goes with the winds. If you find her, ask her to give me a ring. I like her more than I expected to."

"I know what you mean. I've found a new beau myself."

"That will break Jerry's heart. He really had a thing for you."

"I cared about Jerry, but I needed a man who understands the writer in me, not just the female body parts."

Santa Claus didn't know what to make of that. "TMI, honey."

After we hung up, I called Austin police to ask what to do if a person goes missing, but with Pamela's history of traveling for business, the policewoman I spoke to shrugged off my fears of foul play.

Carter tries to reassure me. I had been reluctant to have him stay overnight, worried what my kids would think. So, I asked their permission one night over dinner.

Nora told me, "Mom, if he's the best you can do, maybe you should get a facelift."

Oh, to be a smart-ass freshman in college.

Claire's answer was, "I don't know why anyone would ever want to have sex."

Hypocrite. Claire's pin-up of Han Solo proves that she does like guys, even older ones like Harrison Ford.

Scottie was my only child who seemed uncomfortable, likely an oedipal complex about a guy doodling his mother.

That's why, before Carter's first sleepover, he made the effort to do manly things with Scottie. He took him to see how the newspaper runs on the huge web presses and took Scottie to a play at Pecan Street Theater. Carter even used a quote from Scottie in a review. "The play was pretty good, but one lady overdid it with too much shrieking."

After seeing his name in the paper, Scottie announced that he might become a journalist. He signed up to work on his school newspaper this semester.

Carter was thrilled that his efforts succeeded. "He's a cool kid. You've done a good job, Merry, but guys need a mentor sometimes."

With this kind of familial bonding going on, Carter has hinted about marriage, but I have avoided that conversation. I cannot imagine planning a wedding, or becoming his wife, when every fiber of my writer identity remains on alert for news from Lyle Davis and Warner Brothers.

I have a good feeling this time.

Love,
Merry

SCENE 37

EXT. MERRY'S DUPLEX — 1990 — NIGHT

IN THE DRIVEWAY

Merry pulls in and parks beside Nora's van.
Merry gets out, then goes to the front door.

INT. MERRY'S DUPLEX — NIGHT

Merry enters and tosses KEYS on a foyer table.

> MERRY
> Nora, I'm home. It's time for you
> to pick up Claire and Scottie.
> Remember? You said you would pick
> them up so I could get dinner going.

FROM DOWN THE HALLWAY

Merry hears muffled SCREAMS and THUMPS.

> MERRY
> Nora? Is that you?

Merry runs down the hall to investigate.

AT NORA'S BEDROOM DOOR

Merry hears more THUMPS and muffled SCREAMS.
Merry opens the door.

IN NORA'S BEDROOM

Nora is nude on her back, her hands tied to
bedposts by pink ribbons. Her mouth is duct-
taped shut. Eyes wide in terror, Nora kicks
and struggles as Glenn, nude, holds his gun to
Nora's throat as he rapes her. He's panting so
hard he doesn't hear the door open.

                    NORA
            (muffled screams)
        Help me! Help me!

                    MERRY
        You son of a bitch!

Shocked, Glenn turns to look.

Merry rushes forward, trying to pull Glenn off
Nora, but he pushes her away.

In the process, Glenn's gun falls to the floor.

Merry kicks the gun far under Nora's bed, then
Merry runs out and down the hall.

Glenn jumps off, kneels, tries to reach the gun
but can't. He struggles to stretch under.

Nora keeps trying to get loose.

IN MERRY'S OFFICE

Merry opens the file cabinet and grabs her
father's Glock 27. Hands shaking, she manages
to put in a clip and cock it.

IN NORA'S BEDROOM

Glenn, wiggles out from under Nora's bed. He
stands and aims his pistol at Nora, who is
still tied but struggling.

                    GLENN
        Sorry, love, this one is for you.

At the doorway, Merry fires SIX SHOTS at Glenn.

Glenn collapses in a bloody heap across Nora.

Merry desperately pulls him off her daughter.

Glenn's body lands on the floor. His eyes are
glassy, as blood pours out of his body.

On the bed, Nora's eyes are also glassy.

Merry tries to rouse Nora but finds a huge spot
of blood gushing from a wound in Nora's neck,
caused when a bullet passes through Glenn.

                    MERRY
        Nora! No! Oh no! Nora!

Merry sobs deeply, grabs the bed sheet, and
tries to stop the bleeding, but she cannot
reverse the truth. Nora is dead.

                    MERRY
        This can't be true. Nora, Nora!
        Oh, God, no. Oh no! This can't be
        happening.

In anguish, Merry desperately hugs her
daughter.

On the nightstand there is a BOUQUET of ROSES
and a NOTE CARD addressed in a male hand to
"Nora."

SCENE 38

INT. AUSTIN POLICE STATION — 1990 — NIGHT

SIGN: "City of Austin Police Facility"

In a dingy interview room, a hotshot young
DETECTIVE paces in front of a distraught MERRY
MAYFIELD, 38, still pretty with black bobbed
hair. She sobs into her quivering hands.

> DETECTIVE
> Ms. Mayfield ... I realize this is a
> trying situation, but I need you to
> calm down.

Merry valiantly tries to stop crying.

Detective hands Merry a box of tissues.

She blows, then inhales in a deep shudder.

> MERRY
> A nightmare of nights ... I'd give
> anything for you to go away.

> DETECTIVE
> You mean me, or what happened
> tonight?

MERRY
Too many nights. But especially
tonight. Oh, my baby ...

DETECTIVE
Ms. Mayfield, you said the man you
killed was a stalker?

MERRY
Yes. And a rapist! He has a record.
Did you look into that?

DETECTIVE
This case will be thoroughly
investigated.

MERRY
The rape case was in Alaska. He told
me about it ... statutory rape. A
fifteen year old.

DETECTIVE
Why would you date a rapist?

MERRY
He said the girl lied about her age.
He and I only dated briefly. I broke
it off. He was angry, so he probably
stalked Nora. I wasn't happy when
she started seeing him. He was too
old for her, but she eventually
broke it off.

DETECTIVE
But why was there a bouquet?

>   MERRY
> A bouquet?

>   DETECTIVE
> Yes, a rose bouquet with this note
> to your daughter.

Detective shows Merry the note card addressed
to Nora. She hesitates to take it.

>   DETECTIVE
> We've dusted and taken the prints.

Merry opens the note and haltingly reads
Glenn's scrawl.

>   MERRY
> "There is more beauty in youth than
> in the regret of age. I look forward
> to our future together. Love,
> Glenn."

>   DETECTIVE
> I never heard of a rapist who
> brought flowers and a love note.

>   MERRY
> But he had her tied ...

>   DETECTIVE
> Maybe your daughter liked it kinky.

>   MERRY
> Kinky?! She'd never had sex before.

Detective's smirk says he isn't buying it.

                    DETECTIVE
She was eighteen, ma'am.

                     MERRY
Are you saying anyone who's eighteen
can't still be a virgin?

                    DETECTIVE
Actually, I'm wondering ... you're,
what, forty? Seems like this young
guy ditched you for your daughter.

                     MERRY
He was raping her! And for the fifth
time, Glenn didn't ditch me. I broke
it off because he was too young and
pushy. He kept calling. Showing up
at my door. Following me.

                    DETECTIVE
Ma'am, as I said, this case will be
investigated, but you've killed two
people. I've got to find out why.

                     MERRY
            (screaming)
I was trying to protect her, not
kill her. You've got to believe me.
And if you don't, I need to call a
lawyer or somebody who knows a good
one.

SCENE 39

INT. MERRY'S LIVING ROOM — 1990 — NIGHT

Carter consoles Merry on a sofa as she cries.

Scottie and Claire enter. Claire pats Merry, sits beside her, collapses, and cries too.

Scottie pats his Mom's shoulder, then sits in a chair, sniffles.

                    CARTER
          Merry, do you want to call Brandon?

                    MERRY
          No! I don't want anything to do with
          those people.

                    CARTER
          Surely, he's heard the news.

                    MERRY
          Let him leave messages. And if
          Deanna drives over here, do not open
          the door. Those two do not want to
          help. Like the police, they want to
          damn me.

                    CARTER
I've got a pal who's a darn good
attorney. I'll give him a call.

                    MERRY
What's his name?

                    CARTER
Lloyd Garner. He's an Austin good
ol' boy, but I've heard he's the
best.

                    MERRY
I hope so. Otherwise, I'll need
divine intervention, but not from
Deanna.

Letter Thirty-Six
February 14, 1990

Dear Roland,

Because of all that's happened over the past months, I've not been able to sleep, although Carter is snoring quite peacefully on my waterbed. And, although my fanatical yearning for you has diminished, my need to set down my emotions has not. Especially tonight, *My Dear Diary.*

Carter took me to Jeffrey's for Valentine's dinner. He and I had not been there together because of the expense.

But he insisted, "Let's dress up and step out. Forget the money. It's your favorite restaurant, isn't it?"

He wore his best navy-blue suit and even a tie. Bless him, all spiffed up, he looked as handsome as any lover I could imagine.

All through appetizers and dinner, Carter seemed a bit cautious, something I attributed to his not having been to Jeffrey's often. But as we sipped our cappuccinos, Carter extended his hand across the white tablecloth, caressed my fingers, and curled my palm inside his.

"I want you to know you can count on me, Merry. Your family has been through a lot. But I promise to take care of you and your children. I am dedicated to you and always will be."

Then he presented a small red velvet box with a ring inside, a classic wide band with an elevated pear-shaped diamond. That made me weep, as you can imagine, not about the gorgeous cathedral setting, but having someone dedicate his life to me and my family.

I accepted his proposal but told him I could not set a wedding date, what with my future hanging on someone else's decision. I call and call, hoping for answers. As I told Carter, "It seems I'm always waiting for a verdict over which I have no control. I hope you understand."

He agreed, but tears brimmed in his big brown eyes. I worried that he was upset by my need to wait, but he interrupted me.

"It's not that, Merry. I just never thought I would have a beautiful, brilliant woman like you as my wife. I will do everything I can to make your life happier."

Take that, Professor Brilliance. I have moved into another zone.

Love,
Merry

SCENE 40

INT. LLOYD GARNER'S OFFICE — 1990 — DAY

IN THE HALLWAY

A sign on the door says, "Lloyd Garner & Associates, Attorneys at Law"

Merry and Carter nervously open the door.

INSIDE LLOYD'S OFFICE

Merry and Carter greet LLOYD GARNER, a well-seasoned defense attorney with a Texas twang.

All take a chair.

                    CARTER
          Any news from the district attorney?
          Are they going to charge Merry?

                    LLOYD GARNER
          Murder cases don't happen on our
          timelines. I need details for our
          side of the investigation. Tell me,
          Merry, other than what we've already
          spoken about, is there something I
          might have investigators look at?

Something unusual in the past? If
you didn't kill your daughter, we've
got to prove Glenn is who you say he
was.

Merry looks to Carter, then to Lloyd.

                    MERRY
I don't know if this is connected,
but my neighbor Pamela has been
missing. I've phoned and left
messages. I even called police, but
they blew me off because she travels
for business. Her boyfriend can't
reach her, either.

                 LLOYD GARNER
As they say, 'Trust your gut.' Tell
me more about your friend Pamela.

                    MERRY
She told me one time about a guy she
caught peeping in our windows. He
lied and said he was 'Harry Windsor'
with some bug company. Looking back,
and from her description, I think
that was Glenn.

SCENE 41

EXT. LAJITAS RESORT GOLF COURSE — 1990 — DAY

In a sand trap, a GOLF BALL sits almost
buried.

GOLFER steps in with his sand wedge. He grinds
his spiked shoes to steady his stance, but
his spikes hit something. He adjusts, grinds,
can't get a good stance. Finally, he takes a
swing at the ball, but his sand wedge misses
the ball and hits something that goes THUD.

Standing nearby, his golf buddy CODY laughs.

GOLFER leans to see what he hit. He dusts away
sand, then sees part of Pamela's gaunt bent
knees. He wipes more sand away and sees more
of her legs.

                    GOLFER
          Holy shit, Cody. Look at this.

SCENE 42

INT. LLOYD GARNER'S OFFICE — 1990 — DAY

SUPER: Two months later ...

Merry and Carter sit in front of Lloyd
Garner's desk. He's got a smug grin.

                    LLOYD
        Guess who is not going to trial.

                    MERRY
        Am I in the clear?

                    LLOYD
        Well, it took some convincing to
        get that Brewster County sheriff to
        pay for a newfangled DNA test on
        the scrapings from under Pamela's
        fingernails. Turns out she scratched
        the shit out of her attacker. Those
        new tests can identify people by
        squiggles and lines, you've seen
        them? Well, my threat of a lawsuit
        persuaded the sheriff.

With teary eyes, Merry looks at Carter.

                    MERRY
I hate to think what Pamela went
through.

                    LLOYD
It's a sad story for sure, but
there's good news. About a year ago,
the D.A. in Anchorage, Alaska, was
gung-ho about taking DNA swabs from
sex offenders.

                    MERRY
And?

                    LLOYD
Austin police looked into your claim
that Glenn had a rape charge. They
called Anchorage police and found
two warrants, one for rape, another
for capital murder. Teenage girl.

                    MERRY
Oh no! What did I do by screwing
some guy I didn't even ... Oh, my
poor baby!

Merry cries uncontrollably under the weight of
her daughter's death.

                    CARTER
Merry, none of this is your fault.

                    LLOYD
Carter's right. Life gives you
blows. Too many, sometimes. I
sympathize over the loss of your

friend and especially your daughter,
and I don't mean to diminish that
loss, but you are now free to live
your life. You see, Glenn's DNA in
Alaska matched the DNA from Pamela's
nails. And Austin police found all
sorts of photos of you and Nora
inside Glenn's trailer. You were
right. He was the bug guy Pamela saw
outside your window.

Merry cries out in anguished relief.

                    CARTER
     I don't know how to repay you.

                    LLOYD
     Invite me to the wedding ... if you
     can afford it after you get my bill.

Lloyd grins, but only Carter returns a smile.

                    MERRY
               (still sobbing)
     I only wish my Nora ...

Carter tries to soothe Merry, but she remains
in tears. Carter looks to Lloyd for help.

                    LLOYD
     Carter, I've been in this business a
     long time. There is no happy ending
     for a woman who's lost a child.

Letter Thirty-Seven
May 24, 1990

Dear Roland,

It's been several months since I've written you. I seem to be letting go of my little Raven gang, although I did call Sigrid this week. Like always, we slogged through our low points, with each offering support for the other, although Sigrid's low points have never been as low as mine. But I must not quantify. Her pains are as real to her as mine are to me, no matter how tragic or superfluous. But after our mutual therapy session, I told Sigrid my news about Carter proposing and ... drum roll ... even more wonderful news that you will hear from Sigrid in person, when you meet at the Raven tonight.

Warner Brothers optioned my screenplay! Not only optioned it, but I am under contract for a rather large sum. Six figures. Flush with bucks! Yes, I now can call myself writer because I'm making over $100,000 doing it. Better yet, I don't have to call myself real estate advertising manager anymore, much to Erica Cooke's chagrin.

What a turn! A short time ago, I was drowning in despair. But on June 1, Carter and I will fly to L.A. for the first project meeting. I cannot believe I just said that. I'm heading to Hollywood. Oh, how I wish that my ... but no, even success does not reverse all disappointment and loss.

Have I called Brandon? No. When the only living member of your birth family blames you for the troubles and sorrows life sometimes brings, you must choose whether to allow this person in your life. Although my rift with him tears my heart, I will maintain that boundary. He will never disparage me again, at least not in person. As for his bizarre Deanna, she has not resurfaced. Like me, she probably has given up on our being sisters.

And so, my family is now of my making, my children, plus Carter and his children, his parents who are wonderfully warm and witty people, and his funny sister Helen and her four children in Dallas.

By phone, Sigrid was so relieved to hear of my movie deal, she promised to lay it on thick when she sees you and Jillian tonight.

I cannot wait to hear the details.

Love,
Merry

Letter Thirty-Eight
May 30, 1990

Dear Roland,

Sigrid called me this afternoon to describe your reactions when she told you my news.

"You would have been proud, Merry. I played it cool. We were at the Raven last Thursday, downing a few. Roland asked, like he always does, 'Any news from our Texas pal?' That's when I hit them with your deal."

"Priceless. Any reactions?"

"Well, first off, I only told them the part about your engagement. Roland's face fell as if someone had died, but our dear Jillian had this look I can only describe as smug relief."

"I don't blame her. She's rid of me. The threat of me."

"Then Roland launched into his *shtick* about relationships, zones, and can men and women ever be happy in marriage—you know how he is. Then he ordered another round, while I waited until he brought up your name again. That was when I told him that you'd landed a huge contract with Warner Brothers. Six figures."

"Oh, tell me every grimace and frown."

"Roland seemed truly pleased. He slammed his palm on the table as if saying, 'All right!' But Jillian, I have to say, that's the first time I've witnessed a crack in the woman's facade. She scowled in dismay, harrumphed, and then said sarcastically, 'We'll see if her movie deal ever gets off the cutting room floor.'"

"Should I invite her to the premiere?"

Sigrid laughed. "Probably not. But you'd better invite me. And to the wedding. That will give me an excuse to visit you. I've missed our friendship. Being single in Manhattan is not easy."

"You and Frank forever through?"

"Last I heard, he and the actress broke up, so he moved in with his mother up in Kingston. I hear he's writing a play and will produce it himself. Mommy is his backer."

"If you two really are through, why don't you move here and teach at the university. I know a cute set designer named Nick, who's about your age."

Sigrid laughed. "Let me see what Austin is like before I order the moving van. Oh, and before I forget. Roland's wife filed for divorce."

I went silent with that bomb. It hurt me to know you will then make things official with Jillian. I eventually replied, "A suitable denouement."

"Maybe so … but one more thing about my evening with Roland and Jillian. After she said her snarky line about your film not getting off the cutting room floor, Roland gave her a shitty look and said, 'Well, I hope it does. Merry's not like us schmucks, sitting in a campus bar and dreaming of success. Let's raise a glass to her fortune.' Then, while he and I toasted, Jillian sulked and pouted. Can you believe how petty? I ignored her and toasted Roland back. I told him, 'You taught Merry everything she knows.'"

"What did he say to that?"

"Those who can't do, teach. Those who try are the true existential heroes."

That familiar refrain reminded me what I always hoped you would come to know, and I would have the courage to say. Although you may not have been the greatest playwright or screenwriter, or even financially successful at either, you, Sir, were a brilliant and inspirational teacher. Beyond my infatuation for your startling eyes, riotous humor, and rapscallion charms, I fell in love with your amazing ability to express the thoughts and emotions I had pent up inside.

You called me a "writer," therefore I am. Genet taught me to act, not react. You taught me how. And for that, Roland, I give you my admiration.

Love,
Merry

AFTERWORD

Important Update about Meredith Mayfield:

After Meredith Mayfield died of a sudden heart attack at age seventy-one, her adult children—Nora, Claire, and Scottie—discovered their mother's unsent letters in the back of a file cabinet. Because the envelopes were sealed and addressed to Roland Holmes, the siblings wanted to respect Merry's privacy. Her estate attorney mailed them to Professor Holmes at Columbia University. Although he retired from teaching, the office forwarded them on.

As readers may note, Nora's name is included above. At this writing, she is alive and well—a successful film actress living in Hollywood.

In the *Foreword* of this collection, we alerted readers that most segments are in prose format, while others appear in screenplay format. To resolve any confusion, all scenes presented in screenplay format did not, as far as we know, occur in reality, but stemmed from Merry's "hidden river" of imagination. Meanwhile, the prose accounts are Merry's reality, or as she called them, *My Dear Diary*.

The entire work encompasses the backstory behind Merry's first hit film, *Those Who Try*, produced in 1991 by Warner Brothers and nominated for an Academy Award for best original screenplay that following year. From 1990 on, Merry, her husband, Carter Abrams, and Merry's three children relocated to Los Angeles where she became a prosperous screenwriter for decades. She received her first of three Oscars in 1998 for her third film, *The Redheaded Evangelist*.

We were asked not to include many characters' true names in this work, although the children's names are indeed real. Rest assured, Merry's good friend known as "Pamela" was in the audience to see Merry accept her first Oscar, as were Merry's proud children and her collegiate friend known as "Sigrid."

As to Pamela's whereabouts during the months of Merry's concern, Pamela claims to have been stuck in a grain elevator in Oklahoma, but that was said with a wry tone. Thankfully, she was not murdered and then buried in a West Texas sand trap.

As for the killer named "Glenn," Merry's daughter Nora tells us that a man with a statutory rape conviction dated Merry briefly and also dated Nora. The women were never sure if he had stalked them, but Merry used his criminal background as fodder for her film's thriller plot.

When Roland Holmes received Merry's lost narratives, he was so overwhelmed by their heartfelt revelations, he thought the collection worthy of publication as a memoir. Publishers, however, required the inclusion of selected scenes from Merry's screenplay.

As she herself heard so often, "No plot, my dear, no story."

The screenplay scenes have been edited to clarify differing timelines and environment. Otherwise, they are verbatim from Merry's script.

We hope readers enjoy these insights and especially find relief that Nora and Pamela did not die.

As for Merry's brother, known in this story as "Brandon," we were told that the two siblings remained estranged.

Yours,
Roland and Jillian Holmes
Editors

ACKNOWLEDGMENTS

The author and publisher wish to thank the following "beta" readers who contributed to the final draft of this work. These bright women provided input on the first draft and enabled the author to edit with an eye to reader preferences.

Marilyn Davis, Lakeway, Texas
Toni Knight, Denver, Colorado
Debbie Matern Lofland, New Braunfels, Texas
Sheila Niles, Lakeway, Texas
Pamela Boyd Roberts, Arlington, Texas

In addition, Ms. Roberts above, who is a freelance designer, served as creative director for the novel's cover.

Many thanks also go to Lindsey Nelson of ExactEdits.com for editing and proofreading early drafts, as well as to BookBub.com for a round of proofing on the final draft.

Although this novel has been edited and proofread several times, please use the contact form at patdunlapevans.com if you identify typos or misspellings. In this digital era, mistakes are easy to rectify, and we appreciate your help in achieving perfection.

The author also wishes to thank her husband Dr. Bill Evans for his ongoing patience and support during the creation of a novel, which he has learned is never finished.

ABOUT THE AUTHOR

Pat Dunlap Evans was born in Michigan but at age two, her family moved to San Antonio and later Dallas, Texas, where she was an age-group swimming champ. At South Oak Cliff High School, Pat won a scholarship to attend Southern Methodist University.

An early marriage and the birth of three children plunged Pat into the world of motherhood, until the kids were mature enough for her to complete her bachelor's and master's degrees in English at University of Missouri, Kansas City. The master's degree program offered an emphasis in creative writing. Pat quickly fell in love with the craft of creating characters, predicaments, twists, and turns.

Pat's first husband was a quarterback with the SuperBowl-winning Kansas City Chiefs. She used her experiences as an NFL wife for background in the novel *Out and In*: a mystery-thriller. After the marriage ended, Pat stressed through a career in advertising, PR, and marketing in Dallas and Austin. A second marriage to Dr. Bill Evans of Austin enabled Pat to focus on her true love of writing novels.

Pat has published three titles: *To Leave a Memory*: a warm coming together; *Out and In*: a mystery-thriller, and *Backstory*: behind the scenes of a famous film-thriller. A sequel to *Out and In* releases in 2024. Titled *Ice and Fire*, the mystery is set on the Big Island of Hawaii, where Pat and Bill resided for three years. The pair eventually returned to the Mainland, choosing Las Vegas, Nevada, as their new home.

Please follow Pat on Amazon, BookBub, Goodreads, and her website blog, where you can keep up with Pat's raves and rants.